EDGE OF COLLAPSE

AN EMP POST-APOCALYPTIC SURVIVAL PREPPER SERIES

ALEX GUNWICK

Cover Design by Jacqueline Sweet

outside of New York City.

A shaky video shot through a maze of tall buildings captured a mushroom cloud in the distance. His stomach dropped. Adrenaline spiked through his veins. He forced himself to take calming breaths. Assess then react.

A second image flashed on the screen as the ribbon of terror scrolled on.

We have live video of what appears to be a nuclear bomb explosion over New York. An ABC News chopper captured the detonation from Princeton, New Jersey. UPDATE: LOS ANGELES has been hit.

Shit!

On September 11, all planes had been immediately grounded. A nuclear attack meant his flight would be delayed indefinitely. If he didn't act now, he'd be stuck in San Jose without transportation.

Luke headed toward the exit at a fast clip. He didn't want to start a stampede, but he had to get his gun. He took the escalator stairs three at a time. When he hit the ground floor, he jogged toward the counter where he'd dropped off his luggage.

"Excuse me," he said. "I need my bag. I dropped it off thirty minutes ago, but my flight's been cancelled."

"Do you have your claim ticket?" she asked.

He thrust it into her hand. She scanned the

barcode on it and squinted at the computer.

"You're in luck. We haven't sent it through security yet. I'll be right back."

As she disappeared into the baggage processing area, he studied the flow of people into the airport. No one seemed alarmed. There weren't any televisions in the area, so they probably hadn't heard the news yet.

"Here you go, sir," the airline representative said. "Can I help you with anything else?"

"No."

As he jogged toward the car rental area, he scanned the options and chose the agency without a line. Alamo. Ironically appropriate.

"I need to rent a car."

"What type would you like?" the agent asked. "We have compact, sedan, four-door, SUV—"

"Anything with a full tank of gas," he said.

"They all have a full tank, sir."

"Anything with four wheel drive?" he asked.

"We have a Range Rover Sport. Are you planning on taking it off road?"

"I don't know," Luke said. "I'll take it."

"There's an extra service charge because it's a—"

"Here's my credit card. I don't care about the price." Luke thrust his card toward the man.

"O...kay. I just need you to fill out the rental

agreement. We have optional full coverage insurance but—"

"I don't need it."

"Oh, sir. I highly recommend—"

"Please just print the paperwork," he said through gritted teeth.

The background noise from various conversations inched up with each passing second. He didn't have much time before the shit hit the fan and everyone started to panic. After scribbling his signature across the paperwork, he grabbed the key.

On the way to the lot, he whipped his phone out and tried to call Liz. When his wife didn't pick up, he sent a text.

"LA hit by nuke. BOL now! Take kids. Coming home. Love U."

He hit send. He repeated the process with his daughter's number. Sierra was a freshman at University of California, Irvine. Hopefully she'd already seen the news. But if she hadn't...

He shook his head to clear it. There was no reason to think they were already dead. Their home and Sierra's apartment were both about forty miles south of LA in Orange County. The explosion wouldn't have reached them, but the fallout could. It was October, so the Santa Ana winds might blow the worst of it into the ocean, if they were lucky.

As he ran down a row of cars, he spotted a red Range Rover. He hadn't thought to ask about the color. Damn. No chance at being inconspicuous with this one, but no time to go back and ask for a different color. The highways would already be gridlocked with commuter traffic, so he couldn't waste time.

He pulled onto Highway 101 and headed south. Immediately slowed by a wall of cars, he tapped a few buttons on the console to turn on the GPS. As he attempted to enter his home address, a flash of light blasted across the side and rearview mirrors. He flinched. His eyes snapped closed. As he opened them, an enormous mushroom cloud ballooned into the sky behind him.

San Francisco.

Gone.

People stopped their cars and got out to stare at the nuclear explosion. He swerved onto the shoulder and drove past the melee. The air blast wouldn't reach San Jose, but if the wind blew this direction, the fallout would blanket the city. He needed to get over a mountain and into the central valley as soon as possible. He took the Alum Rock exit toward Mt. Hamilton. Traffic inched along until he hit Mt. Hamilton road.

As he headed up the two lane road, a view of the

entire valley sprawled out to his left. The mushroom cloud had flattened out near the top. Condensation rings circled the deadly gray plume. Radioactive fallout would cover hundreds of miles depending on how hard the wind blew. The more space he could put between him and the cloud, the better.

The road wound up the mountain in increasingly tight curves. After skidding around the third corner in a row, he eased off the gas. He checked the odometer. Twenty-five miles from the airport. Far enough to let him breathe a bit more, but not far enough to ease the tension in his jaw. He wouldn't be relaxing anytime soon. Not until he reached his family.

LIZ POUNDED a punching bag at the warehouse-style boxing gym. Cardio kickboxing kicked her ass, but she loved it. As she pummeled the bag with her fists, briny sweat poured down her face. Biceps aching, shoulders screaming, lungs burning, she refused to let up. Ten other women toiled under the direction of their instructor, but she easily outkicked all of them.

"Five more," Brad yelled, ever the drill sergeant. "Come on, ladies. I want to see those asses working!"

She grinned as he approached.

"Looking good, Anderson." He preferred using

their last names, probably an old Navy thing. He and her husband had been on the same SEAL team. Hard as granite and in killer shape for men in their mid-forties, they obsessed over their fitness regimens.

"Pretend it's Luke's face when he forgets to take out the trash," Brad yelled.

She snorted, narrowed her eyes, and assaulted the bag. A warm breeze rattled the rolled-up door. Her flushed skin chilled in the brief blast of air. A long ponytail slapped against her back. A green camo tank top clung to her like a second skin. Running shorts fluttered against her upper thighs. Calves burning, abs aching, she wanted more.

Several phones buzzed in duffel bags which were hanging from hooks along the concrete wall. As she paused to wipe her brow, her phone chimed with Luke's ringtone. She jogged over to grab it, but missed the call. A series of text messages covered the screen. As she scrolled through them, her heart kicked and fear sliced through her belly.

Nuclear war?

A group of horrified faces looked up from their phones. Everyone started talking at once.

"Did you see the video?"

"I didn't feel anything. Why didn't we feel anything when they hit LA?"

"Oh my God, we're all gonna die!"

"I have to go." She grabbed her bag and ran toward the door.

"Liz!" Brad called.

"I'll check in with you later. I have to get home. Kyle's with the sitter."

"Call me if you need anything," he said.

"Will do."

She hopped into her Jeep Renegade. On the drive home she tried to call Luke and Sierra, but neither answered their phones. She tried the house phone and got a busy signal. Although she was worried about Luke, the root of all fear sprouted from the threat of losing her children. Every mother's worst nightmare.

Ten minutes later, she pulled into the driveway of her two-story home. Several neighbors had gathered at the end of the cul-de-sac. They turned toward her. She waved but didn't stop moving.

Inside the house, she made a beeline for the living room where the television blared. Brittany, their sixteen-year-old babysitter, sat on the couch watching MTV.

"Hey, what's up, Mrs. Anderson?"

"Where's Kyle?" Liz asked.

"Upstairs playing video games."

"Kyle!" Liz hollered upstairs. "Come down here."

"He probably has his headset on," Brittany said.

"Have you heard the news?"

"What news?"

"About the nuclear bombs."

"Bombs?" Brittany's already pale skin turned white.

"Hand me the remote, please."

After Brittany handed it to her, Liz flipped to CBS.

A static bright red screen displayed the message: *Emergency Alert System. An attack on America is underway. This is an emergency action notification. Seek shelter immediately. Threat Level: Critical.*

Reports indicate that a nuclear attack has occurred in multiple cities across America. Additional strikes are imminent. We are under attack. Take shelter immediately. Please stay tuned for any additional information. This message will repeat.

"Seriously?" Brittany asked, her eyebrows knitting together.

"Yes, seriously."

"I need to get home."

"Do you need a ride home?" Liz asked.

"No, I rode my bike."

"Be careful out there. We're not close enough to be in the fallout zone from LA, but if they try to hit the power plant at San Onofre—"

"They?"

"Whoever's bombing us," Liz said.

"Oh, God. I have to go."

Liz paid her and walked her to the door.

"Be careful on your way home. Everyone seems calm so far, but they may not stay that way."

"I will."

"Kyle!" Liz yelled. "Get down here."

When he didn't appear at the top of the stairs, she huffed and headed up to get him. His bedroom door was closed. She knocked and waited. The last time she'd walked in unannounced, he'd been getting dressed for football practice. He'd nearly lost his mind screaming about privacy. She'd had to remind him that he was still a child and therefore wasn't entitled to absolute privacy. Although, she did agree to knock in the future.

"Open up, Kyle."

After banging on the door again, she listened for movement. Nothing. She cracked open the door.

"I'm coming in."

She entered the room. Empty. There was no sign of Kyle. The computer screen was dark and the bed was unmade. Nothing unusual about that. She checked the closet, but he wasn't hiding inside.

Her throat constricted. So he'd chosen today, of all days, to sneak out?

Really?

She picked up the phone on his desk and punched in his best friend's number.

"We're sorry. All circuits are busy right now. Please hang up and try your call again later."

"Great." She hit the end button and set it on the desk.

There was no need to panic. He was probably over at Josh's house. She hurried downstairs and grabbed the car keys off of the key rack by the front door.

When she arrived at Josh's house, she rang the doorbell.

"Oh, hello Liz," Connie said as she wiped her hands on a lemon-yellow apron. "The boys are playing upstairs. I was just pulling some scones out of the oven. Would you like some tea?"

Relief flooded her. At least he was safe.

"How long has he been over here?" Liz followed Josh's mom into the kitchen.

"A couple of hours. I made blueberry today. They go great with ginger peach tea."

"I'm guessing you haven't heard the news?" Liz asked.

"About the bombings?"

Liz nodded.

"Oh sure," Connie said. "We've always known this day would come."

"What?"

"Well, it talks about it in Revelation. Our souls are prepared for the end of days."

Her nonchalant attitude stunned Liz. Connie and her husband had asked her to join them at church, but they'd never mentioned details about their belief system. They were welcoming without being pushy.

"Aren't you scared?" Liz asked.

"No." Connie set a tea kettle on the stove. "But I do hope the angels come to lift us up before things get really bad."

"You know, I forgot that I have an appointment tonight," Liz said. "I really should be going."

"Are you sure? The scones are so much better when they're warm."

"I could take one to go," Liz said, not wanting to hurt the other woman's feelings. Crazy or not, the woman's baked goods were heavenly.

"I'll pack a doggie bag for you," Connie said.

Kyle and Josh bounded down the stairs like a pair of wild animals.

"We smelled cookies," Josh said.

"Hey Mom," Kyle said with a sheepish grin.

"You're in big trouble," she said.

"I tried to call you, but the phones weren't working," Kyle said.

"And I suppose you couldn't stop long enough to tell Brittany you were leaving?"

"Uh..." He pigeon-toed his tennis shoes and stared at them.

"We'll talk about this when we get home." Liz turned to Connie. "Thank you for watching him. I hope he wasn't a bother."

"Not at all. I'm just happy Josh finally made a friend."

Josh's plump face turned pink. He shoved a scone into his mouth.

"Bye, Kyle," he said, crumbs flying out of his mouth.

"See ya," Kyle said.

Liz waited until the car doors closed.

"You do not leave the house without telling someone where you're going," she snapped. "Do you understand me?"

"Sure."

"Kyle, I'm serious. You're grounded."

"You're grounding me during the end of the world?" he asked in a tone of disbelief.

"The world isn't ending. At least I don't think it is," she said. "But until we know what's going on, we're staying in the house. If I catch you sneaking out again, you'll wish the world *had* ended."

was telling the truth. Her vision narrowed, darkness pushing in from every side.

"Sit down. Have a beer." Lonnie pulled a can from a small ice chest.

She sat on an overturned bucket and took the drink. She popped it open with trembling fingers. After taking several long swigs, she turned away from the others. Her father had told her time and again that if nuclear war ever broke out, she should head to the cabin. She'd always laughed it off as paranoia. All of her dad's prepping seemed like a ridiculous waste of time and money, but maybe he'd been right. She whipped out her phone and tried to call him.

"We're sorry but all circuits are busy right now. Please hang up and try again later."

"Dammit."

"What?" Nina asked.

"Phone isn't working."

"I tried to call my dad earlier," Cameron said. "Couldn't get through."

"Should we even be out here?" Nina asked.

"We're too far away to get hit with radiation," Lonnie said. "I watched a documentary about how they made the bomb we dropped on Hiroshima. Unless the wind changes, we should be fine."

"My dad's in San Jose right now," Sierra said as she punched in the number for her mom's phone. The call didn't go through to her cell or the home number. "I'm supposed to be going to our Bug Out Location."

"Your what?" Cameron asked.

"My dad's into prepping, so we have a bunch of food and water at our cabin. He has these monthly family meeting safety drills." She rolled her eyes. "I'm supposed to go to the cabin if we have a huge earthquake or nukes start blowing stuff up."

"Where is it?" Nina asked.

"Up in the mountains."

"How are you going to get there?" Lonnie asked.

"Ride my bike. It's about twenty miles away." Ugh. It would take forever to get there.

"Too bad you don't have a car," Nina said.

"My parents couldn't afford one," Sierra said. "But I don't really need one right now. Everything I need is a bike ride away."

"True. Parking sucks here anyway," Cameron said.

"I guess I should get going before it gets dark," Sierra said.

"You're seriously going to leave?" Nina looked at her as if she'd lost her mind. "Are you sure? Maybe your mom will come pick you up. If you leave, how's she supposed to find you?"

"I doubt she'd try it. We're all supposed to head to the cabin without waiting for anyone else."

A shrill beep emanated from their phones. Sierra

pulled hers out of her back pocket and read a text message from campus security.

President Grayson has declared Martial Law. Mandatory curfew will begin at sunset and last until seven a.m. All students should shelter in place until further instructions are available.

"Guess I'm not going anywhere," Sierra said.

"Not tonight," Cameron said.

"I hope my family's okay. Isn't it weird that they could text us even though we can't call out?" Sierra asked.

"Maybe texting works." Lonnie bent over his phone and tapped furiously.

Sierra texted her mom, dad, and brother. Maybe one of them would get back to her and tell her what to do. In the meantime, she'd have to wait out the apocalypse.

As Luke drove across the California Aqueduct toward the small town of Patterson, he scanned Highway 5. Long-haul trucks lined up like dominos rolled down the road. Cars weaved in and out of the two-lane road as they raced toward their destinations. Up ahead, cars and trucks were crammed into the turnoff for a roadside shopping center. For a brief moment, he considered getting gas farther down the road, but he couldn't risk running out.

He zippered into the snaking line of vehicles headed for the gas station. There were only two options: one on either side of the road. He chose the one to the left. It would be easier to get in and out because it had multiple access points to the main drag. The line inched forward at a snail's pace.

Across the parking lot, an increasingly large crowd waited to enter the small store attached to the gas station. Their gazes wandered and they shifted from side to side. Several men rested their hands near bulging pockets in their jeans. They were probably packing. The central valley was full of people who believed in their Second Amendment right to bear arms. They'd exercise their right if provoked, so he kept a wary eye on them.

Ten minutes later, he reached the pump. He'd only used a third of a tank, so it didn't take long to fill up. He'd spotted several people carrying red plastic gas cans out of the store. If there were any left, he'd buy them all.

The line to get inside had grown by another twenty people in the time it took him to find a parking space. He'd had to backtrack farther into the shopping center to park at a fast food restaurant. Signs on the window indicated that the hamburger joint was out of food. Apparently they'd had a run on food, not surprising considering the circumstances.

"It's a hell of mess," a trucker said as he got in line behind Luke.

"Where are you headed?"

"Modesto. Went through the 152 junction on the 5 about thirty minutes ago. Took me over an hour to go two miles."

"Why?" Luke asked. He turned toward the trucker.

"Hell of a wreck down there. I didn't think highway patrol was going to let folks through."

"What happened?"

"Tanker truck turned over. The whole damn place was on fire."

"And they let you through?" Luke asked.

"It was on the southbound side. They closed one of the northbound lanes, but they were still letting people go past it. You can't see the smoke from here, but it was black as night trying to drive past."

"Are both of the southbound lanes closed?"

"Yup," the trucker said. "I'm guessing they'll close northbound so they can get a cleanup crew up there. With the whole world going to shit, they're going to have to keep the 5 open."

"I was headed south," Luke said.

"Not gonna happen anytime soon. If you're in a

hurry to get home, you should try 33 to 140 to 165. Take that south and you'll pass through Los Banos. You can connect back up to the 5 about ten miles after Los Banos."

"Thank you."

"No problem. You got a radio with you?" the trucker asked.

"I've got a small one."

"Keep it on." The trucker leaned in and whispered. "I heard they're already rationing gas in Nevada and Arizona. I bet you anything we're next."

"Damn, already?" Luke ran his hand across the back of his neck.

"Shit hit the fan. It's only a matter of time until all hell breaks loose. After I drop off my load in Modesto, I'm hauling ass back to Bakersfield."

"Good luck."

"You too," the trucker said.

The line moved forward. A man dressed in a gas station uniform stood inside the entrance. He held a shotgun by his side.

"You had any trouble?" Luke asked.

"Not yet, but it's coming. I can smell it. Desperation. There's a trailer park down the road. As soon as they figure out the world's ending, they'll be down here looting." The man lowered his voice. "I give it an hour. Two max."

Luke nodded, but didn't respond. He had to get the hell out of there as quickly as possible. While he waited to be let into the store, he scanned the shelves. Half of the goods were already gone. Candy bars and trampled bags of chips littered the aisle. A half-melted electric-green Slurpee had tipped over, its content spilling across the filthy tile.

Water. Protein. Carbs.

He'd have to grab as much as he could to supplement the three-day supply in his Bug Out Bag. Although LA wasn't more than a few hours away, he wouldn't be able to drive straight down. LA would be covered in radioactive fallout. He'd have to head inland and find a route around the city center. Any deviation in his plan could cost him a day, so it was better to be well-supplied.

After a large group of men in motorcycle gear left the store, the guard waved Luke in. He didn't waste any time. He headed for the refrigerated section and grabbed four of the largest bottles of water he could find. If he'd been able to make trips in and out of the store, he would have taken it all, but there wasn't enough time. Chaos could break out any minute.

He entered the snack aisle. Most of the beef jerky was already gone, but he found a few bags on the bottom shelf. He tucked his shirt in and started dropping energy bars, bags of trail mix, bags of nuts, and candy bars down his shirt. When he couldn't carry one more thing, he headed toward the counter. The female cashier arched a brow.

"Hungry?" she asked as she rang up the items.

"A little."

"Mm-hmm."

He kept his mouth shut. The more talking they did, the slower she'd ring up the purchases.

A loud crash shook the windows. Everyone in the store turned toward the sound. The front end of a pickup truck had smashed into the concrete wall. Was the guy trying to ram his way in?

The guard ran out and pointed his shotgun at the man in the truck. The driver got out and started yelling at the guard.

"Dammit, Jimmy. He's gonna end up killing someone someday," the cashier grumbled. "Total comes to $130.45. Cash or credit?"

"Credit. Can I get cash back?" he asked.

"Sure. But only forty dollars."

"I'll take it."

The more cash he could get now, the better. Who knew how long the grid would hold up. If the nuclear attacks were planned to take down the grid, the amount of money he had in his account wouldn't make a damn difference. He had about four hundred dollars in his Get Home Bag, but another forty wouldn't hurt.

After the cashier had crammed everything into four plastic bags, he carried it to the truck. He didn't slow down or make eye contact with anyone. He used his peripheral vision to scan for threats. As he tossed everything into the truck, a shot rang out. He reached for his gun. By the time the second shot punched through the air, he had it in his hand.

3

Liz didn't smell the smoke until the fire alarm blasted. She hurried through the kitchen to drag the pan of burning oil off the stove. After opening the windows and the sliding glass door in the living room, she grabbed a broom and waved it at the screaming smoke alarm.

"Is the house on fire?" Kyle yelled down from upstairs.

"No. I was cooking. Can you come down here?" she asked.

Kyle bounded down the stairs. Justice, their one-year-old golden retriever, followed him. Both boy and dog sniffed the air when they entered the kitchen.

"What did you burn?" Kyle asked.

"Oil. I was going to fry chicken."

"Can we order pizza instead?"

"We can't even call out," she said. "And even if we could, I don't think they're delivering right now."

"Why not?"

"The bombs."

"We drove past Pizza Hut on the way home. They looked open," he said.

"If you can get through, we'll order pizza."

He grabbed the house phone off the wall and dialed. The grin on his face faltered, then faded. He hung up.

"Couldn't get through."

"Busy signal?"

"Call can't be completed as dialed. Same as before," he said.

"There's a frozen pizza in the outside freezer."

"I'll get it."

As he headed toward the garage, Justice followed. The dog never left his side. Initially, Luke had wanted a dog for additional security. She'd been against it, not wanting to have to vacuum up fur all the time. But Luke had insisted. Now she couldn't imagine life without the little fur beast.

"Mom!" Kyle ran into the room without the pizza. "There's a cop car outside. They're saying something with the loudspeaker."

Liz checked to make sure the fire was completely

extinguished before heading outside. She waved at her neighbor Jennifer whose house was directly across from hers.

A sheriff's department black SUV rolled down the cul-de-sac. A message blared from the speakers.

"President Grayson has declared Martial Law. Mandatory curfew is in effect beginning at sundown and ending at seven a.m. Anyone found outside after sunset will be arrested. Please stay inside and lock your doors and windows."

A chill ran down her spine. Martial Law? Already? Not that she had any point of reference as to when it should be declared. But still, it seemed extreme. Did they think something else was going to happen?

She ran into the middle of the street to flag down the sheriff's deputy. He rolled down the window, a grim expression on his face.

"Ma'am, please don't run into the middle of the street," he said.

"I'm sorry. I wanted to make sure you'd stop."

"Do you need assistance?"

"No. But, Martial Law? Isn't that a last resort? Do they think there will be more bombings? Did radiation blow down here from LA? Are we safe?"

"You will be safe as long as you follow instructions. That is all the information I have at this time."

When he moved to raise the window, she grabbed the edge of the door.

"Wait. What aren't you telling me?"

"Ma'am, you will be safe if you obey the law. Right now that means locking yourself inside your house at sundown. When we have more information, we'll come back through with another announcement."

"Please, just tell me if we're in danger of radiation poisoning. We have someplace else we can go," she said. "I need to know if I should leave."

The sheriff's deputy sighed. He stared at her for a moment before pinching his nose and closing his eyes. He opened them and gave her a sympathetic look.

"As far as I know, the radiation hasn't reached Orange County. We have a radiation meter at the station and so far it's not picking anything up. We think the Santa Ana winds will blow the fallout into the ocean. That's all I know. I understand your fear, believe me. I have a family to worry about too. Right now, I can't give you more information because we don't have any."

"Thank you." She released her grip on the door and took a step back.

The sheriff raised the window halfway.

"You can't go wrong staying inside," he said. "Stay safe."

"You too," she said.

She continued to stand in the middle of the road after the sheriff left. Jennifer joined her. Although they weren't close friends, all of the neighbors knew each other and liked each other enough to coordinate an annual Fourth of July party.

"What did he say?" Jennifer asked.

"Nothing more than the message he was broadcasting. He told me the safest place to be is locked inside the house."

"That's some horseshit," Kent said as he joined them. The recently retired man never had a nice word to say about anything or anyone, so she wasn't surprised by his comment.

"You're in a good mood today," Liz said.

"I've got to make dinner for the kids. I'll come over *later*," Jennifer said as she fled the group.

"I knew this administration was going to find a reason to take our guns," Kent grumbled.

"Take your guns? Nobody said anything about taking guns."

"They're going to have to pry them from my cold, dead hands."

"What kind of guns do you have?"

"Couple of .45s, an AR-15, a shotgun."

"Aren't AR-15s illegal now?" she asked.

"May as well be. You need a fixed magazine. Can't hold more'en ten rounds, at least until they change the damn laws again. Heard they're taking it to the Supreme Court to get it sorted. Supposed to remove the pistol grip too. It's all nanny state horseshit."

"I thought you could register them as-is if you owned them before a certain date," she said.

"Register them? You think I want the damn sheriff knocking on my door fixin' to steal my guns when shit hits the fan? No way. Easier to make 'em compliant."

"I hope you have gun locks on them."

"Why?" he asked, genuinely perplexed.

"So someone doesn't accidentally shoot themselves."

"I live alone. If anyone shoots themselves with one of my guns, they deserve it for breakin' in."

"You know that's illegal too, right?"

"Breakin' and enterin'?"

"No. Leaving guns sitting around without gun locks."

"How am I supposed to defend myself in the middle of the night when some punk breaks in if I have a gun lock on my shotgun?" he asked.

"Try calling 911 instead?"

He laughed until he'd doubled over and his face turned beet red.

"Liz, you're killin' me. You think the government's gonna help us when we're in the middle of nuclear war?"

"The sheriff was just here. They're helping us now."

"He give you any good intel?"

"Basically said to stay inside and lock the doors," she said.

"Damn right lock your doors. And line up your guns while you're at it. You can't even call out right now. If someone breaks in at night, you'd better be ready to take 'em out. Don't wait around for the law to save ya. We're in a WROL situation."

"What's a WROL?" she asked.

"Without Rule Of Law. Mark my words, the government can't help you now. Only you can save yourself and your family. Where's Luke?"

"San Jose."

"Damn."

"Yeah."

"Well, lock up tight tonight and hope he finds a way home. Last I heard they grounded all planes."

"Where did you hear that?" she asked.

"Ham radio. Made contact with a fella up in Las

Vegas. Nothing's going in or out of McCarran. They've been scrambling fighters out of Nellis though."

"The Air Force base?"

"Yup."

"Have you heard anything else?" she asked. "I haven't been able to get anything on TV other than the shelter in place message. Internet's down too."

"Bet they did that too," he said.

"They?"

"The FCC. I bet they've got a kill switch they can use to keep people in the dark. Probably trying to avoid riots."

"I would think they would want people to have more information, not less."

"You're still thinkin' like we're in the real world. The world we knew is gone. People don't realize it yet, but this is World War III."

"How do you know we're at war?" she asked.

"We got hit by nukes. Of course we're at war. I hope we blow the damn Chinese off the map."

"Did someone say China did this?" she asked.

"Didn't have to. Only a handful of countries have the capability."

"What about Russia?"

"Could have been them too. Doesn't matter. Either way, we're screwed. I've got to head back. Just came out to see what all the fuss was about." He turned to leave, then stopped and looked back. "I like your family, Liz. I know you got guns and know what to do with 'em. Talked to Luke about home defense a bunch of times. Be careful. Don't trust anyone."

"Even you?" she joked.

"Even me," he said solemnly before heading home.

She cocked her head to one side. Kent was nuttier than an acorn tree in September, but she'd never considered him dangerous. The comments he'd made about not being able to call 911, and about how riots would eventually break out made her gut churn. Tonight, she'd sleep with a loaded shotgun by her side. Just in case.

SIERRA ELBOWED through the growing crowd in her apartment. Since word of the nuclear attack had spread through campus, everyone she knew had gravitated to her place. It wasn't the biggest apartment, but nobody seemed to mind. Flowing beer and thumping music had attracted even more people. The party had been raging for hours, but now it was getting on her last nerve.

Fortunately, the alcohol supply was running low.

She wasn't looking forward to cleaning up the mess. Red cups of beer dominated every flat surface in the kitchen and living room. The balcony was overrun with pot-smoking freshmen. The sickly sweet scent wafted in to mingle with the scent of spilled beer. She'd have to leave the windows open overnight to get the smell out.

Nina approached her, a pissed-off expression pinching her features. She said something Sierra couldn't make out over the electronica music blasting from the speakers.

"What?" Sierra yelled.

"This party's getting out of control."

"I know. I hope they leave soon."

"What?"

"I hope they leave soon," Nina hollered.

Several partygoers cast her angry looks, as if they had every right to be there, trashing their apartment.

"They're your friends," Nina said. "Get rid of them."

"Yours are here too," Sierra said, annoyed that her roommate was trying to pin the disaster on her.

"Fine. How do we get rid of them?"

"Throw the rest of the beer into the hall?"

"Problem, Ladies?" Donovan Parker's voice sent shivers of lust down her spine. "You *need* anything?"

Sierra took a sip to buy time, almost choking on

her beer in the process. Oh she needed something all right—him. All six feet of his dirty-hot, tatted-up body. She'd caught glimpses of tattoos on his arms. He even had a green and blue snake coiled up one calf. The ink must have cost a fortune. Not that he'd have to think about money, ever. He was filthy rich.

"Hey Donovan." She flashed her most dazzling smile. "Who invited you?"

"Do I need an invitation?" He licked his bottom lip and narrowed his eyes as if he wanted to devour her. Warmth flooded her cheeks.

"No," she murmured.

Lonnie and Cameron walked in behind Donovan. They grinned at her as they headed for the makeshift bar someone had constructed on the kitchen table.

"We're trying to figure out how to get rid of everyone," Nina said.

"Why? The party's raging," Donovan said.

"It's getting out of control," Sierra said.

"Maybe that's exactly what you need." Donovan put his hands on her hips and started to gyrate to the techno beat.

As he pulled her into a tight embrace, Sierra gasped. She'd never expected him to be so aggressive. But why not? He could have anyone he wanted, and apparently, he wanted her. She banged into another girl who gave her a dirty look before turning back to her boyfriend.

"You never know where they're going to drop the next bomb. We should live it up while we can," Donovan said.

"What if 'they' don't drop a bomb on our heads? Who's going to clean this up?" she asked.

"I'll help."

"Really?"

"It's the least I can do. Besides, I'll be here in the morning anyway," he said with a sly grin.

"You're cocky."

"But I'm right, right?"

"Wrong."

She broke free of his embrace and headed for the bar. She wasn't a one-night-stand piece of ass. If he wanted to get laid, he needed to find someone else. She didn't need that kind of reputation no matter how cute and connected he was.

"Hey." He grabbed her arm and yanked her toward him.

"Ouch!"

"I was just kidding."

"My head is killing me. It's after ten p.m., and someone's going to call the cops. I don't feel like getting busted tonight."

"I have a great idea," Donovan said.

"What?" Nina elbowed past him to stand between him and Sierra. She crossed her arms over her chest and glared at him. Apparently she'd been watching the exchange.

"We'll move the party to my place," he said. "It's bigger and it's off campus so no one's going to care if we're up partying. Besides, the cops will be too worried about the nuke attacks to do anything about a party."

"Sounds great," Sierra said, ready to agree to almost anything to get rid of the partygoers.

"But I have one condition," he said, a sly grin splitting his face.

"What?"

"You two have to come with us."

"Why?" Nina asked. "It's going to take us at least an hour to clean up this place. And I want to go to bed."

"I could arrange that," Cameron said as he inserted himself between Sierra and Nina. He handed Nina a red cup.

"No thanks," she said. "I already feel a headache coming on."

"Okay then." He glanced at Donovan before turning to Sierra. "You try it."

Donovan smiled and strolled past her. He

returned a moment later with a bottle of beer. He held it aloft as he made a toast.

"To the end of the world," he said.

One of the other women at the party stumbled toward him.

"Hey, Donnie. Come dance with me, baby," she cooed.

"Duty calls." He winked at Sierra as he moved toward the other woman.

"Wait," she said. "What about moving the party?"

"If you come with us, we'll move it. If not, eh, you've got a good thing going already."

"Ugh! Fine. We'll go to your place," she said.

Nina groaned.

"We'll only stay a few minutes, then we'll come back and clean this hellhole up," Sierra whispered.

"We make a break for it as soon as we can," Nina said.

"Sounds like a plan." Sierra took a sip of the unidentifiable drink. "What is this?"

"Jungle juice," Cameron said. "It's my own special blend."

"It's really sweet."

She took another sip. It wasn't the worst thing she'd ever drunk, but it wouldn't be her first choice. Typically she preferred a more sophisticated drink like a martini or a cosmopolitan. But she'd settle for anything a bartender would give her while looking the other way. An eighteen-year-old with blonde hair, blue eyes, and a low-cut shirt didn't have to worry about getting carded. And if she did, she'd just have one of her friends hook her up instead.

"Party's moving to Casa Donnie," Cameron hollered.

A cheer went up as people filed out the front door.

"Ladies?" Donovan looped an arm around her and Nina and led them toward the door.

"Are you going to do it to her too?" A woman she didn't recognize stepped in front of them.

"Go home, Audrey. You're drunk," Donovan said.

"You can't buy me off," she said. "You think you have power because of who your dad is, but you don't. I could tell everyone what you did."

"Excuse me," Donovan said as he grabbed Audrey's upper arm and hauled her into the hall.

"What's she talking about?" Sierra asked.

"Who knows," Cameron said. "He'll meet us when he's done talking to her. Let's head out."

She waited until everyone had cleared out of the apartment. As she and Nina followed Cameron into the hall, she spotted Donovan. He towered over Audrey, waving his hand through the air in agitated animation.

Although she couldn't hear what they were saying, it looked like a fight. Audrey wasn't his ex, so Sierra couldn't imagine what they were fighting about. For a second she considered intervening, but it was none of her business. They'd have to work out whatever issue they had on their own.

4

Luke ducked behind the truck as a second gunshot rang out. He inched toward the corner and peeked out. Back at the well-lit gas station, the man who'd rammed his truck into the store's wall lay on the ground, facedown, with his arm twisted at an unnatural angle. A dark red pool of blood oozed from under the dead man's body. The guard stood over him. He held his shotgun in the air and hollered something Luke couldn't make out. Order was degrading fast. He had to get on the road before a gunfight broke out.

He quickly skirted the edge of his truck and hopped into the driver's seat. He held onto his gun with one hand and drove with the other.

After exiting the shopping center, he turned left

onto Sperry Avenue. As he passed through the center of town, people who were gathered in groups in the parking lots of other stores turned to watch him. Men holding crowbars bashed in windows at a pharmacy. A woman carrying a baby dashed across the road, narrowly dodging cross-traffic as she fled the mob.

At the next intersection, an angry group of men wearing white tank tops and matching blue bandanas shot up a police car. So much for Rule of Law. He'd expected societal norms to break down, but he'd hoped it would have taken longer than a few hours. Society operated on a thin veil of law and order, but any cracks in the system could shatter it in a matter of hours.

When the gang set the police car on fire, he flashed back to the 1992 riots in LA. He'd been in Afghanistan in '92, but news of the riots had traveled fast. He couldn't believe how fast the city had dissolved into chaos. And in some parts of LA, the police weren't even bothering to respond to calls.

The light turned green. He punched the gas and flew past the mob. He couldn't afford to get caught in the melee. After he was safely out of range, he slowed to check the street signs. He turned right onto Highway 33 and sped out of town.

Open fields stretched on for miles. Fortunately, twilight blanketed the landscape. Darkness stretched across the fields, giving him some cover. He'd only traveled down this road once before, so he wasn't sure how many miles it was to Highway 140. He vaguely remembered the turnoff being on the other side of a small town, but he couldn't recall any particular landmarks.

Rather than risk getting lost in the dark, he turned onto an unmarked dirt road. He parked behind a cluster of bushes and killed the lights. He grabbed his Get Home Bag from the backseat and hauled it into the passenger side. Since leaving San Jose, he hadn't stopped to eat or drink anything. He tore into a packet of beef jerky and washed it down with a full bottle of water. His parched throat demanded more.

After draining a second bottle, he dug through his bag and found a laminated map of central California. He traveled up to San Jose a couple of times a month for his work as a defense consultant. After serving his country for a decade as a Navy SEAL, he'd left to join the private sector. Sometimes he regretted his decision to leave the service, but with a baby on the way, he'd left for the sake of his family.

He carried detailed maps of central California in case he ever needed to use an alternate route to get home. It didn't take much to shut down the 5. Anything from a car accident to a gas spill could send him miles off of his route. He always wanted a minimum of three main routes home. But with three hundred miles to go, he might be in for a few more detours.

After studying the map, he shoved it back into his bag. He grabbed a bag of trail mix and set it in the cup holder. He tossed the two empty water bottles into the backseat. They might come in handy later.

He pulled out his phone and checked the battery. Still holding up, but he should keep it charged. He plugged the charging cord into the cigarette lighter. He checked for any messages from his family.

Nothing. No calls. No texts.

Since the bombs started dropping, he hadn't heard anything from them. He tried to place a call.

"All circuits are busy. Please try your call again later."

He cursed and ended the call. After setting his phone to charge, he pulled his wallet out of his back pocket. He flipped it open and fished out a picture of his family. He traced his finger across the worn photograph and sighed. Come hell or high water, he'd make it back to them.

Although he had total faith in his wife's ability to take care of the kids, he couldn't help but worry about their safety. Even if everything went as planned, a thousand variables were in play. Anything could go wrong at any time. He shut down the incoming flood of horrifying possibilities. Wallowing in fear wouldn't help him get home. Action would.

Rehydrated and refueled, he was ready to drive the rest of the way home. Even if it took all night.

Miles later, he'd traveled Highway 140 to the 165. He crossed the San Joaquin River and skirted the edge of Great Valley Grasslands State Park. Everything was going well until he spotted lights blazing at the next bridge. He hadn't passed another car in miles. Had there been a wreck on the bridge?

As he cautiously rolled forward, the hair on the back of his neck stood on end. Something wasn't right. Three cars were parked side by side in the middle of the road. Their headlights cut through the darkness.

The shadow of a man passed in front of the truck. Luke spotted the profile of a shotgun slung over his shoulder. He put the truck in reverse and executed a screeching turn. It wasn't fast enough. The back window shattered.

He floored the gas and skidded off into the darkness only to get blinded by a row of headlights perched atop an oncoming truck.

Shit!

He must have passed it without noticing it.

As he veered around the truck, his wheels caught

gravel. It bounced off the undercarriage like automatic rifle fire. He struggled to control the skid. The wheels caught the pavement and he roared forward, fishtailing wildly.

A gunshot rang out. The truck jolted and before he could react, the truck careened over the edge of the road, smashed through a line of bushes, and splashed into the river. It floated for a few seconds before slowly sinking into the water.

He grabbed a small window-breaking hammer from his Get Home Bag. After breaking the window, he pulled himself through it. As he struggled to escape, shouting from down the road drew closer. The growl of a truck's engine grew louder. He only had seconds until they were on him.

He reached in and grabbed his bag. Leaving it would be a disastrous decision. Without it, he was as good as dead.

As he yanked it out, the truck pursuing him skidded to a halt. He waded across the river, fighting the current until he reached the other side. He scrambled up the bank. Shots blasted the earth around him. Dirt rained down, pelting his skin.

His SEAL training kicked in. He dropped to the ground and crawled. Elbow. Hip. Elbow. Hip.

When he reached a patch of dense grass, he moved even faster. If he had any chance of escaping, he'd have to get to the next tree line before they gave chase.

In the pitch-black night, he missed the change in terrain and rolled down an embankment. With cat-like reflexes, he landed on his feet in a crouched position. He splashed through a small stream, ran up the other side, and rushed into the tree line.

With only a hint of faint moonlight to guide his way, he navigated through the thin patch of trees flanking the river. Flat fields of wild grass spread out on either side, giving him no other option but to follow the river.

If he could get far enough away from them, he had a camo tarp in his bag. He ran at full speed and dove into a thicket of bushes. Face down, pressed against the earth, he unzipped his pack and dug through it. His fingers brushed across the tarp. He grabbed it, whipped it open, and threw it over his head. If this didn't work, he was a dead man.

SIERRA STUMBLED down a long hallway on the second floor of Donovan's house. She'd never been inside such a confusing maze of rooms before. Each one blended into the next. As she pushed open a door into a dark room, giggling and kissing sounds flowed out.

"Room's taken," a man yelled from inside.

She quickly closed the door and continued on her quest to find Nina. She couldn't remember if she'd already checked the room at the far end of the hall or not. Had she already been in this wing? Everything was so hazy.

Her leaden feet carried her toward another room. There seemed to be a three-second delay between each step. Her foot would move forward, but she wouldn't feel the movement until she'd already taken the next step. Something was wrong. Probably exhaustion.

Although she didn't want to abandon Nina at the party, she wouldn't be able to stay on her feet much longer.

"Nina," she called. "Are you up here?"

A couple emerged from one of the rooms. Kissing and groping each other, they pushed passed her, completely ignoring her in the process.

"Assholes," she mumbled.

She shuffled into the next room and tried to turn on the light. She felt along the wall until she banged into a lamp. It toppled over. After setting it upright, she turned the light on.

A dull yellow glow illuminated a five foot area around the table. A king-size bed sat next to a large dresser. Across the room, light from a streetlamp cast a hazy glow over a sitting area complete with two wingback chairs. Another table held up an enormous arrangement of fake lilies.

Her eyelids drooped.

So tired.

If she could lie down for a few minutes, she might have the strength to keep looking for her friend.

She climbed onto the bed and kicked off her shoes. After stuffing a pillow under her head, she closed her eyes and drifted off.

In the strange realm between semi-consciousness and sleep, voices drifted like wraiths through a haunted mansion.

"Is she out?" a man asked.

"Looks like it," a second man said.

"Where's Donovan?"

"Downstairs with Rachel. He's trying to bang her too."

"Go tell him she's up here. He wanted her tonight. The other chick can wait. She's willing anyway."

"Are you sure she's not awake?" the second man asked.

"I don't think so. Figure it out while I go get him."

She tried to raise her head, but the room spun on its axis.

"Hey," the second man poked her shoulder. "You awake?"

When she moaned a response, he jumped back.

"Shit."

"Where's Nina?" she slurred.

"She left. Went home."

"I have to go home, but I can't move," she paused. Speaking every word had taken a Herculean effort. Why couldn't she move? "Where's Nina?"

"Shit."

The man headed toward the open door. He stopped inside the room and turned to face her. Light from the hall backlit his figure. His face was shadowed, fuzzy, unrecognizable.

"I have to leave," she whispered.

Two more figures pushed past him into the room. One of them closed the door.

"She's a wreck," the second man said. "I don't know about this."

"She won't remember a thing."

"Donovan?" she mumbled. She tried to lift her head, but it weighed a thousand pounds.

"Shit, are you sure? She knows who I am."

"I put enough in her drink. If she remembers anything I'll be surprised."

"All right," Donovan said. "You stand guard."

"What if someone comes?"

"Get rid of them," Donovan said as he pulled his shirt out of his jeans.

"Whasss going on?" she said.

"What you always wanted," he said with a sneer.

As he moved to unbuckle his jeans, warning bells went off. She struggled to formulate a thought, but as soon as she could get a few words to coalesce, they'd dissolve into oblivion.

Donovan dropped his pants. He walked toward the bed. In a rush of realization, she choked out a strangled sound. No! This couldn't be happening.

He climbed onto the bed. She tried to ball her hands into fists, but the muscles refused to contract.

"Shut up," he snarled. "You've wanted this from the moment you met me."

"No." It came out a whisper, barely registering above his gruff breaths.

She closed her eyes, unable to move. Unable to fight back. Completely helpless and alone, her worst nightmare was about to come true.

A commotion at the door caught Donovan's attention. He eased off the bed and stomped over. As angry, unidentifiable words bounced around the room, she summoned every ounce of strength and rolled toward the edge of the bed. The momentum pitched her over the side. Without the ability to use her muscles, she flopped onto the floor like a dead fish.

"Jesus. Sierra? Is that you?"

"Nina?"

Sierra tried to raise her head off the floor. A solid lead ball would have weighed less.

"Help," she whispered.

"What the fuck were you guys doing?" Nina spun toward the men. "I'm calling campus security. What the hell did you give her?"

Nina dropped to her knees and rolled Sierra onto her side. A wave of nausea rolled up from her belly. She vomited all over the floor.

"Grant!" Nina screamed. "One of you go get him or I swear to God I'm going to hack your fucking dicks off myself."

The pulse of retreating footsteps echoed against the wood. With her ear to the floor, Sierra recognized a second set of footsteps. Then a third. Some arrived while others left. In the haze of it all, she lay there, unmoving.

A minute or an hour passed. Strong hands gripped her arms and someone lifted her over his shoulder. She flopped against him like a rag doll.

"You're okay," Nina said. "We're taking you home."

"Home?"

"Yes. Let's go, Grant," Nina said. "I'm calling the police. You fuckers will not get away with this."

"She's drunk," Donovan said. "It's her word against ours."

The sound of a fist hitting flesh was followed by a deep grunt. She wasn't sure who hit who, but someone was down. She lifted her head enough to see Donovan splayed out on the floor.

"I'll press charges, you bitch," Donovan snarled.

"Dude, she just coldcocked you," one of his friends said.

"Shut the fuck up."

The voices faded as she drifted back into a foggy world of misshapen faces and unrecognizable sound.

When she came to, she was in her own bed. Nina hovered over her with a glass of water in one hand and a couple of pills in the other.

"You need to drink this," she said. "And take these. I don't know what they gave you, but it might help."

"Hurts," Sierra mumbled. Her stomach cramped with every breath.

"You've been throwing up on and off for the last two hours. I tried to call 911 but the lines are still down. Grant went out to see if he could find anyone from campus security."

Sierra lifted her head off the pillow and tried to grasp the water. As the glass started to slip, Nina steadied it.

"I'll hold it. You sip," she said.

The water felt like heaven against her parched lips. She gulped down a mouthful. When it hit the back of her throat, she coughed and sputtered.

"Slowly," Nina said.

Sierra sipped more water. She held her head up as long as possible before weakness forced her back against the bed.

"That's enough for now," Nina said. "We'll try for more in a few minutes. Maybe you'll be able to take some aspirin later."

"Thank you." Tears formed in her eyes.

"Don't cry. You're already dehydrated."

"How did this happen?" Sierra asked, more to herself than to Nina.

"Donovan's an asshole. I shouldn't have left you alone at that party. Something didn't feel right, but I chalked it up to all the drunk assholes playing beer pong in the living room. I should have stayed by your side."

Sierra reached for her friend's hand and tried to squeeze it. Nina sat next to her on the bed. She held her hand and told her not to worry. But Sierra couldn't stop thinking about what had almost happened. She'd almost been raped by Donovan and his friends, and she'd been completely helpless to resist.

As she started to cry, Nina pulled her head into her lap. She stroked her hair like a mother would a child's and promised her she was safe now. But was she? If they couldn't even call the police, how could she possibly be safe?

5

Flashlights danced in the darkness about a hundred yards away. Luke pulled the front of the tarp down. He pressed his body against the damp earth. At this point, his plan would either work, or it wouldn't.

As he waited, his heart pounded. His lungs heaved with the need to replenish his oxygen supply. Footsteps approached. He slowed his breathing rate. A branch cracked a few yards away. His muscles tensed, ready to spring into action if necessary.

"You guys see anything?" a man yelled. He sounded young. Maybe in his early twenties.

"No. Where'd he go?"

"Goddamned ghost," a third man said before

hawking a wad of saliva and spitting. It landed near Luke's feet.

"Let the snakes and coyotes have him," an older man said. "No point in chasing one man when there will be more coming along the road. Move out."

The footsteps receded, but Luke didn't move a muscle. As he waited to make sure they were gone, the sounds of nature took over the night. Small animals scampered through the grasslands; frogs croaked. He was probably alone, but to be sure, he held his position for fifteen minutes.

He slowly pushed the tarp up. His eyes had adjusted to the darkness, but without any towns nearby, there wasn't enough ambient light to illuminate the landscape. Convinced the men were gone, he crawled out from under the tarp. He stood and brushed dirt and muddy leaves off of his shirt.

The temperature had dropped, and although he wasn't uncomfortable, he could have used a jacket. Unfortunately, his was in the wrecked truck. He couldn't go back for it. The truck was totaled and he couldn't risk running into the men again.

He needed to get away from the road and find a safe place to hide for the night. It was too dark to read his map without a flashlight, so he used the tree line as a guide. It paralleled the road for about a mile. The river turned, taking him away from the road. He didn't want to wander too far away from it until he could get his map out.

As he plodded through the muddy riverbank, he scanned the shadowy landscape. When he spotted a bridge up ahead, he picked up the pace. It wasn't the same bridge he'd tried to cross, so hopefully the makeshift highwaymen hadn't blockaded it too.

He approached with the stealthy pace of a SEAL. He hadn't been in combat in years, but muscle memory took over.

About ten yards out, he hid behind a tree so he could scout the location. He set his pack on the ground and slowly unzipped it. After shifting a couple of items, he pulled out a Bestguarder 6x50mm HD Digital Night Vision Monocular. It wasn't military grade by any means, but it did the job. He held it to one eye. Night turned to day.

As he scanned the bridge, the black and white contrast gave him a two-hundred-yard view. Much farther than he needed, but nice for the added security.

The vacant bridge stood out in light gray contrast to the dark gray sky. He searched for any sign of man or animal, but found nothing. Perfect.

He unzipped an outer pocket and placed the monocular in it for easy access. He'd have to rearrange his pack now that he was on foot. But plotting a new route took precedence.

After scrambling up the bank, he found a dry spot on the embankment under the bridge. He set his pack down then squatted in front of it. He pulled out a laminated, waterproof map of central California. Although he'd never expected to end up on foot, he'd packed several sets of California maps just in case.

He unrolled his tarp and used it as cover over his head and pack. He retrieved a small Fenix PD35TAC Tactical Edition flashlight which was clipped to his pocket. After laying the map out, he cupped his fingers over the flashlight. No point in broadcasting his location. Even with the tarp cover, if someone else had night vision, they'd easily spot him. The faster he moved, the better.

As he traced his finger down Highway 165, he groaned. He had to be at least three hundred miles away from home. And that was if he took a straight line through LA, which would be impossible.

The slow burn of frustration gnawing at his gut intensified when he calculated how many days it would take to walk home. At ten miles a day, it would take a solid month to get home. Minimum. If he ran into any more problems, it would take even longer.

He hadn't planned a route around LA yet because he'd expected to make it to Buttonwillow within a few hours of leaving San Jose. But with the detour and now the loss of his vehicle, he'd be lucky to make it there within two weeks. He was still one hundred and fifty miles away from his first real planned stop.

He turned off the flashlight. Going back for the truck wouldn't work. He'd hit the trees hard. The engine had to be permanently damaged. There were other supplies in the truck, but he could only carry so much. He'd also have to contend with the people who'd shot at him. Overall, it wasn't worth it to try to salvage anything.

At least he'd grabbed his Bug Out Bag. Most of the equipment he'd need for a long trip home was in the bag, but he'd still have to stop for food and water. Trying to plot out more than a day's trip at a time would only increase his frustration. He'd have to take it ten miles at a time.

If the terrain was easy enough, he'd try to get closer to twenty, but with so many potential factors to consider, it didn't make sense to over-plan.

He could go longer without food, but he wouldn't last more than three days without water. He'd have to stay within range of a river or lake the whole way home. Unless…

He flicked on the flashlight and studied the map. The California Aqueduct crossed under Highway 5 close to the 152 cutoff. He'd planned on heading in that general direction anyway, so he could continue on the same route, then follow the aqueduct down to LA. He'd have an endless supply of water. If he needed food, there were plenty of farms up and down the highway. And who could forget the fetid stench of cattle near the Coalinga cutoff? "Cow-linga" as he preferred to call it.

The situation was still total bullshit, but at least he had a plan. Maintaining a good attitude would go a long way toward making the journey home less arduous. He'd have enough to deal with from a physical standpoint, so he needed to keep his mindset on point.

Situational awareness and adaptability were two of his greatest strengths. He'd use every skill in his arsenal for the express purpose of getting back to his family. Sure, the journey would take much longer than he'd expected, but he'd make it home eventually.

In the meantime, Liz was more than capable of taking care of the kids. He'd married the strongest, smartest woman he'd ever met, and had no doubt she had everything under control back home.

But then again, he'd thought he had everything under control and now he was hiding out under a bridge. He couldn't help but worry about his wife and kids.

Since leaving the gas station, he hadn't been able

to tune into any live radio stations. They all seemed to be broadcasting the same emergency message. He had a small hand-crank radio in his pack, but didn't want to risk using it and giving away his location. Maybe he'd have a chance to try it out tomorrow.

With too much adrenaline flowing through his veins, he wasn't ready to sleep. The more ground he could cover at night, the better. He'd have to watch out for snakes and coyotes—humans too—but he couldn't sit around all night.

After drinking a bottle of water, he refilled it with water from the stream. Once the bottle was full, he screwed the top on. When he ran out of fresh water, he could use the Lifestraw Water Filter in his gear to make the stream water drinkable. It wouldn't be the best-tasting thing he'd ever drunk, but it sure beat getting the runs.

LIZ PERCHED on the edge of her bed and dialed Luke's number for the fifth time in an hour. Phone lines were still down. She'd sent several texts to both Sierra and Luke. Neither had responded. They were probably trying to reach her too, but couldn't get through. She'd been tossing and turning for the last two hours. Trying to sleep was pointless. Worry clung to her like Spanish moss to a southern oak.

The shotgun lay by her side where Luke should have been. Her heart jumped with fear. What if he wasn't safe? How was he going to get home? Was he even still alive?

She slipped out of bed and tightened the robe around her waist. Even with the hot, September wind blowing through her window, she couldn't get warm. Fresh air usually helped her mood and her bedroom was on the second floor, so it was unlikely someone would try to climb through it. Hopefully, she wouldn't end up glowing in the dark.

According to the sheriff, they were safe from radiation. She believed him. She'd caught Luke playing with a nuclear blast simulator online once. The fallout zone for a direct hit in downtown LA would extend out as far as North Orange County, but it wouldn't blow south unless the prevailing wind changed directions. The Santa Ana winds would reverse the normal airflow and would blow the fallout into the ocean. Not ideal, but really, was there an ideal place for nuclear fallout?

Maybe a cup of herbal tea would help her get to sleep. She padded down the hall to check on Kyle. His door was closed. She listened for a few seconds before heading downstairs. In the kitchen, she put a kettle on the stove.

While she waited, she tried calling out on the land line. Nothing.

The teapot whistled. She filled a mug with boiling water. A chamomile teabag followed.

As she headed upstairs, she heard clicking coming from Kyle's room. She knocked on the door.

"Come in."

She found him sitting up in bed reading a comic book.

"Still awake?"

"Can't sleep."

"Why not?"

"I think we should Bug Out."

"Really?" she asked, amused. She took a sip of tea. "What makes you think we should leave?"

"Gunshots."

"What?" Tea sloshed over the rim to burn her trembling hand. "Crap."

She set the mug down and wiped her hand against her robe.

"Need ice?" he asked.

"No, it's not bad. What's this about gunshots?"

"I heard them a few minutes ago. They woke me up."

"Where did you hear them? Close by?"

"I don't think so. Sounded like it was coming from the other side of El Toro Road. From those ugly orange-colored houses."

"Those are condos."

"Same difference." He shrugged. "I haven't heard anything since, but I can't get back to sleep."

"I've been thinking about Bugging Out too," she admitted.

"To the cabin?"

"Yeah. But I think it's too early. So far nothing's any different in the neighborhood. It's safer to stay at home with all of our stuff than risk breaking curfew."

"Do you think they'll really arrest people for going outside?" he asked.

"I'm…I'm not sure."

Was it realistic to arrest people for simply walking around? She could see it if they were breaking the law, but if they weren't, it seemed a bit extreme. It wasn't like there were huge mobs of people running around firing off shotguns with one hand while holding blazing makeshift torches in the other. As far as she knew, there weren't any machete-wielding maniacs—yet.

But would there be? The possibility of a lawless world seemed unfathomable when she'd woken up that morning; now, she wasn't so sure.

The *pop-pop-pop* of gunshots broke through the silence.

"Did you hear that?" Kyle asked, eyes wide.

"Yeah."

She moved to stand next to his window. Although the shots sounded like they were coming from several blocks away, she positioned her body to one side of the glass before peering out. She couldn't see anything but other houses and rooftops. She squinted and considered getting Luke's night vision goggles from the garage.

Another round of shots splintered through the night.

"See? It's coming from those orange houses," Kyle said.

"Sounds like it."

"We should Bug Out. Dad would have bugged out already."

"We can't. Not tonight. We might get arrested. I don't want to take the chance. Why don't we wait until morning to decide? Maybe we can find out what happened over there."

Kyle furrowed his brow. He ground his lips together before reaching for his comic book.

"I've got Dad's shotgun and the alarm system is on," she said. "I know hearing those shots is scary, but we'll be safe tonight. I promise."

"How can you promise we're safe when we don't even know what's happening outside?"

"If anyone tries to get in through the windows or doors, the alarm system will go off. I've got the shotgun and I'll use it if necessary," she said.

"We should get my rifle out of the gun safe," he said. "I can help guard the house."

"No," she said in a tone that left no room for negotiation. "The guns stay in the safe unless we're going to the range."

"Or when we Bug Out."

"Or when we Bug Out," she agreed.

"I still think we should leave. What if Dad's already there? Didn't he tell us to go to the cabin if any nukes were ever dropped on LA?"

"He did, but he was assuming all hell would be breaking loose. Other than those gunshots, nothing has happened. I think we're a lot safer at home where we have an alarm system and a big supply of food and water."

"We have food and water at the cabin," he said.

"True. But look, we're safe for now. No one's coming in the house tonight. Whatever's going on over there is over a mile away."

"Not very far. I could walk there in twenty minutes."

She sighed, unsure of how to convince him not to be afraid when she was worried herself.

"If you want, I can stand guard at the top of the stairs while you sleep," she said.

"I'd feel better if I could have my rifle."

"Not tonight."

"Tomorrow night?" His eyes lit up.

"Maybe. Depends on what we find out in the morning. Hopefully someone knows what happened."

She used to be able to turn on the news or go online to find out what was going on in real time. The neighborhood even had its own Twitter hashtag and Facebook account. Now she'd have to settle for in-person communication. Not the fastest way to get information, and probably not the most accurate way either. But without any other options, she'd have to wait until sunrise to find out why someone was shooting their gun in the middle of the night.

6

Sierra dragged herself across the cold tile floor in her bathroom. She'd spent the whole night praying to the porcelain gods. The shriveled up, empty core of her stomach ached from all the barfing. Her mouth tasted like raw sewage and she stunk.

As she dragged herself into the bathtub, she considered calling out to get Nina's help. Her friend had been by her side all night. She'd only left to open the door to Grant who'd come at dawn to check on her. Nina knew him from high school, so she'd asked for his help in getting Sierra home from the disastrous party.

Sierra had refused to let him into the bathroom to see her. She'd lied and told him she was perfectly fine when in truth, she didn't know if she'd ever be okay again.

After plugging the bathtub, she turned the hot water on. Even though Donovan hadn't touched her, the slimy aura of his malicious intent still clung to her. She couldn't wait to wash off the evil.

How could she have been so infatuated with a monster? Was she really so blind that she couldn't see beyond his charm? She'd always considered herself a good judge of character. But after last night, she wouldn't be so quick to trust anyone no matter how handsome and charming they appeared.

The scalding water lapped at her legs. She turned on the cold faucet so she wouldn't be burned. As the tub filled, she added bubble bath the way her mom used to do when she was young. She'd tried calling her again, but the phone lines were still down.

It was probably better that way. Her mom would never let her out of her sight if she found out about the party. She'd probably lecture her on being careful. Situational awareness, she called it. A term picked up from her dad's prepping books.

How many times had her dad told to be careful about meeting new people? How many times had he lectured her on why she should always be aware of her surroundings? He'd tried to drill situational awareness into her head, but had she listened?

No.

She hung her head in shame. Humiliated by her stupidity, she wasn't sure how she'd ever face Nina again. Her friend probably thought she was a complete moron for ending up in the bedroom with Donovan and his friends. And could she really blame her?

As tension coiled up her spine, the pounding in her head increased. She sank down into the water and closed her eyes. When the water turned cold, she toweled off and dressed in a pair of loose-fitting pants and a baggy shirt. The clothes had no shape, but no one was going to see her today. She wasn't stepping foot out of the apartment until she was sure the world was safe.

After making a cup of mint tea, she sat on the couch. She clicked on the TV and flipped past the red alert screens. One of the cable news channels was broadcasting from the Hollywood Hills sign. A female reporter in a hazmat suit stood with her back to what was left of Los Angeles. Smoke rose up from the ashes. The cameraman zoomed in on toppled skyscrapers which lay in ruin in downtown LA.

Sierra couldn't stand the images. She changed the input so she could watch a romantic comedy. As she flipped through the options, a key scraped into the front door.

Nina walked in with Grant by her side. They were covered in dirt and ashes. Crusty stains of what looked suspiciously like blood dotted their shirts and jeans.

"What happened?" Sierra asked.

"Nothing," Nina said sharply while glaring at Grant.

"We should tell her," Grant said.

"Tell me what?"

"Nothing." Nina faced Grant, her tone morphed into a low growl. "I told you to keep your mouth shut. If you tell anyone—anyone—you won't be able to justify what you did."

"What did you do?" Sierra asked softly.

Nina and Grant were silent for a moment, glaring at each other.

"Nothing," Grant said.

"Exactly. Go home. Burn your clothes. And keep your mouth shut. No one will find out unless you tell someone," Nina said.

"You better keep your mouth shut too," Grant snapped.

"There's no way in hell I'm telling anyone about what happened."

Grant strode toward the front door. He opened it, and paused long enough to cast an angry glance back at Nina before heading out. He slammed the door behind him.

"What was that all about?" Sierra asked.

"He made a stupid, crazy decision about something and now he probably regrets it. I was hoping you'd still be asleep when we got back."

"What did he do?"

"It's better if you don't know," Nina said. "Plausible deniability."

"Does it have anything to do with last night?"

"I'm taking a shower."

"Wait." Sierra jumped up and blocked the entrance to the hall. "We don't keep secrets. You can tell me anything and I won't say a word."

"You don't want to know, trust me."

"I feel so bad about last night. It's all my fault."

"No." Nina grabbed her hand and squeezed it gently. "I know you think the whole world revolves around you, but it doesn't. Last night wasn't your fault, so don't wallow in self-pity. Even if you made some bad choices, it doesn't excuse what he tried to do. Please tell me you understand at least that much…"

"I—"

"—I know you want to be liked," Nina continued. "You want to be popular. The center of attention. Envied by all of the other women on campus.

But you're letting your need to be liked cloud your judgment."

"You just said it wasn't my fault."

"It wasn't, but the minute you realized something wasn't right, you should have left the party."

"I was trying to find you," Sierra said. "I didn't want to leave you there alone."

"I can take care of myself."

"And you're saying I can't?"

"All I'm saying is that you need to be more cautious about people. There are a lot of terrible people walking around who were very good at hiding their true natures before the bombs dropped. They knew the cops were a phone call away so that kept them in line."

"But now we can't call the cops," Sierra said.

"Exactly. So you need to be even more vigilant. Don't go anywhere alone. Don't trust anyone you don't really know."

"Donovan's the Chem TA. I *knew* him."

"Not really," Nina said. "You only knew him on a superficial level."

"I figured he wasn't a bad guy because everyone else seemed to know him too. How am I supposed to tell good from evil if they're so good at hiding it?"

"There were signs."

"Like what?"

"He wouldn't take 'no' for an answer. Huge red flag," Nina said.

"I thought he liked me."

Nina sighed.

"You've been sheltered your whole life. You've never seen evil before, but it's rising up now. People are starting to realize they can get away with things they couldn't before the bombs. There are no rules anymore. There are no laws. A person could…" Nina swallowed audibly. "A person could get away with almost anything right now."

"Did Grant do something bad?" Sierra asked.

"It's better that you never find out. I'm taking a shower. When I get out, I don't want to talk about the last twenty-four hours ever again."

As Nina headed down the hall, Sierra stared after her. Nina had never scolded her before. Even though she'd repeatedly told Sierra what had happened wasn't her fault, Sierra couldn't stop a fresh wave of guilt from dragging her under.

UNDER COVER OF DARKNESS, Luke hiked through the night. He stayed away from the main road, instead using cover wherever he could find it. With so many wide-open fields, he'd been exposed more often than not.

Although the last ten miles had passed without incident, he would have to stop before he reached Los Banos. Sunrise couldn't be more than an hour or two away. Trying to walk through town in broad daylight was asking for trouble. He'd need to find a place to hunker down and rest. He hadn't slept all night. If he could find an abandoned shed or barn, he'd stay there until sundown. He could rest, take stock of his water supply, and then be on his way after nightfall.

Another mile passed before he spotted a farmhouse on the other side of a huge field of tomatoes. Adjacent to the tomato field, a large orchard of almond trees stood up against the night sky. He skirted the tomato field and entered the first row of trees. Using them for cover, he continued toward a collection of buildings around the farmhouse. With any luck, they'd have a loft he could hide out in. At the end of October, almond harvesting season would be over for the most part, so there shouldn't be many workers on the farm.

A long dirt road cut through the center of the orchard. As he continued toward it, the low rumble of a pickup truck came from farther down the road. He fell in behind a tree and pulled his monocular out.

Three men sat sandwiched together in the front seat. Two more sat in the back of the truck. The red glow of cigarettes flared. He lowered the scope and pulled back as the truck rolled to a stop about ten yards away. The men got out and stood in a semicircle around one man. In the still of the night, their words carried.

"Are you sure the old man is home alone?" the man at the center of the circle asked.

"The wife might be there too," a second man said. "I couldn't watch the place all day."

"We get to keep her, sí?" a third man asked.

The group laughed.

"Nah, ese," the second man said. "Our old ladies would cut off our cajones if we brought a woman home."

"If la esposa está aquí, we kill her," the first man said. "We take the jewelry, the cars, el dinero, eso es todo. Entiendes?"

"Sí, Carlos."

"Vámanos. I want to be home before the sun comes up," Carlos said. "You two go around back and get the cars. Juan and Ricardo go with me to la casa."

The two men headed off into the night. As they passed his position, Luke held his breath. Moonlight glinted across the butts of pistols they'd shoved into their waistbands. One man also carried an AR-15 on a single-point bungee sling angled across his chest.

They continued on, oblivious to his presence. Carlos, Juan, and Ricardo slipped into the orchard on the opposite side of the road and trekked toward the farmhouse.

A litany of silent curses blasted through Luke's head. This wasn't his problem. Hell, he should steal their truck and use it to get as far south as possible.

He walked over to the driver's side and slowly opened the door. He reached in and found the keys dangling from the ignition. Clearly they hadn't expected there'd be anyone hiding in the orchard in the middle of the night.

He lifted his foot up to the running board then stopped. He hung his head, at war with the part of him desperate to get home as soon as possible. His family came first, but leaving another family outnumbered and presumably outgunned didn't sit well. What kind of man would leave innocent people to be slaughtered?

As he stepped down, he reached for his P938. He pulled three additional magazines from his Get Home Bag and shoved them into his front pocket. Each held six rounds. If he couldn't take out five targets with eighteen rounds, he deserved to get shot.

He approached the front of the house. He'd take out the three men inside first, then deal with the two who were tasked with stealing the cars after he'd secured the homeowners.

As he reached the tree line, Carlos's leg disappeared through a front window. Since he hadn't heard the crack of glass, the intruder had probably breached the house through an unlocked window.

Luke waited until Carlos disappeared before running fast and low across the open space between the orchard and the house. When he reached the window, he stood to the left side. Right now he had the element of surprise on his side. But as soon as he entered the home, he'd be faced with an unknown layout. He considered pulling out his night vision, but it wasn't hands-free and it wouldn't do much if the enemy wasn't in the room.

He took a quick peek around the edge of the window frame into the house. The dim glow of a nightlight from the hallway gave him enough light to make out a couch, a TV, and several chairs. Moving in a semicircle, he took small steps while scanning for Carlos and his buddies.

After clearing the room, he climbed through the window. He pressed his back against the wall. He held his gun out as he rescanned the room.

Still empty, he slowly walked across the wood floor. As he took another step, the floor creaked. He froze. Footsteps sounded from near the rear of the house. He quickly pressed himself against the wall next to the door to the hall. One of the men walked past the room without looking inside.

Luke stepped into the doorway. After a fast scan to make sure they were alone, he rushed the man from behind. He slammed the butt of his gun into the man's skull, knocking him down. He dropped to the floor. As he landed, a resounding thump echoed down the hall.

A scurry of footsteps came from somewhere upstairs.

"Juan?" Carlos whispered.

Luke stood motionless with his gun pointed at the top of the stairs.

Footsteps from another room downstairs caught his attention. Before he could change positions, another man stepped into the hall. He startled and reached for his AR-15, but it was too late. Luke put two shots in his heart and advanced to put another between his eyes as he fell.

Upstairs, a woman screamed.

Luke rushed to check the man on the floor. He was dead. Luke grabbed the AR-15 while stuffing his SIG in his waistband. He pulled back the bolt to make sure a round was chambered then headed for the stairs.

A gunshot rang out.

Using the sight, he swept up the stairs. The area was clear, so he moved as quickly and quietly as possible. Unfortunately, the old house creaked and squeaked. Warped boards at the top of the stairs didn't help.

Since Carlos already knew his location, he expected a hail of bullets when he glanced around the corner into the hall. Nothing happened.

He pressed his back to the wall and headed in the direction from which he'd heard the scream. Several doors were closed. Falling back on his tactical training, he opened the first door and swept from left to right until he'd cleared the room. He stepped inside to check under the bed and inside the closets. Empty.

As he returned to the door, pounding footsteps approached. A woman in a white nightgown ran past, screaming when she spotted him. He leveled the AR and waited for Carlos. When he didn't follow, Luke risked a glance down the hall. The woman peeked out from the last room on the right.

"Where is he?" Luke asked.

"My husband. Oh my God!" she shrieked.

"Where?"

The woman pointed down the hall in the direction from which she'd run. Not very helpful.

As he stepped into the hall, he pointed the gun

toward the next door. He opened it and swept the room while trying to keep an eye on the hall.

A blast of gunfire sounded from the stairwell. He spun into the room, clearing the doorframe as bullets chipped away at the wood. Two sets of footsteps pounded into the hall. He'd completely forgotten about the two men outside. Of course they'd come running when they'd heard the first shots.

The woman shrieked.

Luke took a breath before peeking out. One man had an arm around her neck. He held a gun to her head. The second man stood a few feet in front of them. Without hesitation, Luke put a round through his chest. The man stumbled before falling down the stairs.

"Cabrón! Come out or I kill her," the other man snarled.

He didn't move. They planned on killing everyone anyway, but he hadn't shot her yet. He couldn't take him out with the AR without risking hitting her so he switched to the SIG.

"Carlos?" the man called.

"Down here," Carlos said from the opposite end of the hall. "Who the hell is shooting?"

"I don't know. Where's the husband?"

"Knocked out. They have a safe. He wouldn't tell me the combo," Carlos said.

"Maybe she can tell us."

The woman screamed.

"What's the number bitch?" the man asked.

"I don't know. I don't know."

"Liar!"

"He didn't tell me," she wailed.

"Bring her to me," Carlos said.

"What about the other guy?"

"Pendejo! Kill him!" Carlos muttered a string of words Luke couldn't make out.

Luke risked a glance. The man dragged the woman down the hall. Luke waited until they were closer. He raised the pistol and closed his non-dominant eye. He couldn't risk missing. After blowing out a breath, he took the shot.

The man's brains exploded against the wall. He crumbled to the floor. The woman screamed and flung herself at Luke. He pulled her into the room behind him.

"You have to save my husband," she screamed and grabbed his shoulders.

He shook her off.

"Step back," he said gruffly.

"I can't breathe. I can't breathe." She slid down the wall and sat at his feet.

"Which bedroom are they in?"

"On the right. At the end."

Before he could step into the hall, another gunshot blasted. Luke knew he didn't have much time, if any. He checked the hall. It was empty, so he pressed his back against the wall and hurried down toward the open door.

"Surrender and I'll let you live," Luke lied.

Carlos's laughter skirted the edge of madness. He leapt into the hall and fired off two shots before Luke could react.

Searing pain radiated out from the center of his right shoulder. He staggered forward and raised his gun.

"Get down," the woman screamed.

As he dropped down, the loud boom of a shotgun blast cut through the air. His face hit the floor and darkness sucked him under.

7

Liz scraped the last few granules of French roast out of the tin on the kitchen counter. After dumping them into the percolator, she turned on the machine and waited. There seemed to be an inverse relationship between how much sleep she'd had to how long it took to brew coffee. Less sleep, longer brew time.

The doorbell rang. After checking through the peephole to see who it was, she opened the door to Jennifer.

"Sorry I split on you yesterday," she said. "I knew Kent was going to launch into his conspiracy theory crap and I didn't have the patience for it."

"He's got some interesting ideas. Coffee?" Liz asked.

"Sure."

While Liz grabbed two coffee mugs from the cupboard, Jennifer sat at the kitchen table.

"What was it this time? Aliens? Government mind control?"

"Martial Law to take all of his guns," Liz said. "Cream? Sugar?"

"Both if you have it."

"I hate to admit it, but I'm worried. Did you hear the gunshots last night?"

"Yeah. Woke me and Frank up around three a.m."

"What's he think about all of this?" Liz asked.

"He thinks we should go to the grocery store and stock up just in case."

The doorbell rang.

"I'll get it," Kyle yelled as he bounded down the stairs.

"Make sure you know who it is before you open it," Liz called.

Jennifer's husband Frank walked into the kitchen a few seconds later. His normally smiling lips formed a thin line. The leathery skin on his forehead scrunched up. He pulled a chair close to his wife. As he sat, he wrapped a protective arm around her.

"Ran into Kent a few minutes ago," Frank said.

"He still ranting about the government?" Liz asked.

"No. He has a police scanner. Apparently a group of people were looting the grocery store last night. Sheriff's deputies shot and killed two of them."

"They shot people for stealing?" Liz sat in a chair across the table from them.

"Yeah. Isn't that crazy?" Frank asked.

"It seems like…well, for lack of a better word, overkill," Jennifer said.

Frank groaned.

"Well, what else would you call it?" she demanded.

"Excessive force, maybe?" Liz said.

"Whatever you want to call it doesn't matter," he said. "If people are already trying to loot places, we need to get to the store and stock up before everything's gone."

"Should we go together?" Liz asked.

"It might be safer," he said. "Strength in numbers."

"When do you want to go?" Jennifer asked.

"Now, before more people decide to stock up," he said.

"Kyle!" Liz called. "Do you want to go to the store with us?"

"No." He yelled from the living room. "I'm watching a movie."

"Okay."

Frank offered to drive his work van so they'd have plenty of room for everything. As they pulled into the parking lot, Liz's eyes widened. The outside of the grocery store looked like it had been hit by a tornado.

"The windows are all broken," she said.

"There are cops at the front door," Jennifer said.

"I wish I'd brought my gun with me. Just in case," Frank quickly added.

"Let's get in and out as quickly as possible," Liz said.

"There are a ton of people in line waiting to get inside," Jennifer said. "This isn't going to be an in and out job."

"I hope there's enough food left," he said.

The line to get inside snaked along the side of the building. Four deputies carrying AR-15s stood three feet apart at the front of the store. They were letting groups of ten customers in at a time.

"We might not get another chance at this," Frank said. "Grab as much food as you can. Get a lot of canned stuff too. Don't get all fresh. It won't last very long. Don't waste time on water. We still have that at home. Although, we should probably fill up extra bottles just in case."

"Got it," Liz said as Jennifer nodded.

Thirty minutes later, they were the next group to

go inside. A stone-faced deputy handed one small hand basket to each person.

"You have ten minutes to shop. You can only purchase what will fit in the basket and in your hands."

As she entered the store, she sucked in a breath. Broken glass and sticky, spilled soda covered most of the aisles. Crushed red roses littered the floor of a small flower shop at the front of the store. In the fresh fruit and vegetable section, bruised peaches and crushed corn cobs created a sea of small tripping obstacles. She carefully checked before each step, grateful she'd worn her boots instead of tennis shoes.

Liz ignored bags of chips and disheveled rows of candy bars, instead heading straight for the canned chili. She checked the labels for cans containing the most calories and added those to her basket. As she continued down the aisle, she grabbed bags of beans, cans of mixed vegetables, and the biggest bag of rice she could manage.

The carefully balanced pile in her basket teetered to one side. She dropped the bag of rice while trying to balance the weight. Fortunately it didn't break.

On her way to the checkout stand, she added a few candy bars to the pile. Sure, they were nutritionally worthless, but they'd give her a quick burst of energy and would help morale if things got even worse.

As she waited in line, she tried not to think about all the ways things could get worse. She didn't have to wait long. When she reached the counter, the cashier was taping a sign to the credit card reader. *Cash Only.*

"What's wrong with the machines?" Liz asked.

"Can't get the authorizations to go through. Lines are down."

"Okay. I'm not sure how much cash I have."

"I'll ring it all up while you count. If you don't have enough, we'll put some back."

"How are you able to ring things up if the computers aren't working?" Liz asked.

"All the pricing data is downloaded at midnight for the next day's specials. So we're working off yesterday's prices."

"It didn't download this morning?"

"Nope. Comes to $75.87."

Liz dug through her purse. She managed to scrounge together $55.35. Over twenty dollars short. She kicked herself for not grabbing extra cash from her Bug Out Bag. Luke had always said cash would become the only accepted tender if there was a power failure. She'd encountered the same problem three months ago when a hacker had taken down several banking systems for several hours.

"I'm twenty dollars short," she said.

"What do you want to put back?"

"Is there any way you can hold everything for me while I go home to get more cash?"

The cashier looked at her as if she'd grown three eyes and green tentacles.

"Have you seen this place? I'm surprised we're even open. I can't promise your stuff will still be here in the next five minutes. It'll be gone for sure in another half hour or so. Probably sooner."

"Fine. Put the candy back, and…" she studied the pile of food. "The bag of rice." She had a giant container of rice at home, so it wasn't a terrible loss, but it still hurt.

After paying the cashier, she dropped her remaining fifteen cents into her coin purse. She grabbed the bags of groceries and headed toward the van. Jennifer and Frank were loading their groceries. They'd been able to get a lot more because they were given one basket each. Apparently they also carried a lot of cash.

"Let's get out of here," Jennifer said. "I don't like the way people are eyeing us right now."

"Agreed," Liz said.

She stuffed her groceries in the back of the van, hopped in, and yanked the door closed. Frank fired up the engine one second before the pulse of semi-automatic gunfire shattered the air.

SIERRA HADN'T SPOKEN MORE than five words to Nina all afternoon. They'd watched two romantic comedies in a row without laughing, joking, or even speaking to each other. A ball of worry rolled around in Sierra's gut. Nina refused to tell her anything about why she'd come home covered in ashes and blood. In some ways, Sierra didn't want to know, but she was sure it had something to do with Grant.

A knock sounded on the door. Nina froze. Her head turned slowly toward the door.

"Expecting anyone?" she asked.

"No," Sierra said.

"Wait here."

Nina went into the kitchen and walked out with a knife from the butcher's block. She held it behind her back as she went to answer the door. Sierra's eyes went wide. What was she so afraid of?

"Who is it?" Nina asked.

"Holly. Oh my God, let me in. Have you guys heard the news about Donnie's house?"

When Nina opened the door, Holly spilled in as if

she'd been pressed up against it. Nina closed the door behind her.

"His house burned down last night," Holly said, breathlessly, as if it were the most exciting thing she'd ever heard. "The fire department didn't come because no one could call them so it burnt to the ground. Three people died!"

"Who died?" Sierra asked while watching Nina out of the corner of her eye.

"Donovan, Cameron, and Lonnie."

As Nina paled, a cold fissure of dread snaked through Sierra's belly.

"How did they die?" Sierra asked.

"At first everyone thought they'd burned to death, but when people went in to search for survivors, they noticed they were covered in stab wounds."

Sierra forced her gaze to stay on Holly. She couldn't let it drift to the knife still held behind Nina's back. Had Nina stabbed them?

"That's not even everything," Holly said.

Sierra's spine went rigid.

"There's a rumor going around that Donnie tried to rape someone. No one seems to know who, but someone from the party. You guys were there, right?" Holly asked.

"Not for very long," Sierra said while casting a sideways glance at Nina.

"I wonder who it was," Holly said.

"Who's spreading the rumor?" Nina asked.

"It doesn't matter," Sierra said quickly. "Does anyone know who killed them?"

Nina's gaze snapped to Sierra. A flash of warning blazed in her eyes.

"No, but I bet it has something to do with the rape," Holly said.

"Attempted rape," Nina said.

"Right." Holly frowned slightly.

"Did the cops ever come?" Nina asked.

"No. I heard they're all over at the Spectrum shopping center. Apparently a riot broke out last night. Ten people were shot."

"By cops?" Sierra asked.

"No, by other people. It's crazy out there. I'm afraid to leave my apartment," Holly said.

"And yet you're here," Nina said.

"I thought you'd want to know," Holly said, an edge of frustration in her tone.

"Thanks for stopping by," Sierra said as she ushered her toward the door. "If you hear anything else, let us know."

"I will."

After closing the door, she turned to face Nina. Her friend strolled into the kitchen and returned the knife to the block. Without saying a word, she walked back to the couch, resumed her position, and hit "Play" on the movie.

"We're not going to talk about this?" Sierra asked.

"Nothing to talk about."

"Did you… Did Grant…" She couldn't bring herself to ask the question.

"Meg Ryan is so good in this, don't you think?" Nina asked.

"What?"

"They had it coming."

Sierra's breath hitched.

"Please tell me it wasn't you," she whispered.

"Of course not. Grant became unhinged. I've never seen him so crazy," Nina said.

"Has everyone lost their minds?"

"Probably. Everyone thinks the world's coming to an end. They're all turning into wild animals."

"Maybe I should go to the cabin."

"If your family's going to be there, then maybe you should. I don't know if anyone will ever figure out that I was with Grant, but if they do, you could be in danger too."

"I can't believe Grant killed them," Sierra said.

"Me either. It was crazy. Anyway, I don't want to talk about it anymore. I'm tired. I just want to watch a movie and chill."

"Okay."

Sierra walked down the hall to her bedroom and closed the door. She stood in the center of the room, trying to decide what to do. Her head pounded and blood pulsed through her ears. Staying on campus wasn't safe. The cabin was about twenty miles away. If she left when it was dark, no one would see her go. She could safely get away from all the insanity on campus.

And maybe her family was already at the cabin waiting for her. Maybe they were worried that she hadn't arrived yet.

Sierra grabbed her phone from her nightstand and punched in her dad's number. She got a busy signal. At least it wasn't the usual message that the call couldn't be completed. Maybe her dad was talking to her mom. Maybe he was trying to call her. He'd know what to do.

After waiting several minutes, she tried again.

"We're sorry, but your call can't be completed as dialed."

"Shit!"

"Everything okay in there?"

Sierra jumped. Nina's voice came from directly on the other side of the door.

"Fine," she said as she opened the door.

"You're not going to tell anyone, are you?" Nina asked.

"No. But I think I'm going to leave tonight."

"That's probably the right thing to do."

"You should come with me. We have enough food at the cabin," Sierra said.

"No thanks. I'm sure things will get back to normal as soon as they stop dropping bombs."

"It might take a long time. What if they hit the power grid or something?"

"You sound so paranoid," Nina said.

"It could happen."

"Whatever. Anyway, if you're taking off later, good luck. If I'm asleep, don't wake me up. I'm super tired."

"Okay."

As she waited for night to fall, she couldn't stop thinking about how crazy things were getting. In an unpredictable world, she couldn't count on anyone anymore. Except her family. She needed to go home as soon as possible. Her dad had always said to go to the cabin if there was ever an evacuation-level emergency. This certainly counted.

The Bug Out Bag her father had insisted she take sat in the back of her closet. After digging it out from under a pile of clothes, she opened the olive-green backpack. She dug through the supplies until she found a waterproof map. Behind it, she grabbed a clear overlay with multiple zigzagging trails.

For OPSEC purposes, her dad had told her to ditch the overlay if she ever got captured so that her captors couldn't find the cabin. At the time, she'd laughed at the fictional scenario. Now, she shuddered.

They'd mapped out several routes to the cabin, some more direct than others. Since she didn't have a car, she'd have to ride her bike. She traced her finger over the bike trail, making a mental note of which roads to turn on. If she took the most direct route, she'd only have to travel about twenty miles, most of it on bike trails and sidewalks. She couldn't see any reason why she couldn't go directly to the cabin.

She stood and walked over to the window. Outside, everything seemed normal. People were sitting around talking and laughing. Cars were flowing in and out of the parking lot. The whole thing seemed like a bad dream, but it wasn't. She had to leave.

After hauling the backpack onto her bed, she searched for a flashlight. She dug through a variety of gadgets and contraptions. They'd come in handy in case she got stuck overnight. She wasn't planning on stopping once she got started. Although she'd never biked twenty miles in a row before, she had enough adrenaline pumping through her to propel her across the country if necessary. With any luck, she'd be at the cabin before midnight.

8

Luke groaned as searing pain shot down his shoulder. He cracked one eye open. Yellow wallpaper blurred and swirled before settling into view. He lay on a quilt-covered bed in a room he didn't recognize. As he tried to sit up, lighting-sharp pain fired along the nerves in his arm.

"He's awake." A woman's face hovered over him.

"Give him some water," a man said.

The woman held a blue plastic cup up to his lips. She slid her arm behind his neck and helped him tilt forward. Cool water splashed against parched lips. It trickled into his mouth, slid down the column of his throat, and pooled in his belly.

He opened his mouth wider and gulped another mouthful. When he'd finished the whole cup, his head fell back against a pillow. The synapses in his brain fired and slowly the events of the night coalesced. He was in the farmer's house. The farmer and his wife stood over him.

"What happened?" A sour film glued his lips together.

"You saved our lives," the farmer said.

"Are they dead?" Luke asked.

"Yes. We buried them in the backyard with a backhoe," the farmer said. "I'm Bob. This is my wife Mary."

"I'm Luke." He couldn't move his left arm, so he used his right to try to sit up. A fresh wave of molten lava burned through his nerves.

"Try to stay still," Mary said. "The man holding Bob hostage shot you before I could shoot him. I'm sorry I didn't get to you sooner. I forgot about the shotgun we keep in the closet in our spare bedroom."

"Better late than never," Luke said with a grimace. "How long was I out?"

"About six hours," Bob said.

Luke turned toward the window. White lace curtains covered most of it, but plenty of sunlight shone through. It had to be noon, at least. Maybe later.

"What time is it?" Luke asked.

"Almost one p.m." Bob pulled a wooden chair

next to the bed. As he settled his barrel-chested frame into the chair, denim coveralls and a white T-shirt shifted around his bulk. He regarded Luke with steely gray eyes. A large gray beard covered his weather-beaten skin. Balding on top, he'd cropped his remaining hair short. "Now I don't want to get into it with you, but what were you doing in my house?"

Luke had no doubt the man could see right through a lie, so he went with the truth.

"I was passing through the orchard when a pickup truck full of men stopped a few yards away. It was dark so they didn't see me. I heard them planning to attack your family, so I waited until they'd split up before heading inside."

"How did you get in?" Mary asked.

"Same way they did. You left a window unlocked."

"Dammit, Mary. How many times have I told you to keep the windows locked at night?" Bob asked.

"You told me you'd checked them last night so I didn't bother," she said. "Don't try blaming this on me."

"Neither of you did anything wrong," Luke said. "You didn't know a gang of thugs were going to break in."

"If I'd known, I would have been waiting at the top of the stairs with the shotgun," Bob growled.

"Are you hungry?" Mary asked.

"Starving," Luke said.

"I'll get you some stew."

After she left the room, Bob stood and paced at the end of the bed.

"The whole world's gone to shit ever since the bombs dropped," he said. "I thought we'd be safe on the farm, but last night we found people trying to raid the fields. We already sold off our crops for the season, but it didn't stop thieves from trying to break into our almond stores. I rigged up a bunch of trip-wire and flares around the barn. I don't know how well it's going to work, but I had to try something. Things are only going to get worse as people start to realize how dependent we are on outside food supplies. Sure, we're surrounded by farms, but the harvest is over. Whatever's left in the fields will be rotten within a month."

"You might want to move all of the food into the house," Luke said. "Easier to guard it."

"Good point." Bob stopped at the window. He moved the curtain aside and looked out. "I tried to find your vehicle. I found the pickup those guys came in, but nothing else."

"I was on foot."

"Why?"

"Ran into a militia up the road. They took my truck."

"Sons of bitches," Bob said.

"I'm trying to get home to my family. I was on a business trip in San Jose when San Francisco was hit."

"Where's home?"

"Orange County."

"That's a good three hundred miles from here," Bob said.

"I know."

"And you were heading out on foot?"

"I didn't have a choice. I can't leave them alone," Luke said. The pain of knowing that he was so far away from his family hit him in the gut. When he tried to move, his shoulder screamed. "How bad is it?"

"Nicked the outer edge of your shoulder. Bit off a chunk of flesh, but you're one lucky sonofabitch. It didn't hit any bone. No arteries. It was only a .22."

"A .22? I never saw it," Luke said.

"It was mine. Walther P22. Kept it on the nightstand. He found it. You're lucky he missed bone. You were bleeding like a stuck pig, but Mary patched you up."

"Stitches?"

"Five." Mary walked in with a large, steaming

bowl of stew. "Nothing fancy, but you'll live. They'll need to be cut out in about a week."

"It hurts like hell." Luke used his good arm to pull himself into a seated position.

"Well, you *were* shot," Mary said with a slight smirk. "Eat up before it gets cold."

The first mouthful of stew tasted better than a lobster and steak dinner. Perfectly seasoned with just the right mix of meat and potatoes, he couldn't shovel it into his mouth fast enough. Who knew when he'd get another meal like this. He'd have to eat up while he could.

"I'll be gone by nightfall," Luke said between bites.

"You're staying the night with us," Mary said. "You shouldn't be outside after dark. It's not safe."

"I don't want to trouble you folks."

"Trouble us?" Bob crossed his arms over his chest. "You saved our lives. You're welcome to stay here as long as you need. I know you're in a rush to get home to your family, but if that wound gets infected, you'll be dead in a week."

"The hospitals are a mess," Mary said. "I went past Memorial Hospital on the way to Walmart in Los Banos. They had triage set up in the parking lot."

"Why? Did a bomb hit near here?" Luke asked.

"No. But last night a gang tore through town, burning down houses and shooting people," she said.

"And it hasn't even been twenty-four hours," Bob grumbled.

"I wonder if it was the same guys from last night," Luke said.

"No. It was more than one group," she said.

"How were things at Walmart?" Luke asked.

"Shelves were stripped bare. I managed to get some canned food, but it wasn't much. We do a lot of canning ourselves, so we've got a good supply. You never know when you'll have a bad crop and with the cost of water skyrocketing, well, we've had to stockpile food for the leaner times."

"I figure we can go about eight months on the stuff we got stored in the basement," Bob said.

"Don't let anyone know you have extra food," Luke said. "If the grid goes down, we might not get resupplied for months."

"My parents started a small Victory Garden during World War II. We've been canning from that land ever since. Never turned it over for commercial use," Bob said with pride.

"Everyone should have a garden. Even if it's just a couple of tomato plants or some strawberries. It might not feed the family for months on end, but it helps cut down on the food bill," Luke said.

"If you've got extra, your family should be okay while you work your way home," Bob said.

"We've got a Bug Out Location too," Luke said. "A cabin in the mountains. My family should be there already if they're following the emergency plan."

"I'm sure they are," Mary said. "Get some rest. We'll see how you feel in the morning."

After the couple left the room, Luke lay back and closed his eyes. A wave of frustration tensed his muscles. A new wave of pain shot straight to his hand. Hopefully he didn't have permanent nerve damage. He flexed his hand slightly, noting a low level of numbness. Not a good sign. If he lost use of his hand, it would make the trek home even harder, and he was already facing a torturous journey.

LIZ TWISTED to look back through the rear window of the van. An angry mob closed in on the sheriff's deputies who stood guard at the front of the store. Gunshots rang out as Frank peeled out of the parking lot. Up ahead, the street signal turned yellow. He hit the gas. As they flew through the intersection, the light turned red.

"We got out of there in the nick of time," Frank said. "I knew they wouldn't be able to hold the line for very long, I'm glad we got out of there when we did."

"Me too. Did you guys get everything you needed?" Liz asked.

"Not everything," Jennifer said. "We ran out of cash."

"Same here."

"I hope you have reserves stashed at home," Frank said.

Liz almost responded with the truth, but after seeing the chaos at the store, she didn't want anyone to know how much cash she had on hand. Especially not her neighbors. Although they were as friendly as neighbors could be, they weren't family. And protecting her family until Luke could get home was her number one priority.

Frank was watching her in the rearview mirror.

"I could probably scrounge up another twenty dollars if I searched the house," she said.

For a split second, his eyes narrowed as if he didn't believe her, then his face relaxed.

"We don't have much at home either," he said, probably lying too. Not that she blamed him.

In truth, she had hid a total of three hundred dollars in secret compartments around the house. Hopefully she'd still be able to remember all the hiding places.

"Do you have enough food and water to get you through a few weeks?" she asked.

"Two weeks' worth," Jennifer said. "After the last big earthquake, we decided to store some food and water in case we had another earthquake."

"Us too," she said. Again, lying about the extent of their supplies.

They had stored a six-month supply of rice and beans in five-gallon buckets in the garage. The prep had cost about one hundred and twenty dollars total. They'd bought the beans and rice in bulk bags at the Asian market when they were running an especially good sale. They'd purchased five, five-gallon buckets from Home Depot. Mylar bags and oxygen absorbers for dried food and long-term storage had come from Amazon.

She'd helped Luke put the emergency food reserves together a few months earlier. Ever since they'd taken action, she'd felt a lot better about how they'd fare if the grid ever went down after a large earthquake. And if they ran out of food or had to bug out, they had a second supply at their cabin.

Frank pulled into the driveway at his house.

"Thanks for the ride," she said.

"Sure thing," Frank said. "Do you need any help carrying anything in?"

"No, I got it."

After they'd said their goodbyes, she carried the groceries into the house.

"Kyle, can you lock the door behind me?" she asked.

"Yeah. I think we should barricade it too."

He walked into the foyer from the living room to lock the door. He followed her into the kitchen.

"Why would we need to barricade the door?" she asked.

"The news came on."

"Oh!"

She dropped the groceries on the counter and headed into the living room. She hadn't bought anything perishable, so they could wait. Any news from the outside was better than no news.

She picked up the remote and flipped through the usual news stations. All were still playing the red emergency broadcast message.

"Which channel was it on?"

"One of the cable channels," Kyle said.

She scrolled through the list until she found one broadcasting news.

"You're looking at the first photos out of Washington, D.C. The White House was hit sometime in the early morning hours. All that remains is a pile of rubble. The president has been moved to an undisclosed location. We're not sure if he's in Air Force One, or if he's under-

ground, but he plans on addressing the nation later tonight. In the meantime, we'll stay on the air until the nuclear crisis is averted.

"In other news, power has been out in San Francisco since a nuclear bomb destroyed several power stations. All citizens should consider storing water as soon as possible—"

She clicked off the TV. Her legs went out from under her and she plopped down on the sofa. If San Francisco had been hit, could Luke have survived? He was thirty or so miles south of the city, but if the fallout blew in the right direction, he was as good as dead.

"That's bad, right? Mom?"

"Yeah, it's bad," she said, unable to sugarcoat it.

"Is Dad dead?"

"What? No," she said, more harshly than she'd intended. "Your dad is the smartest person I know. He's probably going to walk in any minute now. He probably got stuck in traffic driving from San Jose."

If he'd managed to rent a car. *If* he'd been able to avoid the air blast. *If* he wasn't already irradiated by fallout. So many "*ifs*." So much could have gone wrong between San Jose and here. And even if he had a car and had made it to the Grapevine, how could he get through LA? The city had been devastated by the bomb.

She pushed all the horrifying possibilities out of her mind. Freaking out wouldn't do any good. She needed to think about what to do next.

"Are we going to Bug Out now?" Kyle asked, as if privy to her thoughts.

"Not yet. I still think we're safer at home than we would be at the cabin. But we need to fill all of the water jugs in the garage. Just in case."

"What about the WaterBOB? Should we set it up in the guest bathroom?" Kyle asked.

"I forgot we had it."

"Dad told me if we ever looked like we might run out of water, we should fill it up first."

"You're right," she said, impressed by his initiative. Normally it would take multiple tries and lots of squabbling to get him to do anything not on his usual chore list.

"I'll go fill it."

"While you do that, I'll start filling the other five-gallon jugs in the garage."

After filling twenty, five-gallon jugs and capping them, she walked over to the outside pantry. Luke had built a great system so they could store a lot of food, but could still rotate it out so it wouldn't go bad. He'd built several large cabinets which ran the length of one side of the garage. Inside the cabinets, he'd built angled shelves. The oldest cans would roll to the front, while the newest could be easily loaded from the back. They only stored food they already ate, so they never had to worry about food sitting around unused.

It had taken her a year to stock the extra pantry. Instead of spending a fortune to buy everything at once, she'd wait until canned food went on sale. Each week, she'd spend an extra $5-10 on whatever happened to be the best deal. Using this method, she'd hadn't needed to give up anything other than an overpriced latte or two.

"Bathtub's full," Kyle announced as he strolled into the garage.

"Jugs are full, and we've got plenty of food."

"Now what should we do?"

"Wait, I guess. I don't want to leave unless absolutely necessary. I'd hate to miss Dad and Sierra if we leave too soon."

"Are you sure Dad and Sierra aren't at the cabin already?" he asked.

"They would have used the Ham radio to call Kent."

"Has he been listening?"

"Kent's always listening to his radio. If he'd heard from Dad, he would have told us."

"We should go to the cabin and check," he said.

"If it seems safe enough, we can check tomorrow.

When we were at the grocery store, things weren't going well."

"But you got groceries."

"Some, but everything will be gone by tomorrow. Probably today, if people managed to get past the police."

"I should have gone with you," he said.

"I'm actually glad you didn't. I don't want you anywhere near a shootout. Which reminds me, until things get back to normal, I don't want you wandering off. If we do need to bug out, I want to be ready to go in five minutes."

"Five minutes? We haven't even packed anything."

"Good point. Go get Dad's Bug Out checklist and let's see what we need to do."

"Where is it?"

"The red binder in his office."

"Okay."

As he opened the door to go into the house, Justice came flying out. The dog yipped once before trotting over to a plastic bin full of dog food.

"I already fed you today," she said.

"Woof!"

"You can't have any more food until dinner."

The dog lay down with his front paws pointing forward and his rear legs splayed out. He flashed his most dejected puppy dog look.

"You are such a con artist," she said.

Justice rolled onto his back and let out a pitiful moan.

"Belly rubs, hmm?"

As she moved to rub his tummy, he jumped to all fours and ran over to a small container of dog treats. He barked once then sat on his hind legs. He cocked his head to one side and stared at her until she couldn't resist.

"One cookie. That's all you get."

He yipped and spun in a circle. She grabbed a peanut butter-flavored treat and waited. When Justice resumed his sitting position, she leaned down to give it to him. He gingerly took it from her hand before chomping on it.

As he ate, she petted his furry head. She wasn't sure how long they'd be able to stay at the house, but she wanted to retain as much normalcy as possible. She had a feeling things were going to get much worse before they got better. But for now, she'd wait it out at home. Hopefully she wasn't making a huge mistake by staying.

9

Sierra teetered to one side as she exited her bedroom. Her Bug Out Bag weighed at least fifteen pounds, but she'd had plenty of time to adjust the straps across her hips and shoulders until the weight was evenly balanced.

She headed toward the living room. Nina lay sleeping on the couch. Since she'd specifically told Sierra not to wake her, Sierra tried to be as quiet as possible. She moved past the couch toward the front door.

"Are you going?" Nina asked in a groggy tone.

"Yes. I'm heading out now. I should get there around midnight."

"Good luck. Watch out for the crazies."

"I will. Are you sure you don't want to come?" Sierra asked.

"I'm good here," Nina said. "I'll barricade the door if I need to."

"What will you do when you run out of food?"

"We've got plenty of food in the cabinet. I can go down to Albertson's if I need more."

"By the time you go, there might not be anything left," Sierra said. "If people haven't already made a run on the grocery stores, they will. Within a few hours, the shelves will probably be empty."

"Then I'll be on the apocalypse diet." Nina grinned. "Best diet ever. When the hot as hell Marines roll in to save us, I'll be able to squeeze into my skinny jeans. I'm sure I'll be saved first."

Sierra shook her head. Trying to reason with her was a pointless waste of time, so why bother?

"See you around," Sierra said.

"Have fun in your secret bunker or whatever."

"Stay safe."

"You too. Hopefully things get back to normal soon."

"I hope so too."

Sierra's phone buzzed, scaring her half to death. She pulled it out of her back pocket and a text message from her dad appeared.

"Get to the BOL. Don't stop. Don't tell anyone about the location. I love you."

She quickly pounded a message into the phone.

"On my way. Won't stop. Won't tell. Love U."

"Who was it?" Nina asked.

"My dad. He's alive." Her throat constricted. "I have to go."

She hurried downstairs to the parking garage to unlock her bicycle. Her first year at UCI was going to cost a fortune, so she hadn't wanted to pressure her parents into buying a car. She hadn't needed one because everything she needed was within walking distance. But sometimes she wished she had one. Now was one of those times.

After unlocking the bike, she swung her leg over and climbed on. Outside, a golden twilight hung over the city. The hills at the base of Saddleback Mountain gleamed in the fading light. She'd have to bike to the mountain, then find the trail that led to the cabin. It was about twenty-five miles, give or take, depending on which route she took. If she took Campus Drive to the university bike trail, followed the trail along the 405 freeway, and crossed to Sand Canyon Avenue, she could avoid a lot of traffic and get to the foothills in a couple of hours max. Maybe an hour if she didn't have to slow down for anything.

She adjusted the straps on her backpack to secure

the bag against her body. At five feet three and one hundred and twenty pounds, her fifteen-pound bag wasn't light by any means, but it wasn't so heavy that she'd consider leaving it. Her dad had drilled it into her head that if she ever had to leave during an emergency, she had to bring the bag no matter what.

As she pulled out into the parking lot, she passed several students who were standing around with beer cans in their hands.

"Where you headed?" one of them called.

She ignored them and continued pedaling to get momentum. The sooner she got back to her family the better. Her dad would have things completely under control. She had absolutely nothing to worry about.

The ride to Campus Drive took less than a minute. She continued past the Albertson's shopping center and briefly considered stopping for Starbucks. Who knew how long it would be before she could get another Frappuccino?

As she coasted past the entrance to the parking lot, a car nearly hit her. It blared its horn. She skidded to a stop on the sidewalk and turned to glare at the occupant. A young Asian man yelled obscenities at her. Jerk.

Another car turned immediately after his and then another. She frowned as more cars formed a line.

The parking lot was almost full, but people kept honking. Near the entrance to the grocery store, two men argued loud enough for their conversation to carry across the parking lot.

"I got here first. It's my cart."

"I don't give a shit."

The second man shoved past the first and pushed his way through a throng of people streaming into the store. A woman carrying a baby yelled as someone running past knocked her shoulder. The crowd surged forward, pushing and vying for a closer space to the entrance. A man in a store uniform approached the seething group and tried to maintain order. It lasted about ten seconds before the group stampeded into the store.

Sierra shivered. Things were already getting bad. Getting coffee fell off of her priority list the second someone came barreling out of the store with a cart full of water.

"You have to pay for that," a man screamed from inside the store.

A gunshot rang out. The crowd screamed and ran in every direction. Sierra peddled furiously to get away. The sooner she got onto the bike trail the better. People were already losing their minds and only a couple of days had passed. What would they be like once darkness fell?

As a dusky sky blanketed the farm, Luke joined Mary and Bob at the dinner table. Green beans, smashed potatoes, and a roasted chicken sat in matching white and blue cornflower Corningware dishes. Mary had offered to bring his dinner up, but he needed to get on his feet sooner than later. He settled into a cushion-covered, wickerback chair.

Steam wafted up from basket of fresh-baked rolls to ignite his taste buds. It looked and smelled exactly like his mother's cooking. She'd been gone for three years now and not a day went by that he didn't think of her. He couldn't have asked for a better mother, or a better wife. He'd truly been blessed by the women in his life.

When the couple bowed their heads to pray, he added a silent prayer to keep his family safe. After finishing the prayer, Bob used a lemon-yellow potholder to pick up the green beans. He spooned some onto Luke's plate.

"I hope you don't mind me dishing everything out for you," Bob said. "But if you drop Mary's dishes, she might smother you in your sleep."

Luke laughed while Mary scowled at her husband.

"I wouldn't smother him, honey," she said indignantly. "I'd get the shotgun. No point in making him suffer."

Bob roared with laughter. Luke checked to make sure she was kidding and was greeted with a sassy smile.

"That's my girl," Bob said.

"How long have you been married?" Luke asked.

"Twenty-eight years and going strong." Bob puffed out his chest. "I married the prettiest woman in the world."

"Oh, honey." Mary blushed.

"I say that about Liz all the time," Luke said. "We've been married almost twenty years. We were supposed to go to Fiji next year to celebrate."

"We renewed our vows on our twenty-fifth anniversary in Hawaii," Mary said. "Paradise."

As she and her husband gazed into each other's eyes, Luke averted his. He'd have given anything to be able to look at Liz and get confirmation she was okay. He just hoped Kyle and Sierra were with her.

"Do you have kids?" Luke asked.

"Three. We haven't had anyone join us for dinner in a long time," Mary said wistfully. "They're all grown with their own lives now. They come back for holidays and birthdays, but it's not enough."

"Our youngest son moved to Sacramento for school," Bob said. "He's studying economics. Thinks it'll help him run the farm. I don't know. I think I've done a damn good job running it without a fancy education."

"You run it as good as your daddy did," Mary said.

"Thanks, honey."

As Bob leaned over to give her a peck on the cheek, Luke took a bite out of the dinner roll. It melted in his mouth. He eyed the basket.

"Eat as much as you want," she said. "We've got a hundred pounds of flour stored up. We won't be running out of biscuits anytime soon."

"You made them from scratch?" Luke asked.

"I make everything from scratch," she said. "You can't trust all the processed junk they try to pass off as food these days. Mono-un-glycolated-crap."

"Don't get her started," Bob said.

"Do you want to get Alzheimer's?" she demanded. "They haven't proved it yet, but all those chemicals and pesticides can't be good for your brain."

"Our farm's organic," Bob said.

"Yep. They should outlaw the stuff that's killing all the bees and destroying our farmland. We keep poisoning the soil expecting it to recover, but one day it won't. One day this will be a nuclear dust bowl."

Everyone at the table went still.

"I didn't mean it like that," she whispered.

"Oversalinization's going to get us first," Bob said.

"I read an article about that last year. The plants suck up all the irrigation water, leaving the salt behind."

"It happens through evaporation too. We pour millions of gallons onto fields and over time the extra water evaporates and we're left with fields full of salt. It's been accumulating for decades. The whole central valley is going to turn into a huge salt flat if we're not careful," Bob said.

"Farmers can use better drainage systems to drain the excess salt," Mary said. "There are other ways of doing it too, but a good drainage system is the easiest to implement quickly."

"Bet you never thought you'd get a lecture on soil conditions today, did you?" Bob asked.

"Nope. Can't say that I did," Luke said.

"There's a lot more to farming than throwing some seeds in the ground and dumping water on them," Mary said.

"Sure is," Bob said. "Luke, I've been thinking…"

Luke looked up and set his fork down.

"You know that pickup those guys left out in the grove?" Bob asked.

"Yeah."

"I want you to have it," Bob said.

"I couldn't take that from you," Luke said. "The

fuel alone will become a valuable commodity if they start rationing."

"We insist," Mary said. "You saved our lives. We don't need another vehicle. We're not going anywhere anyway."

Luke's heart soared. He'd be able to drive the rest of the way home. His transportation problem would be solved.

"I should leave tonight," he said.

"Stay the night," Bob said. "Let Mary change your dressing in the morning. Give it a full twenty-four hours before you head out."

"Please stay," she said, a wobble in her tone.

Luke nodded slowly. They didn't just want to check on him, they wanted another person around to protect the house. A valid concern. And at this point Liz and the kids would already be at the cabin, so another few hours wouldn't make much of a difference.

"Okay," he said.

"Great," Bob said.

After dinner, they sat around the television in the living room. The emergency broadcast message appeared on every channel and they didn't have cable. Bob switched off the TV.

"I'm going out to check the flares," Bob said.

"Mind if I come with you?" Luke asked.

"I don't want you straining your arm," Mary said.

"I won't let him lift anything," Bob said.

"Okay. But hurry back. My peach cobbler's about to come out of the oven," she said.

"Cobbler?" Although Luke had already stuffed himself fuller than a chubby kid at a buffet, he always had room for dessert.

"She spoils me." Bob grinned.

"I might not want to leave after all," Luke joked.

"You're welcome to stay," Bob said.

"Thanks, but I do need to get on the road tomorrow."

Outside, darkness pressed in from the fields. Shadowy pockets around bushes seemed to twist and move as Luke followed Bob toward the barn. After the events of last night, his imagination had run wild at every squeak in the house.

They passed a freshly dug pile of dirt. Probably the graves.

"Why did you bury them instead of call the police?" Luke asked.

"No phones."

"You could have gone into town to get them."

"Honestly? I didn't want to deal with the questions and paperwork. A few years ago we caught someone stealing almonds. They'd backed a truck up to the edge of our property, cut the fence line, and they were gathering up our nuts. I held them at gunpoint until the sheriff arrived. Wish I'd shot them. Would have been less paperwork."

Luke raised a brow.

"You probably think I'm heartless, killing in cold blood," Bob said.

"It's…a bit extreme."

"They were trespassing." Bob spit on the ground. "This is my land. My family's livelihood. And if those punks thought they could steal from me, they had another thing coming."

In a lawful world, Luke would have had more qualms about his story. But now that everything was changing, he wondered if he wouldn't do the same thing. When lawlessness took over, did it change a man's moral compass? Did the rules of society still apply when there was no one around to enforce them? Did anarchy give him every right to defend both his life and his property? Could he kill if it wasn't in self-defense? He hoped he'd never have to find out.

10

Liz found Kyle in the office sitting in his dad's chair. The red binder lay open on the desk, but he wasn't reading it. His hunched shoulders and vacant stare stopped her mid-stride.

"What's wrong?" she asked.

"I used to make fun of Dad's safety meetings," Kyle said, his voice cracking. "But now I wish I'd paid attention."

"Don't worry, Dad left us a list of what to do in case of a nuclear attack." She could hardly get the last two words out. Even in her worst nightmares, she'd never imagined a nuclear attack on US soil.

"What should we do first?" Kyle asked.

"Go upstairs and get your Bug Out Bag. It's in the back of your closet. Don't bring anything else. If we lose the car, we're going to have to hike up the mountain."

"Why would we lose the car?"

"We won't lose the car. Forget I said that."

"Is someone going to take it from us?" he asked.

"No. No one's taking anything. I'm a good shot."

"I need my rifle."

"No," she said. "I'll be able to protect us. I don't want you to worry."

"I know how to shoot. Dad took me hunting last summer," Kyle said, a hint of indignation in his tone.

"Shooting an animal and shooting a human aren't the same. I need you to help me get everything piled up so we'll be ready if we need to leave."

"Fine," he grumbled.

"Don't pout."

"I'm not pouting…Can I bring Rocky?" Kyle asked, referring to the stuffed animal monkey he'd had since he was a baby.

"Of course."

"What about Justice?"

Upon hearing his name, their golden retriever bounded into the room. The massive ball of shiny fur skidded to a halt at her feet. He wagged his tail and sat back on his haunches to beg for another treat.

"Of course we can bring the fur beast." She leaned down to scratch behind Justice's ears. "Sorry, buddy.

No more treats until we get to the Bug Out Location. Come on, bring it in, group hug," she said as she drew him into a tight hug with the dog. She told herself she was doing it to reassure them, but truthfully, she needed a hug.

"Mooom!"

When she released him, he made a face. She sighed. The teenage years were going to suck. Hopefully they'd live long enough to see them.

As Kyle headed upstairs to get his bag, she grabbed the red folder off the desk. She opened it to the first laminated page and checked the table of contents. Luke had listed the possible disasters in order of likelihood. Nuclear attack was dead last.

She flipped to that section and began reading the steps he'd outlined. For the last year, they'd held a monthly family meeting to review the safety procedures list. They'd spent most of their time focused on what to do in the event of an earthquake, but had briefly touched on other possibilities. They all knew how to handle everything from a gas leak to a house fire, but she'd never expected to need to use any of it. Now she was glad they were prepared.

Step 1: Grab the Bug Out Bags

Already in motion.

Step 2: Unload the gun safe. Take all of the guns with you.

Okay.

Step 3: Grab all of the gas cans in the garage and load the car.

Yep.

Step 4: Check traffic maps if still able.

She tried to load a realtime map on her phone but the connection failed.

Step 5: Bug Out. Do not wait for anyone else. Everyone knows the plan.

The last step had kept her up all night. Luke and Sierra could already be at the cabin waiting for her. Although she had no way of knowing where they were, every instinct in her body screamed stay and wait for them. Luke had warned her this would happen. A mother's instinct to protect her children would override any rational thought. Even knowing this, she couldn't make herself leave the house. Not yet. Not until the situation became too dire to stay.

Kyle returned with his backpack on. Justice followed him into the office.

"Now what?"

"I'll back the car into the garage so we can load up. I need your help with the gas cans. They're heavy."

"Pfft," he said. "I've been pumping iron with Dad. I got this."

To prove his point, he flexed his bicep. She smiled

as he beamed with pride. He was his father's son and took every opportunity to present himself as a younger version of his dad. She loved them both beyond words. Her throat constricted. She cleared it as she headed out to move the truck.

After backing in, she shut the garage door. No point in broadcasting her plan to the neighbors. She wanted everything packed and ready to move as soon as possible.

Near the back of the garage, a large steel gun safe was bolted to the concrete. She entered the numeric combination and waited. It didn't open. She punched in the number again.

Nothing.

She checked the electrical outlet to make sure it was plugged in. It was. Strange. The number should have worked.

The safe had a backup dial lock which didn't require a power supply. She tried the combination, but the door wouldn't budge.

She frowned. Had Luke changed the code?

As she started to try the number again, she remembered a conversation they'd had the previous week. Luke had been concerned about Kyle getting into the safe, so he'd reset the door so that it would require a key in addition to the code.

At first she couldn't remember where he'd said he

put the key, but then she spotted a rusted coffee can on the top shelf of his work bench. Bingo!

She opened the safe and started pulling out guns. As she slowly packed them into their cases, she checked to make sure they were clear. She didn't want a bag full of loaded guns sitting out where Kyle could get to them. Although they'd drilled the principles of gun safety into their son, he was only thirteen years old. Trusting a kid to follow rules at that age was asking for trouble.

After packing all of the rifles, she pulled the handguns out starting with the Ruger GP100. If she had to shoot her way out of the cul-de-sac, she'd need something she could reload fast. A revolver wasn't the best gun for the job. She packed a Smith & Wesson Model 686, followed by an M&P22 Compact. Technically a .22 would work in a pinch, but it wasn't her preferred firearm.

For self-defense, she'd typically want the Mossberg 500. But trying to maneuver a shotgun while driving up a mountain wasn't a good plan. She couldn't find a case for it, so she grabbed a duffel bag and placed the shotgun in the bottom. She added a Glock 34 and a Sig Sauer P229.

Finally, she took out her favorite handgun, an HK P2000. After shooting thousands of practice rounds with this gun, it felt like an extension of her own hand. She could hit a moving target at twenty-five yards. At first she'd been afraid to learn how to shoot, but after finding out about shooting competitions, her competitive spirit had taken over. It hadn't taken long for her to become adept at taking down targets.

The door from the garage to the house opened. Kyle stepped out with Justice on his heels.

"I packed the guns. Let's load the truck. We'll start with the full gas cans, then the water jugs, then the empty cans. The ammo crates are next."

"What about the guns?"

"I'll put them in the back seat. Where is your Bug Out Bag?" she asked.

"In the hall. I grabbed yours and Dad's too."

"Great! Get those and put them on the floor in the back seat."

As he followed her instructions, the seriousness of his expression filled her with a mixture of pride and fear. They were all alone in the world. She didn't know if Luke had made it out of San Jose. She hadn't heard from Sierra either. For all she knew, they could be dead already.

As darkness fell, Liz closed all of the blinds in the house. The distinct feeling of being watched followed her as she moved from room to room. Probably paranoia, but who could blame her? After listening to the radio all day, reports of widespread power outages and looting had her on edge. Jennifer and Frank had tried to go to several other grocery stores across town, but they'd returned empty-handed. The looters had taken everything.

When she returned to the living room, Kyle turned on the TV.

"Can we watch a movie or something?"

"Let's see if there's any more news," she said.

He flipped from channel to channel. They all displayed the same red emergency broadcast screen.

"Red screen of death," Kyle said.

"Don't say that."

"Why not? It's true."

Before she could get into an argument with him, the doorbell rang. Kyle launched himself off the couch and ran toward the door.

"Maybe Dad's home," he yelled.

"Stop!"

She raced forward and grabbed his hand as he reached for the doorknob.

"We don't know who's out there," she whispered.

The doorbell rang again. Justice's claws clattered across the tile floor as he scampered toward them. After sniffing the bottom of the door, he barked and snarled. She gestured for Kyle to come closer.

"Who's out there?" he asked.

"Shh! I don't know."

"Hey, Liz," Kent yelled. "Open the damn door." The paranoid neighbor punched the doorbell repeatedly. "I need to tell you something."

Something about his tone raised the hairs on the back of her neck. There was no way in hell she would open the door for him at night. Maybe during the day in full view of the neighbors, but not right now.

"Come back in the morning," she yelled.

"Dammit, Liz. Open this door right now."

"NO!"

Through the peephole, she watched him back up. He kicked the door.

Kyle ran upstairs.

"I've got my shotgun," she lied. "Go away or I'll be forced to use it."

"You're not gonna shoot an unarmed man," Kent said.

"You've got a 9mm in your waistband."

"It's not loaded."

"I'm not an idiot."

Kyle ran down the stairs with the Mossberg 500.

"I told you not to touch the guns," she hissed.

"Seriously? He's about to kick down the door."

He had a point.

She grabbed the shotgun and switched the safety off. As she held the gun up to the window over the door, she pumped a shell into the barrel.

Click-clack.

"You're crazy," Kent snapped.

"I'll come see you in the morning," she said.

As he left, he tromped through her rose bushes.

"Asshole," she muttered.

"Is he gone?" Kyle asked.

"For now."

"Is he going to come back?"

"I don't know."

She chewed on the edge of her lip. Curiosity warred with self-preservation. She wanted to know why Kent had insisted on talking to her, but at the same time, he could have told her through the door. He didn't need to come inside. And hadn't he already warned her not to trust anyone, including him?

Ratatatat.... Ratatatat...

"What was that?" Kyle asked, eyes wide.

"Sounded like a full-auto."

"It was close."

"Next block over."

"We should leave. It's not safe here anymore," Kyle said.

"We'll leave at first light," she said.

"Why not now?"

"Curfew. We might get arrested."

"Who cares? We're going to get killed if we stay

here. Either Kent's going to come back or whoever is shooting out there will come for us."

The edge of hysteria in his voice forced her own fear down. She needed to stay calm so he wouldn't panic.

"We'll leave in the morning. I'll stay up and guard the house tonight while you sleep," she said.

"Sleep? Are you crazy?"

"We don't have a choice right now. Go upstairs and try to get some sleep. I'll wake you up when it's time to leave."

"No way. I'm staying down here with you. And I want my rifle. I'm getting it."

He stomped off toward the garage.

"Get back here."

She didn't move away from the door. When Kyle returned with the rifle, she pressed her lips together. Screaming at him wouldn't do any good at this point.

"I won't shoot myself by accident," he said.

"Don't shoot me either."

"Why…wow, you think I'm a dumb kid. I get it. If Dad were here, he would have *handed* me the rifle. You're treating me like I'm still ten."

"You're only thirteen."

"Yeah, and I'm in high school."

"A freshman."

"Whatever," he waved a hand dismissively. "I'll

sleep on the couch. We can take turns guarding the door. You should probably set the alarm too. Not that the cops will come. But at least it's loud enough to scare someone away."

She punched their security code into the alarm box on the wall by the front door.

"It's armed. But let's be perfectly clear about something. You are the child, I'm the adult. You will listen to me and follow my instructions. Are we clear?"

"Sure," he said in a surly, noncommittal tone.

She didn't know what else to do.

After standing by the door for over an hour, she pulled a chair from the kitchen into the foyer. She sat down with the shotgun in her lap and faced the door. Kent probably wouldn't be coming back, but she couldn't assume anything. The world was falling apart. As far as she was concerned, everyone was a potential threat unless proven otherwise.

11

Sierra road her bike past University High School and onto the Turtle Rock trail. When she reached University trail, she turned onto the dirt path. Light from a full moon cast sinister shadows across the trail. Thick scrub brush and trees lined the Sand Canyon Wash, cutting off visibility from cars passing by on University Drive. The sound of whizzing cars and the occasional blare of a passing radio helped keep her fear at bay.

She hated the dark. Always had. But never more so than when she'd been trapped in the room with the drunk guys. If Nina hadn't been there to rescue her… She shuddered. She had no intention of ever getting drunk again. One close call was enough.

As she turned a corner in the path, laughter

carried from somewhere in the distance. She slowed as several figures came into view. Three men, probably in their early twenties, stood around a small fire. As she drifted closer, flames from the fire lit their demonic faces. They leered at her.

"Hey, baby. You're not gonna be able to outrun the Russians on that thing. Where you headed?"

She hit the brake and put her foot out to balance.

"Just passing through." She tried to keep her voice steady. Showing fear was out of the question.

"Why don't you come party with us a while?" Second Guy snickered. "We've got beer."

"I don't drink."

"You don't have to drink," Third Guy said.

"I'm just driving through," she said with less confidence. Maybe she should turn around and backtrack a bit. But she didn't want to waste time.

"She's got a nice rack," First Guy said.

"Nice ass too."

Decision made, she spun in a half circle and pedaled away from the group. Footsteps pounded in the dirt behind her.

"Get that bitch," Second Guy yelled.

Panic gripped her chest. She could hardly catch her breath as she frantically pumped her legs. There had been a trail back to the main road up ahead. If she could reach it in time, she could flag down a passing motorist.

The pack chased her, never more than a few yards behind. They were in better shape than she'd anticipated. She pedaled faster and harder until she spotted the side path back to the road. As she skidded around the corner, she hit a patch of loose gravel. The bike spun out from under her and crashed into the bushes. Branches clawed at her face and arms, tearing her skin. Her hip slammed against a jagged rock. Her head smacked the base of a tree trunk.

In a daze, she willed herself to get up and move, but her brain and body seemed disconnected, as if the message wasn't moving from one part to the next. Three dark shadows blocked the light from passing cars. She wasn't more than ten feet from the edge of the road, but she may as well have been a hundred miles away.

The men moved toward her. One grabbed her legs while the other two hauled her out by her arms. She twisted and writhed and struggled against their powerful grips. She screamed and kicked, fighting like hell to get away. She caught the one holding her legs in the jaw. He dropped her and howled. The other two pulled her to her feet.

"You're gonna pay for that," Second Guy said.

The guy holding her legs glared at her with black

eyes. Even in the darkness, she sensed evil bubbling up inside the man. A wave of pure terror shot through her muscles. She jerked and pulled away from the other two. Sprinting up the small slope, she reached the road. The men caught up with her. One grabbed her hair and yanked her back. She lost her balance and tumbled back down the path. He crawled across her, pinning her to the ground.

She sobbed. Pure terror froze her in place.

This was it; she wasn't going to survive.

A gunshot cracked. One of the men screamed and stumbled into the underbrush.

A second shot sliced through the darkness. Two sets of footsteps pounded in the dirt. One running away from her, one running toward her.

"Get off her," a man yelled.

"This bitch is mine," her assailant snarled.

Bang! Bang!

Her ears buzzed. She couldn't hear anything, but the man on her back fell to the side. Someone lifted her to her feet. A man, probably in his thirties, peered into her face.

"Are you okay?" he asked.

She could hardly make out the words and simply nodded.

"They're gone. You're safe."

She stood on shaky legs. When she spotted the

dead man on the ground, she screamed. Blood and brains blanketed the earth beside him. Half of his head was missing. Gone. Blown away. She kept screaming until her savior clamped his hand over her mouth.

"Shh! One of them got away. Be quiet so I can hear."

Her eyes widened and she nodded vigorously. The man released her. He held a black pistol in his hand, pointed at the ground.

"Where are you headed?" he whispered.

"I'm. Trying. To… Get home," she choked.

"Where's home?"

"I can't tell you."

He turned his attention back to her. He hoisted her backpack off the ground and handed it to her.

"Is this your Bug Out Bag?" he asked.

"Yeah. My dad gave it to me."

"Smart man."

"How many miles do you have to go?" the man asked.

"Only maybe…. Twenty? I'm not sure."

"Do you have a map?"

"Yeah, but I don't need it," she said. "My dad and I rode the path multiple times. He insisted we practice so I wouldn't need the map."

"You might need it. Depends on your route. It's

not safe to be on the road right now. Shit's getting bad out there," he said.

"But I have to keep going. I don't have anywhere I can stay until I get to—" She stopped abruptly. Even though he'd saved her life, she couldn't tell him the plan.

"You don't have to tell me the location," he said. "Which direction are you headed?"

"Saddleback Mountain."

"You and probably half the county," he said. "But I'm guessing your dad has a plan for when shit hits the fan?"

"Yeah." She eyed him warily. Just because he'd saved her from those other men didn't mean he was safe.

"Well, good luck," he said.

As he turned to leave, his backpack came into view.

"Wait!"

"What?"

"Thank you," she said. "If you hadn't been here…"

The man sighed and ran a hand across his buzz-cut hair. He mumbled something under his breath that she didn't catch. He looked her up and down, not in a predatory way, but as if he were assessing her.

"How old are you?" he asked.

"Eighteen. Why?"

"Do you know how to shoot a gun?"

"Yes."

"Build a fire?"

"Yes."

"Your dad take you camping a lot?" he asked.

"All the time when I was a kid."

He laughed.

"What?"

"You're still a kid," he said.

"I am not. I'm in college. I have a driver's license."

"Where's your car?"

"I don't have one."

"Why not?"

"I didn't want to ask my parents. And I didn't need one. Why are you asking me all of this stuff?" she demanded.

He glanced at the sky. Moonlight caught the edge of his strong jawline. A wash of stubble cast shadows across his chin. Lean, powerful muscles bulged against his black T-shirt. The edge of a tattoo peeked out from underneath one sleeve.

"Military?" she asked.

"What?" His gaze snapped back to her.

"Your tattoo."

"Marines. I'm Derek." He held out his hand. She shook it.

"Sierra. My dad was a Navy SEAL."

"No shit?"

"No shit," she said.

"Well, that helped me make my decision."

"What decision?"

"I'm going to Saddleback too. My parents live in Modjeska Canyon. I need to check on them."

"Where's your car?" she asked.

"Stolen."

"Seriously?"

"Right after a nuke hit LA. My car alarm went off, but by the time I got my gun and got downstairs, it was gone."

"LA? How did you get down here so fast?"

"No, I was at home in Newport Beach when the nuke hit LA. I've been walking ever since."

"Do you think they're going to drop more bombs?" she asked.

"They?"

"I don't know. The Russians. The Chinese. North Korea. Who knows. There enough nuclear weapons out there to blow up the whole planet. Maybe the terrorists got a hold of them."

"No," he said. "My guess is the Chinese. But you're right, we don't know."

"I wasn't able to get any news. A shelter in place message was on TV when I got home."

"The last I heard, New York, LA, San Francisco—"

"San Francisco?" Her heart stalled.

"Yeah."

"My dad's in San Jose on business."

"I hope he had a plan to get out of there."

"I'm sure he did," she said softly. "How far can a nuclear explosion reach?"

"Depends on the bomb size. But if he was in San Jose, he probably escaped most of it."

"Most?"

"It's hard to know. I haven't had time to listen to my radio," he said. "I've got to get to my parents before everyone starts to realize how bad things are going to get."

"I hope you get there safely," she said as she righted her bicycle.

"You still plan on biking out of here?" he asked, a hint of amusement in his tone.

"I'll take my chances on the main road from here on out. The bike trail isn't safe."

"You're not going anywhere on that thing," he said.

She pulled the bike into the light. The crossbar was bent. The chain had snapped. Spokes stuck out in all directions. Her bike was wrecked.

"Shit!"

"Yep."

"This isn't funny. I can't walk twenty miles."

"Anyone can walk twenty miles. It might take some time, but you'll get there," he said.

"It will take me two days," she said. "I almost didn't make it two hours."

"It's about ten miles to the foothills. If we start walking now, we'll make it well before sunrise."

"We?"

"Yeah, we. Unless you'd rather take your chances alone."

AT SUNRISE on the second day after the bombing, Luke joined Bob in the large red barn. Newer beams supported the front section of the barn, while plywood boards covered older parts. According to Bob, it had been built in 1908, but he'd added onto it after his father had passed away.

"I want to give you a couple of things for your trip," Bob said.

"You don't need to give me anything," Luke said.

"You're right about that, but I want to. I can't thank you enough for saving me and Mary. We loaded up the back of the truck this morning with some canned food, but I've got beef jerky stored up.

I'd been planning on selling it at the farmer's market, but I doubt I'll be doing that anytime soon."

Bob approached a large white deep freezer with a flip-top lid. He opened it and started piling meat into an old grain sack.

"It won't last too long once it defrosts," Bob said. "Maybe a couple of days. We vacuum sealed it which should buy you time. I also found a small ice chest you can have. Nothing fancy, one of those Styrofoam deals, but it will help keep things cold for a few more days."

"I hope it doesn't take a few days to get home," Luke said. "With the truck, I should be able to get to LA in five or so hours."

"How are you planning on getting through it? The whole city's covered in radioactive fallout by now. It won't be safe to pass through for another two weeks. Even then, I'd try to find a way around it."

Luke hadn't even considered the fallout problem. He'd been so focused on getting home, he'd forgotten that LA sat in a basin with the San Gabriel Mountains on one side and the Pacific Ocean on the other. Even if he tried to follow the 210 freeway through the San Fernando Valley, he'd be downwind from the city center. Pasadena would be directly in the path based on the standard wind patterns. Even if the Santa Ana winds were blowing the radioactive material in the opposite direction out to the ocean, was it worth taking the risk?

"I haven't thought about how to get through it," Luke admitted. "I'm trying to take one day at a time."

"That strategy works until you find yourself at a dead end road," Bob said. "I hope you don't end up in a bad situation for lack of planning."

"I'll figure something out before I get to LA."

"We'll be praying for you. I don't know if we'll ever meet up again, but if you ever end up in our area again, you're welcome to stop by. Just watch out for the tripwire."

"Thank you."

Luke reached to shake the man's hand, but Bob pulled him into a man hug and slapped him on the back.

"You're a good man. Take care of yourself. I hope you get home to your family before the day's out." Bob released him and headed back toward the house. "Mary's been baking up a storm since four a.m. I think she's got something for you too."

As they approached the house, the scent of fresh-baked biscuits wafted out. They'd already stuffed him with a classic country-style breakfast of hash browns, eggs, bacon, and biscuits and gravy. But he sure as heck wasn't going to turn down any food they wanted to give him. Given the events of the last forty-eight hours, he couldn't count on having a smooth ride home. And Bob had made a good point about fallout. How was he going to get around it? He'd have to figure it out later.

"I baked two dozen biscuits," Mary said as she filled several Ziploc bags. "I would have packed gravy too, but there's no way to heat it up."

"I appreciate what you're doing for me," Luke said. "I hope you guys stay safe."

"I've got a stockpile of ammo in the basement," Bob said. "I've hid extra shells all over the house and we've loaded all the guns. Anyone trying to rob us will be in for a rude awakening."

"Even so, keep an eye out for trouble," Luke said.

"We will." Mary handed him steam-shrouded bags full of biscuits. "Let's get you on the road before it gets too late."

"Sounds good."

Luke went outside to the pickup truck. It was an '89 Dodge Ram 150. Underneath a film of dirt, the formerly white, rusted-up cab body wasn't much to look at, perfect for blending in. No one would take a second glance at the pile of crap. Hopefully it would run well enough to get him all the way home.

"I checked your fuel. It's at about half a tank. I wish I could spare some, but gas may become too hard a commodity to come by." Bob rubbed the back of his neck. "She'll probably get about fifteen miles per gallon on the highway, maybe ten or eleven on the streets. I'm guessing she's got about fifteen gallons in a thirty-gallon tank. So you're looking at maybe two hundred miles or so before you need to fill up."

"I'm going to try to top her off as soon as I can find a gas station," Luke said.

"There are a couple of stations up on Highway 33. You might have some luck there," Mary said.

"All right. Well, I guess I'll be on my way," Luke said.

After Mary gave him a hug and Bob shook his hand, Luke climbed into the truck. He fired her up and turned down the dirt road into the orchard. He watched the farmer and his wife wave at him until they became distant specks in the rearview mirror.

With any luck, Bob's makeshift early warning system would give them a leg up on any intruders. They were good people and they deserved to be safe. But in an unsafe world, a few guns and some flares might not be enough to stop criminals from taking everything they had.

12

Liz woke with a start. She grabbed the shotgun and braced it against her shoulder while searching for an imminent threat. A single lamp glowed in the living room. Kyle lay on the couch, sleeping. Outside, the orange light of sunrise irradiated scattered clouds across a gray-blue sky.

Justice trotted in from the doggie door in the kitchen. His dew-drenched paws left a trail on the tile. He sat at her feet and cocked his head to one side as if asking about breakfast.

She stood and checked the peephole. The front yard was empty. No one appeared to be walking around outside, so she abandoned her post to feed Justice. After pouring a cup of kibble into his bowl, she folded up the rest of the fifty-pound sack of food and dragged it into the garage. They'd packed the truck so well that she couldn't find space for the dog food.

Fortunately, they had at least one hundred pounds of kibble stored at the cabin. When they'd planned for a possible Bug Out scenario, they'd included dog food. They'd also stockpiled medicine for fleas and ticks. Justice was part of their family. She'd never consider leaving him behind.

"Are we leaving?" Kyle walked into the garage while rubbing his eyes. His rifle dangled from a strap over his shoulder.

"Yes. I hope the safety's on."

"Yes, Mom." He rolled his eyes.

"Last chance to pack anything else," she said. "We'll leave in ten minutes."

"Okay."

"Make sure you packed a jacket and extra shoes… and bring your photo album."

Upstairs, she pulled her wedding album out of the closet. She flipped open the first page to a photo of her and Luke. They'd planned on celebrating their twentieth anniversary in Fiji next year. Somehow she had a feeling that wouldn't be happening. At this point, she'd be grateful to celebrate it anywhere as long as Luke was still alive. He had to be alive. She couldn't imagine life without him.

They didn't have much room left in the truck, but she found a place to stuff the album. Kyle jammed his album full of pictures into the back seat.

"Ready to head out?" she asked.

"Yeah."

The doorbell rang.

"Now what?" she asked.

She went inside and cautiously approached the front door. She peeked out to find Jennifer standing on the doorstep, alone.

She opened the door.

"Did Kent come to your house last night?" Jennifer asked.

"Yes. Come in so I can close the door."

"He came over around ten last night and was screaming his fool head off. Frank told him to go away."

"Did you find out what he wanted?" Liz asked.

"No. And honestly, I don't care. He's nuts. I don't know why you talk to him anymore."

"Did you hear the gunshots last night?"

"Yeah. I called Tiffany Schuller. Her house backs up to ours. Her neighbor Donald was shot last night. Apparently someone was prowling around and Don tried to call 911. But the phones are still down. Isn't that weird that they're still down? Shouldn't they be up by now?" Jennifer asked.

"This whole thing is crazy," Liz said. "Is Don okay?"

"No. He's dead."

"What?"

"It looks like someone robbed him last night. The house was ransacked. They stole his laptop, TV, all of his food. They even took his wedding ring."

"Where's his wife?" Liz asked.

"They tied her up in the garage. She's still alive."

"Did they…"

"They only tied her up, nothing else. Thank God," Jennifer said. "Ted Olson heard the shots. The robbers fled through the fence on the side yard. He almost caught one of them, but they all got away."

"Did the police ever show up?" Liz asked.

"No. Someone even drove over to the sheriff's station. They said they'd add the break-in to the list of crimes they're following up on today. Can you believe that? They're too damn busy to investigate robbery and murder."

"The system is falling apart."

"It's only been three days," Jennifer said, exasperated.

"It doesn't take much. Look at the LA riots in '92. Cincinnati, 2001. Katrina. Berkeley."

"Berkeley?"

"They riot every time someone sneezes in the wrong direction."

"They have a history of protesting."

"There's a difference between peaceful protests and rioting," Liz said.

"True."

"My point is, we've seen cities fall apart within hours, not days. We have almost no information about what's going on. No internet connection. No phones. People are panicking and it's only going to get worse."

"What can we do to protect ourselves?" Jennifer asked with a frown.

"Stay inside and lock your doors. I don't know what else to tell you," Liz said.

For OPSEC, she wasn't going to tell anyone she and Kyle were leaving, and certainly not where they were headed. In a WROL situation, secrecy could mean the difference between living and dying.

"Have you heard anything from Luke?"

"Nothing."

"I'll pray for his safe return," Jennifer said. "I should be getting home."

"Thank you for the prayers. Stay safe."

After Jennifer left, Liz locked the door and deadbolt. She walked into the kitchen and used the magnetic letters on the fridge to spell BOLK. She jumbled the rest of the letters around it to make it look random. Anyone looking at it wouldn't recognize the code, but if Luke or Sierra came home, they'd know she'd left for the cabin with Kyle.

She took one last look around before heading into the garage. Her heart clenched. They were leaving so much behind to head down an unknown road. She hoped everything would still be there when they came back. *If they came back.*

Kyle opened the passenger door. Justice hopped in and scrambled into the small space they'd left for him in the back seat. As she walked around to the driver's side, she attached a concealed carry holster to her belt. She slipped her HK P2000 into it. Maybe they'd make it to their Bug Out Location without a problem, but she wasn't taking any chances.

She climbed into the truck and hit the garage door opener. As the door slowly raised, shouts coming from a crowd of people caught her attention. She quickly double-tapped the opener to close the door.

"What's going on out there?" Kyle asked.

"I don't know, but we can't leave right now. Not until the crowd is gone."

"Should we go check it out?"

"No. We'll stay here until it's safe to leave. It might take an hour or so, but I don't want an audience when we leave."

Almost twelve hours later, the sun hung low on the western horizon. Liz peered out from behind the curtains in the living room. Several fights had broken out throughout the day. She'd cracked a window to listen to the men argue about whether or not they should pool their resources. The "discussion," if you could call it that, had unraveled and a fistfight had broken out.

Only a few stragglers remained in the cul-de-sac. Everyone else had headed in for the night. Sunset was less than an hour away. Leaving now would put them outside after curfew, but she didn't have a choice. If they didn't leave now, they might not have another chance.

SIERRA'S FEET burned and her back ached from carrying the backpack. They'd been walking for two hours when they reached the intersection of Sand Canyon and Irvine Center Drive. Derek held up his hand. She stopped.

"Movement. Ten yards up, left side," he whispered.

She peered into the darkness. A row of dense bushes lined the road, sectioning off an industrial area. Pockets of lightless black holes hid a multitude of places people could be hiding. Although they'd encountered a handful of people in the industrial area, none of them had been threats. They were just ordinary people trying to get home.

"Let's check it out," he whispered.

"Maybe we should just cross the road."

"If it's a threat, we need to neutralize it."

Neutralize it? She didn't want to know what that would entail. Killing someone who was trying to kill you was one thing, but hunting down a perceived threat was another. She stayed behind him as he stalked forward.

Up ahead, the bushes rustled. A blur of black fur burst out of the leaves. The dog barked and snarled in their direction. She backed up, ready to run if necessary.

"Don't move," Derek said. "If you run, he'll chase you."

She froze. When she was ten years old, the neighbor's dog had escaped the yard and had attacked her on her front lawn. The scars on her arms had faded over time, but the memory of the dog's vicious teeth hadn't.

Derek pulled his gun out of a holster at his waist. Her eyes flashed between the gun and the dog. Was he going to kill it? The dog hadn't even attacked them.

As they inched closer, the dog bared his teeth. He snarled and snapped.

"Go on," Derek yelled. "Get lost, mutt."

"He's coming toward us."

"I see."

When he raised his gun, she grabbed his arm.

"Wait! Don't kill him."

"Let go of my arm," he growled.

She released it. He pointed the gun toward the dog, but angled it toward the sky. He fired a shot. The dog raced into the bushes. Its claws scratched against the asphalt as it took off through the parking lot on the other side of the hedge.

"I wasn't going to kill him," Derek said as he holstered the gun. "But don't you dare grab me again like that. Are we clear?"

"Yes, sir," she said warily.

"We're almost at the Great Park. Let's rest there."

He turned his back on her and took quick strides down the sidewalk. She had to hurry to keep up with him. They didn't speak until they passed under the 5 freeway.

"We need to scope it out first," he said. "I doubt anyone's moved out of their homes yet. The power's still on. But I don't want to take any chances."

"Sure." Still shaken by the incident with the dog, she wasn't about to argue with him.

When his hand dropped to his side, she flinched. He'd saved her from the men who'd attacked her, but why get involved? He could have kept going. And he hadn't shot the dog, so he couldn't be too bad.

"The buildings look unoccupied," he said. "But let's get behind them and stay out of sight of the road."

She followed him. They passed several vacant buildings before reaching the information center building. It was the farthest building back from the road, not counting the unfinished soccer stadium.

"Why aren't we going in there?" She pointed at the stadium.

"Not enough escape routes."

"Yeah, but if no one knows we're there, we won't have anyone to escape from."

"It's not safe enough." He dropped his backpack against the wall and sat down. "We'll rest for twenty minutes then start walking again."

She set her backpack on the ground next to his and sat on the concrete beside him. After fishing out a bottle of water, she took several long swigs. She bathed her parched tongue in the liquid before swallowing.

"I've got a couple of extra MREs," he said. "You hungry?"

"What's an MRE?"

"Meal, Ready-to-Eat." He opened an olive-green vacuum-sealed pouch and grabbed a metal spork from his pack. "This one's chili mac."

"Seriously?"

"It's good stuff." He forked a spoonful into his mouth. "Want some?"

"No thanks."

"Suit yourself."

"Why are you helping me?" she blurted.

"Leave no man behind," he said.

"You don't even know me."

"Doesn't matter. Your dad's ex-military, so you're practically family. If you were my daughter, I would hope someone else would do the same for her."

"Do you have any kids?" she asked as she dug a granola bar out of her pack.

"Nope. Never had the pleasure."

"It's not too late. You're not that old."

"Thanks." He smirked.

"I didn't mean it like that," she stammered.

"It's okay. How about you, any kids?"

"No. I'm not old enough," she said.

"You have a narrow definition for when a person should have children," he said, amusement in his tone.

"I'm still in college. My mom made me swear not to get married until I have my degree."

"Smart mom."

"Have you ever been married?" she asked.

"Once."

When he didn't elaborate, her curiosity got the best of her.

"What happened?"

"Filed divorce papers when I was in Afghanistan."

"That's a shitty thing to do."

"Maybe. But she said she was sick of sitting at home worrying about whether or not officers would show up at her door with their hats in their hands."

"I guess I can understand that," she said. "But I always thought marriage was for life."

"It should be. People give up on it too easily these days. When I said 'until death do us part,' I meant it. But that was years ago. I've moved on."

She finished her granola bar in silence. Her boyfriend of three years had broken up with her right before prom her senior year of high school. The pain had nearly killed her and they weren't even married. She couldn't imagine what it would do to someone who had committed their life to the other person. She planned on waiting for the right man to come along. If she found the right person, she'd never have to get divorced.

"We should get back on the road soon," he said.

"We've got another thirty minutes to an hour before we get to the toll road."

"Sounds good."

When she stood, her swollen feet throbbed in protest. She'd tried to stick to her cardio routine since starting college, but studying seemed to get in the way more often than not. Now she wished she'd kept up her morning jogging routine. Packing on the first ten pounds of the "freshman fifteen" didn't help either.

When all this was over, she vowed to get back into running and eating healthy. Her unhealthy obsession with macaroni and cheese in a cup would have to end too.

As she pulled on her backpack, Derek retrieved a small flashlight from his pack.

"I don't want to have to use it, but I've got it handy just in case."

"I probably have one in my bag too. Should I get it out?" she asked.

"No. We should be fine for now. The sun's down, but the streetlights are still on. We'll reassess when we make it to the hills."

As they headed back toward Sand Canyon Avenue, distant gunfire set her on edge. They were safe for now, but for how long?

13

Luke drove white-knuckled through the intersection of Badger Flat Road and West Pacheco Boulevard. Red flames and black smoke darkened the sky over the shopping center. The Walmart parking lot writhed with looters. Men with bandanas over their noses and mouths shot pistols into the air. Women with overflowing shopping carts elbowed their way through the bands of marauders. Absolute chaos spilled across the street to the Target shopping center.

As Luke continued through the melee, a woman ran into the street directly in front of his car. She held her hands up and hollered at him to stop. He swerved around her, narrowly missing a man with a shotgun. He sped past the group. Trying to get gas in a town overrun with criminals would be impossible. He had enough gas to get to Buttonwillow, provided the 5 was open. If the highway patrol hadn't cleaned up the tanker truck spill, he'd be stuck.

He turned right on Pioneer Road and back-tracked to Highway 33. As he crossed the California Aqueduct, he checked the water level. The recent droughts had decimated California's water supply, but heavy rains earlier in the year had helped a bit. It looked half-full. Not bad. Worst case scenario, he could stop and refill his bottles later.

Two highway patrol cars blocked the northbound ramp of the 5 to Sacramento. They stood with their hands resting on their duty belts. They eyed him as he approached. He continued along the road onto the overpass toward the southbound ramp and another set of squad cars. He pulled to a stop a few feet from them.

The officers approached, one on each side of the car. Luke rolled down the driver's side window.

"Road closed?" Luke asked.

"Yes." The officer's gold plate name badge read *Franklin*.

"I heard there was a tanker truck spill a few days back," Luke said.

"That was cleaned up the same day."

"Why is the road closed now?"

"The National Guard and the military are using the road to send soldiers and supplies to LA. The freeway's closed all the way to LA," Franklin said.

"How long will it be closed?" Luke asked.

"Indefinitely."

"I'm trying to get home to my family in Orange County," Luke said.

"The 99's still open as far as I know. You could try it. But it might be closed off too."

"Can you radio someone and ask?"

"No. Radio communication is strictly emergency only right now," Franklin said.

"This is an emergency. I need to get to my family."

"I understand," Franklin said in a placating tone. "But I can't help you. Take 99 south and see if you can get closer. I doubt they're letting anyone through LA right now. You may want to find a hotel until the roads are open again."

Luke nodded and put the truck in reverse. Intellectually he understood their inability to help him, but emotionally, he wanted to grab their batons and beat the crap out of them until they radioed over to find out if 99 was open.

He drove away before he could enact his violent impulses.

A mile down the road, he pulled over. He took his

map out and began searching for an alternate route. He didn't want to drive fifty miles across to Highway 99. If it was closed, he'd lose a total of a hundred miles backtracking.

With his finger on the map, he drew multiple lines until he found an acceptable path. He could take back roads to cut around the south end of Los Banos and try Highway 33 south. It ran mostly parallel to Highway 5 so it wouldn't put him too far off track. He folded the map and set it on the seat next to him.

After pulling an illegal U-turn, he headed back toward the cutoff to Highway 33. One mile bled into the next as he headed south. He kept an eye on the gas tank gauge. The next big town was Coalinga, about sixty-five miles away. He'd stop there for gas. Running out of gas in the middle of nowhere was the last thing he needed.

With nothing to distract him, his thoughts turned to his family. By now, they had to be at the cabin. Liz was probably worried sick about him. He would have given anything to get one damn phone call through to her. Hearing her voice again would be enough to get him through any obstacle in his path.

They'd been through hard times during his deployments. He'd been in situations in which he couldn't have any communication with his family for weeks at a time. She'd stood by him even though she'd later confessed she'd been terrified he wouldn't come home. But he'd always come home.

In the worst sandbox dump in the worst mountains of Afghanistan, he'd used his family to get through blistery hot days and freezing nights. He'd pictured her face before every mission, silently vowing he'd stay in one piece so he could return home to the woman who kept his soul alive.

He swallowed against the swelling in his throat. The only time he ever got close to breaking was when he pictured his family without him. He shoved the image aside and replaced it with a mental picture of his kids. He was so proud of Sierra. She'd graduated in the top of her class in high school and now she wanted to be a scientist. Although his adorable little girl had grown into a smart young woman, she'd always be his little pumpkin.

And Kyle, a mini replica of him, was growing up too. He'd entered the terrible teens with a vengeance. He'd tried Luke's patience more than once, but his son had a good heart. Kyle was just acting out the way all teenagers did. Hopefully he wasn't giving his mom a hard time.

Luke sighed.

"I'm coming, guys. Just hang on. I'll be there soon," he said.

He gripped the steering wheel and squinted

against the sunlight. It wasn't even noon yet, but the temperature was spiking higher by the minute. He turned on the AC. It spit warm air into the cabin. He waited several minutes before giving up. Apparently the thugs hadn't changed their refrigerant. Ever.

"Assholes," he muttered.

Maybe he could do something about it in Coalinga.

Twenty-five miles north of his target, Highway 33 merged back onto Highway 5. The onramp was blocked by highway patrol. Luke didn't bother stopping. He used South Derrick Avenue to connect back onto Highway 33 fifteen miles south.

Ten miles later, he approached Coalinga. He pulled up to the first streetlight. It was out. Not even flashing. Weird.

He continued down the road toward the center of town. The electric signal at the second intersection was also out. He frowned and turned into a gas station. All of the electronic displays on the gas pumps were dark. A small snack shop attached to the gas station was also dark.

Movement in the store caught his attention. He stuffed his gun in his waistband and approached the front door.

LIZ GRIPPED the steering wheel with white-knuckled hands. As she turned onto El Toro Road, a black BMW blew through the red light in the opposite direction. She slammed on the brakes and skidded out of the reckless driver's way. The other car narrowly missed her before smashing into a light pole. She glanced in the rearview mirror. Normally she would have stopped, but since they'd left their home, people had been driving like it was Saturday night on a holiday weekend.

"That guy almost hit us," Kyle said as he turned to look behind them.

"I know."

"The cops just pulled up. That was fast."

"There's a sheriff's station up the road. They were probably headed to work," she said.

"Probably. People are driving psycho. Are we almost there?" Kyle asked.

In any other circumstance, she would have rolled her eyes, but not today.

"We're about ten minutes to the cutoff," she said.

As they approached Cook's Corner, her stomach rumbled. The scent of greasy French fries and mouth-watering cheeseburgers wafted out of the old-fashioned roadhouse.

In a small parking lot out front, men in motorcycle leathers stood around in groups. They stared at the truck as she drove past. Normally they'd be so engrossed in admiring each other's bikes that a stampede of elephants could pound by without garnering a second glance. The last few days were anything but typical.

She would have given anything to be able to stop for a basket of chili cheese fries. Diet be damned. As far as she was concerned, calories didn't count when all hell was breaking loose.

"Why aren't they at home?" Kyle asked.

"I don't know. Maybe they've got nowhere else to go."

"Everyone has somewhere to go," he said.

She couldn't begin to speculate on their lack of activity and didn't want to get into a debate.

The two-lane road twisted up into the hills. As they passed a neighborhood of million-dollar homes, she noted armed guards standing outside the gate. Interesting. Maybe they'd had a contingency plan in case something like this happened.

"Do you think Dad's okay?" Kyle asked.

"I hope so. If anyone can make it through this, it's your dad."

"What about Sierra?" he asked.

"She's probably at the cabin already."

"How long are we going to have to stay there?"

"At least a few weeks. Maybe longer. It depends

on a lot of things. The weather. The state of the world. How many supplies we have at the cabin. We'll know more when we get there."

"Can we listen to the radio?"

"Sure."

She turned on the car's radio. Static crackled through the speakers. After turning down the volume to a more manageable level, she searched through the FM channels.

"Hmm. Nothing's coming through," she said.

"Maybe we can find some news." He hit a button to change to AM stations. After scrolling through several stations, a weak signal broadcast an emergency broadcast message. "Nothing new there."

"Keep searching."

He cycled through more AM news channels. Several played the emergency broadcast message on repeat. Only one seemed to be broadcasting live.

"An executive order from the President of the United States has restricted gas sales to police and military personnel only. If you're heading out to get gas, turn around and head home. Residents in the vicinity of Los Angeles, San Francisco, New York, Miami, Chicago, Philadelphia, and Houston are advised to stay inside.

"Nuclear fallout will continue to be radioactive for several weeks. Stay inside. A basement or storm shelter is the best option. If you can't go underground, try to get

nine floors above ground level. Close your windows. Do not go outside. Exposure to high amounts of radiation is deadly. Stay safe, and God bless you."

She switched off the radio. Shock made her fingers tingle and her toes lose sensation. At least eight cities had been bombed. Eight! This wasn't an isolated incident. It wasn't just the West Coast. The entire country was under attack.

Sweat broke out on her forehead. She wiped it away with the back of her trembling hand.

"Are you okay, Mom?"

"Yes."

She had to remain calm for his sake. They were following the bug out plan. They'd make it to the cabin safely, and Luke and Sierra would meet them there. It would all work out. She had to stay positive. There was zero evidence that either Luke or Sierra were dead. If she gave in to fear now, she'd have a long road ahead of her.

The turnoff to Silverado Canyon appeared. She took a right at the road and within a minute passed a church. The parking lot was packed with cars and people. A large barbecue sent billowing smoke into the air. A man in an apron flipped burgers as they passed.

She continued down the road toward the Silverado Café. Its old-time Western façade and dirt parking lot was a nod to simpler times when you could head over after church and whittle away a Sunday afternoon amongst friends. Their cinnamon rolls were to die for. Her saliva glands clenched as moisture flooded her mouth. As soon as they got to the cabin, she'd make dinner.

Light faded faster in the canyons. Long, deep shadows stretched across the road. Old, gnarled oaks rose up on either side of the road, helping to hide country-style homes tucked into the hillside.

Up ahead, a handful of trucks barricaded the two-lane road. Five men in military-style gear held rifles or shotguns at their sides. Two more men sat on the tail-gate of a pickup. They all turned toward her as she approached. The men in the truck scrambled to grab their rifles.

"What the hell?" she muttered.

She slowed to five miles an hour. Without making any sudden movements, she reached for the pistol at her side. After carefully moving it into her lap, she pulled her shirt out of her pants and draped it over the gun.

"Don't say a word," she told Kyle. "Let me do all the talking."

"Okay." He nodded, eyes wide.

As she pulled to a stop five yards before the barricade, two of the men strode toward her. She rolled down the window.

"Put your hands up where we can see 'em," the guy with the shotgun said. Dressed in green and tan camo, the man could have stood on the side of the road and had no problem blending into the tree line.

She did as instructed.

"State your business," he said.

"We're headed up to our house." She opted to keep her explanation simple. Without knowing their purpose for barricading the road, she wasn't sure which line to take with them.

"Where do you live?"

"Up the mountain." For OPSEC reasons, she didn't give the exact location. She didn't want visitors later.

"I've never seen you here before," the man said. "You have any proof you live up there? Driver's license?"

"Yes."

As she leaned over to grab her purse, the man stepped back and brought his gun up.

"Slow down there," he said. "Nice and slow."

She frowned as she pulled her purse into her lap. Her driver's license listed the address of the property they owned. Luke had insisted they each carry an ID with a different address in case they ever needed it.

The canyons were prone to wildfires and the fire department wouldn't let non-residents past roadblocks in an evacuation situation. She'd thought he was being paranoid; now she was glad he'd insisted on it.

After handing the ID to the man, she rested her hand on the butt of her gun. He was too busy studying the ID to notice.

"Says it expired last month," he said.

"It did?" she asked, genuinely surprised.

"Yeah. I can't let you back there."

"But it's my house," she said. "You can't stop me from going back there. Are you sheriff's deputies?"

"No."

"Any kind of law enforcement?"

"No." The man snorted. "We're in a without rule of law situation. Haven't you seen the news?"

"Of course I have."

"Well then, you know shit's hit the fan. People are heading for the hills. We're not letting them into the canyon. We've got to protect our own."

She pressed her lips together.

"We'll let you turn around this time, but don't come back. We'll shoot on sight if we catch you up here again," he said. "Are we clear?"

"Crystal."

"All right. Good luck to you."

She bit her tongue and rolled up the window. Assholes. What right did they have to keep her from accessing her own home?

As she made a three-point turn on the narrow road, her chest tightened. She wasn't one to back down from an unfair situation, but they outnumbered her and certainly outgunned her. Even if she could somehow manage to shoot two guns at once, she'd have the firepower of seven men blasting back at her. It wasn't a survivable scenario.

She'd have to find another way to get to the cabin. With twilight descending, she wasn't sure she could find another route up the mountain. If she didn't figure something out soon, they'd be trapped in the dark in the middle of nowhere.

14

Sierra's leaden feet dragged with each step. They'd been walking for several hours when she finally couldn't take another step. She stopped. After dropping her Bug Out Bag on the sidewalk, she leaned back against a block wall.

"I need a break."

"Let's cross the toll road and find the trail, then we can stop," Derek said.

"I can't. My feet are killing me."

"We're too exposed here. We're only a block away from the nearest houses. The toll road is less than a mile away. After we cross it, we'll be at the foothills."

"I can't do another mile," she said. "I'm not sure if I can even go ten more feet."

"If someone from those houses came out with a gun, would you be able to run?" he asked.

"Of course." She didn't want to get shot. What a stupid question.

"Well then you can walk another mile," he snapped. "Pick up the bag and move out."

As she reached for her bag, she grumbled under her breath. Derek hadn't even broken a sweat as far as she could tell. Based on his ripped biceps and thick neck, he probably spent half his day at the gym. He obviously couldn't understand her pain. How could he? The man was a machine.

Step after step, the blisters on her feet sent sharp waves of pain up her legs. By the time they reached the overpass to the toll road, she was ready to ditch him and take her chances alone. She pulled her phone out of her pocket to check the time. Two-thirty a.m.

"The trailhead is on the other side of the bridge," he said.

"Lead the way," she said with as much fake enthusiasm as she could muster.

When they reached the dirt trail, she followed him around the first curve. The coastal sage scrub landscape was comprised mainly of small bushes and long grasses. When she was in high school, she'd come out with some hippy tree-huggers to gather sage for a group project. The hiking part was fun, but after an hour, she'd been ready to head home. If she could have found sage at the mall, she wouldn't have wasted a day searching for it in the hills.

"Let's stop here," Derek said.

"Thank God."

She dropped her pack in the center of the trail and sat down next to it. She pulled a bottle of water out and drank the whole thing. Maybe she should have conserved some, but she was so thirsty.

Derek sat across from her. In the darkness, she couldn't read his expression, but she didn't have to. She could feel his frustration. Guilt niggled at her. If she'd been in better shape, they would have made it farther by now. She was slowing them down.

After a few minutes of silence, Derek unzipped his pack.

"If we kept walking tonight, could you make it another ten miles?" he asked.

"Honestly? No."

"I was hoping to make it farther, but maybe we should camp here for the night. It's a fairly safe location and we're at about the halfway point. We can get up at first light and be home to our families by tomorrow afternoon."

Tears formed in her eyes. She couldn't wait to get to the cabin. Her mom and brother were probably already there. Maybe her dad was there too.

"Do you have a tarp or anything like that in your bag?" he asked.

"Let me check."

She opened her pack and began unloading it. She couldn't see much, so she flicked on her mini LED tactical flashlight and set it face up on the ground. It fell over so she hooked it into the crease of her leg.

"Point it down," he said.

"Why?"

"Someone could see the light."

"Oh."

She laid the flashlight on her thigh and angled the beam toward the ground. She pulled an emergency space blanket out of the pack along with a lightweight tarp. After digging past the first aid kit, she found a roll of 550 paracord. She set it on the tarp.

"I've got stuff to make a tent," she said.

"Do you know how to do it?"

"Yeah. My dad taught me. We need to find a couple of trees."

"Let's see if we can find a small grove. It will give us protection from the wind and help hide us if people come down the trail," he said.

"Okay."

She stood and grabbed the flashlight.

"Here, let me show you how to hold it so that you give off less light," he said.

She handed it to him. He cupped his hand over the top of it, only letting a small shaft of light escape.

"Got it," she said.

"Let's check over there first." He pointed toward a darker spot farther into the hills.

She gathered up her belongings and followed him. After searching for ten minutes, they found a small grove of old California Live Oaks. Some of their gnarled branches dipped down to touch the earth, while others reached out to form a canopy of cover.

"This is perfect," she said.

"Absolutely. Let's use this tree for both tents. There are plenty of good, sturdy branches."

"Okay."

She unloaded her tent-making gear and grabbed the 550 paracord. After tying a taut-line hitch knot around one branch, she secured the other side with a threaded figure eight knot. She walked across the ground, kicking away rocks and any other sharp objects. Satisfied with the ground, she unrolled the tarp and tossed it over the line.

She returned to her pack and searched for tent pegs. When she couldn't find them, she looked over at Derek.

"You don't happen to have extra tent pegs, do you?" she asked.

"No. Try using rocks."

She searched through the pile of rocks she'd kicked out of her way. After grabbing the largest ones, she used them to stake down the edges of the tent. She grabbed the space blanket and laid it on the ground under the tent. It would have to work as a sleeping bag.

She crawled under the tent and dragged her bag to the edge. She retrieved the first aid kit. When she pulled her shoes off, her feet began to swell almost immediately.

"Crap."

"What?" he asked.

"My feet are a wreck."

"Blisters?"

"Yeah."

"Do you have any moleskin?"

"Uh…" She searched through the bag. "Yep."

"If you have antibacterial wipes, use those first then apply the moleskin."

"Okay."

She followed his directions and had the blisters covered in no time. Her feet were still sweaty, so she didn't put her shoes or socks back on.

Derek crawled into his tent.

"You did good today," he said. "Get some rest. Tomorrow we're going home."

"Thanks. And thank you for rescuing me. I don't

know what I would have done if you hadn't come along."

"You'll be much safer when you're with a group. Traveling alone right now is just asking to be robbed, or worse."

"I can't believe everyone's going crazy already," she said.

"It's only been a couple of days. In another week, people will start to realize we're in a bad situation and they will get desperate."

"Won't everything go back to normal once they stop bombing us?" she asked.

"I don't know." He turned off his flashlight. "Goodnight."

"Goodnight."

She lay back on the blanket. It was super thin and did little to cushion her from the ground. Even though she'd cleared the area, small pebbles and pieces of bark poked up. She tossed and turned, trying to find a comfortable position.

Unable to find one, she sat up and rifled through her bag. She found an extra T-shirt and a thin pair of long underwear. She rolled them into a ball and stuffed it under her head. She punched the wad and rolled onto her side. She closed her eyes and waited to fall asleep.

And waited.

And waited.

Derek's soft and steady breaths mocked her. Of course he'd sleep like a baby. He didn't even need it. He could probably walk forty miles and not need a break. She huffed and rolled onto her back. She folded her arms across her chest and glared at the top of the tent.

A week ago her life had been close to perfect. Now she was stuck in a tent, trying to survive the apocalypse. She couldn't wait to get to the cabin. At least she'd have a bed, unlimited access to water, and tons of food. She hadn't realized how much she'd miss civilization once it had been taken away from her. Thank God her dad had turned into a crazy prepper. She shuddered to think of what might have happened if he hadn't.

LUKE PULLED on the door to the gas station's snack shop. It didn't budge. Locked. He cupped his hands together and peered into the darkness. An old man in worn jeans and a loose, gray T-shirt stepped out from one of the aisles. He walked up to the door.

"Power's out," he yelled through the glass. "The pumps and the register are out."

"How long have they been out?" Luke asked.

"An hour or two."

"Any idea what happened?"

"The power plant stopped running. Word is they were hit this morning."

"With what?" Luke asked.

"A bomb. Not a nuke though or we'd all be shadows on the floor."

"They're dropping bombs now?"

"Damn Commies," the man grumbled. "We should have hit first."

"Who is it? Who's attacking us?"

"The Russians. I knew it would be them. Everyone's been going on about North Korea for the last year, but they're a blip on the map compared to Russia."

"I thought it might be the Chinese," Luke said.

"No. They're taking over all our real estate. Much smarter. They don't have to drop a single bomb. All they have to do is keep buying up our land. My daughter can't even buy a place and she's got a good job. The Chinese came in and propped the housing market up so Americans can't afford to buy our own houses. Isn't that some bullshit?"

Luke nodded. He'd had a hell of a time trying to find a house in Orange County. All of the new homes were listed at around a million dollars and the older homes sold faster than you could bid on them. Mostly to investors.

"Anyway, sorry I can't help you out," the man said before turning and walking farther into the store.

"Wait!"

"What?" the man asked as he returned to the door.

"I have cash."

"I still can't get the pumps to work without power."

"Can I get some food and water?"

"Let me see the cash." The man fixed his wary gaze on Luke.

"I'll be right back."

Luke jogged back to the truck and grabbed a hundred dollars from his pack. He had more but didn't want to let on. He couldn't afford to spend it all now, not when he was still hundreds of miles from home.

As he walked back to the store, a teenage boy on a skateboard rolled past. The kid stared at him with narrowed, hawk-like eyes before continuing on his way. A chill ran down Luke's spine. It reminded him of the lookouts he'd encountered in Afghanistan.

Luke hurried back to the store, not wanting to linger.

"Here." Luke discreetly showed him the cash. "I'll only be a minute."

"You alone?"

"Yeah."

The man reached into his pocket to retrieve a key. After unlocking the door, he stepped back to allow Luke to pass. The man locked the door behind them.

"Stick to the inner aisles," the man said. "I don't want people thinking the store's open. I had to shoot at some looters last night."

Luke noted the bags under the man's eyes. He looked as if he hadn't slept in days, which may have been the truth.

"I'll get you a basket."

After the man wandered off, Luke canvassed the store. The usual supply of beef jerky, potato chips, and trail mix greeted him.

"You're lucky the place hasn't been ransacked," Luke said.

"I've got a gun," the man said.

Luke spun around to find the man at the end of the aisle holding a basket. A shotgun attached to a two point configuration sling hung across his shoulder. The muzzle pointed down and to the left, not in a threatening position, but the sudden appearance of the weapon put Luke on high alert. Trusting anyone at this point would be a mistake, so he kept an eye on the shop owner while he took the basket from him.

Jumpy and ready to pull his pistol at the slightest provocation, Luke quickly filled the basket. He took all the high-calorie bags first, then added as many candy bars as he could find. They weren't the best for nutrition, but he'd need the calories. Stopping at McDonald's was out of the question. Even if he found one open, he wouldn't want to wait around for his food. It would put him in too precarious a position if shit went down.

A radio squawked behind the counter at the front of the shop.

"CQ CQ calling CQ this is W7SHTF, Whiskey-Seven-Sierra-Hotel-Tango-Foxtrot. W7SHTF, Whiskey-Seven-Sierra-Hotel-Tango-Foxtrot beaming west from Las Vegas. Over. CQ CQ calling on twenty meters. W7SHTF listening."

The shop owner hurried over to the radio and picked up a large microphone. "Hey, how you are W7SHTF? This is W6NAH, Whiskey-Six-November-Alpha-Hotel. My name's Rick. Romeo-India-Charlie-Kilo. Over."

"Hey Rick! You are five by nine. Name here's Cody. Charlie-Oscar-Delta-Yankee. We're located in Las Vegas. Over."

"You're five by nine. Good signal coming

through. We're located in Coalinga, California, about two hundred miles north of Los Angeles. Over."

"How are things there? Over," Cody said.

"Power's out but can't complain," Rick said. "How about you? Over."

"Haven't been nuked yet. Not holding my breath though. I figured we'd be one of the first to go. Sin city and all. Over."

"Let's hope they ran out of nukes. Over."

"God willing. Over."

Luke half-listened to the men's conversation as he piled his haul onto the counter. He glanced out the window to make sure there wasn't anyone outside. It was still clear, but he didn't want to waste too much time.

After stacking what he guessed to be about a hundred dollars' worth of food and water, he motioned toward Rick.

"Cody, it's been great talking to you, but I've got to run. Keep your family safe. I'll be praying for you. This is W6NAH. Clear."

"This is W7SHTF. Clear."

"I can't scan any of that," Rick said as he set the microphone down. "But I'm guessing it's about right. Let's call it even."

"Sounds good to me. How long have you been an amateur radio operator?" Luke asked.

"My whole life. My dad taught me how after I watched *Pump Up the Volume* with Christian Slater."

"I love that movie. It was one of the last ones I saw before I shipped out to basic training."

"Army?"

"Navy."

"A squid, huh?" Rick teased.

"Hey, at least I'm not a knuckle-dragging jarhead," Luke jabbed back.

"Where'd you serve?"

"A tour in Afghanistan, two in the Sandbox."

"And you still have all your limbs?" Rick asked.

"For the most part. I think I've still got a few pieces of shrapnel where the sun don't shine."

Rick laughed until he doubled over, wiping at his eyes.

"You okay?" Luke asked.

"Yeah. It just brings back memories. I was in before your time."

"'Nam?"

"Yeah."

"Hell of a war."

They fell silent for several seconds, both lost in memories.

"You didn't pick up much water," Rick said as he bagged the snacks.

"Ten gallons should hold me for a few days. I've got a LifeStraw if I need it."

"Grab a few more gallons on the way out. On me."

"You don't have to do that," Luke said.

"Well…" Rick walked around the counter and slapped him on the back. "I figure you're Navy, so you'll need all the help you can get."

Luke laughed until his cheeks hurt. He hadn't found a moment of humor since he'd left San Jose. It felt good to let go of all the stress and fear for a couple of minutes.

As he and Rick loaded the food and water into his truck, his heart felt lighter. He was fully capable of getting home to his family. The government could throw up a hundred roadblocks and he'd still make it, especially now that he was fully supplied.

"You take care," Rick said as he slammed the tailgate.

"You too."

Back on the road, Luke turned onto Jayne Avenue toward Highway 33. Flat, barren fields stretched across both sides of the highway. The road crossed over an old, dried-out river bed. A smattering of dry sagebrush and anemic trees did little to break up the landscape.

A flash of orange in the distance caught his attention. As he drove closer, the bright splotch of color took shape. And when he realized what he was looking at, he grabbed his gun from the passenger seat. He checked to make sure there was a round in the chamber before leveling it at the prisoner in the orange jumpsuit.

15

Liz backtracked past the café until she reached an unmarked dirt road. Gravel rumbled under the truck's tires. The truck's headlights cut through the darkness to illuminate a rocky trail wide enough for a car, but not much else. As she drove past gnarled oaks, she gripped the wheel.

"Keep your eyes out for any other cars," she said.

"What about people?" Kyle asked.

"Them too."

They continued on in silence for the next two miles. She kept the speed under twenty miles per hour so she would not miss the fire road junction. Dry brush and long wild grasses supplied fuel for occasional wildfires.

In October 2007, as many as one million people

had been forced to evacuate their homes as thirty fires burned in the mountains of Southern California. It had taken nineteen days to put out all of the fires. Unmarked access roads for firefighters crisscrossed the mountain. She hoped to make use of them to get to the cabin.

"I'm hungry," Kyle said.

"Me too."

"Is there any food in our bags?"

"Yeah, but do you think you can wait until we get to the house?" she asked.

"I guess."

His dejected tone ignited her motherly instinct. She wasn't about to let her son suffer while she tried to find the right road.

"Grab one of the backpacks," she said.

He hauled one into the front seat.

"Open it up and look for the granola bars. You can have some of those for now. We'll have dinner when we get to the cabin," she said.

"Okay."

He retrieved a bar and tore into it. He'd had a huge growth spurt over the summer and had turned into a little trash compactor. When it came to food, if it wasn't nailed down, he ate it. She didn't mind the extra-large grocery bills. As long as he was healthy, she wasn't worried.

"Whoa!" Kyle pointed toward the right side of the truck. "There's a cabin over there."

She tried to place it, but it didn't look familiar. Even though they were at least a couple of hundred yards away, she could clearly make out the family's movement inside. They had the place lit up like a Christmas tree. Anyone passing by would be able to easily count how many people were inside.

"When we get to the cabin, we have to keep the lights off," she said.

"Why?"

"OPSEC."

"OP-what?"

"Operational Security."

"Sounds like something Dad would say."

"We learned about it together," she said.

"What is it?"

"OPSEC is basically making sure you don't give out any information about your location and resources. You don't want anyone else to know how much you have and where you have it, because if things get bad, those people will come to take your stuff."

"We've got a ton of guns. No one's going to take our stuff," he said.

"Even with guns, we don't want to have to shoot people unless we're in danger. Wouldn't it be better if no one knew where we were, or what we had?"

"I guess so."

"Don't worry. No one knows about the cabin except us. We've taken steps to keep it well hidden."

"What if someone finds it on Google Maps?" he asked.

"Google hasn't sent its fleet of spy cars out into the canyons yet. I doubt they'll be doing it anytime soon either," she said.

"Spy cars? Cool! I want a spy car!"

"We might have to turn this into a spy car soon," she said.

"So people can't see us?"

"Exactly. When did you get so smart?"

"Duh, Mom. I read stuff online."

She suppressed a shudder. God only knew what he'd read online. Although she'd done her best to restrict his internet usage with child-friendly blocking software, some kids were smart enough to bypass the system.

Last month, Kyle had been at a friend's house when one of the other boys had pulled up an adult site. She had already had the birds and the bees talk with her son, but what he'd seen had led to an extremely uncomfortable discussion about sexual consent. He wasn't allowed to spend time with that particular child anymore. His friend's mom had been mortified and had also banned the other child from playing with her son.

As Kyle happily munched on the granola bar, she focused on the road. They had to be close to the second cutoff.

Up ahead, two bright, shining eyes flashed in her headlights. The startled horse galloped off into the darkness. She eased off the gas and rolled forward, checking for other animals. Wild horses didn't live in these hills, but maybe someone's fence was down.

A weed-covered dirt road appeared. She turned onto it and cut the headlights so only the running lights stayed lit. It wasn't the best option for traveling at night, but there were several cabins up ahead, and she didn't want them to see the truck.

When she reached the edge of the property for the first cabin, she studied the dark structure. No lights or movement. Maybe the owners didn't live there year-round. Or maybe they were inside hiding.

She kept moving forward, passing two more unlit cabins before turning onto the final road toward her cabin. She navigated around a thirty-foot-tall natural rock formation that jutted out of the side of the hill. When she and Luke had scouted possible Bug Out Locations, they'd fallen in love with this parcel. Not only did it have a natural wall of protection, but a spring-fed stream ran across the back of the property, giving them unlimited access to water.

As she swerved around the rock wall, a thick, seemingly natural grove of trees came into view. Beyond the trees, they'd cleared a twenty-five foot radius around the cabin both for fire protection, and for visibility. No one could sneak up on them if they had someone on watch.

They'd built the cabin on a patch of higher ground for security purposes, and also to avoid any possible flooding. Although the stream didn't change much through the seasons, all it would take was one good rain to make it overflow its shallow banks.

The cabin didn't come into view until she'd driven through the grove. It was highly unlikely anyone had ever found the cabin, but she wasn't taking any chances.

"Stay in the car while I check on the house," she said.

"Why?"

"I want to make sure it's clear."

"You're so paranoid, Mom. You said no one but us knows about it."

"I know, but I want to check it out anyway," she said.

"Don't shoot Dad or Sierra by accident."

"I won't. Stay here."

"I'm hungry."

"We'll eat after we unload."

"Well hurry up so we can unload this crap."

"Kyle!"

"Stuff."

"That's better."

She flicked off the overhead light switch so that it wouldn't turn on when she opened the car door. Not that it would matter much. If anyone was inside, they'd hear her coming. If it was Luke or Sierra, they'd know to signal her. But if it was someone else, she would be an open target until she could clear the cabin.

In a crouched position, gun in hand, she hurried up the steps and stepped to the left side of the front door. She knocked, then listened for any hint of movement. A squatter wouldn't answer the door, but he would make some kind of sound when he came to investigate.

She waited a full minute. The silent canyon made it easy to hear anything that might be out of place. When she didn't hear anyone, she carefully pulled the key to the cabin from her pocket. She used her non-dominant hand to unlock the door. She held the gun close to her side, ready to begin the sweep.

As she pushed open the door, the muscles in her arms flexed. She flicked on the small flashlight mounted to the gun and pointed it inside. In a slow arc across the door, she swept from right to left. She didn't take another step until she'd thoroughly cleared the first section. Using this process, she was able to clear the main room and the kitchen, leaving the downstairs bedroom and loft.

She slid along the wall as she approached the open bedroom door. After repeating the sweeping process, she cleared the room, under the bed, and the closet. She climbed the stairs to the loft and found it empty. Nothing seemed out of place.

After holstering her gun, she headed out to the truck. Kyle opened the door.

"Find any serial killers?" he joked.

"Nope. All clear."

"Any sign of Dad or Sierra?"

"No," she said softly, not wanting to think about possible implications.

"Can we eat now?"

"Unload first. I want to hide the truck in the shed."

Kyle frowned, but didn't complain. Instead, he opened the back door and let Justice out. The dog had slept through most of the ride, including the stop at the roadblock. So much for an attentive guard dog.

A single pocket flashlight glowed on its lowest setting, giving them just enough light to see the steps.

She and Kyle worked quickly to unload all the gear. Ten minutes later, she set the last bag full of guns down next to the rest of the arsenal in the living room.

"I'm going to move the truck. Don't turn the lights on."

"Then can we eat?"

"Yes. Go look in the cupboard and find some chili."

"Yum!"

She moved the truck into a large shed they'd constructed behind the cabin. From the outside it didn't look like much, but inside, they had everything they needed to stay out here for months. She'd never thought they'd have to use the cabin as a bunker, but now she was grateful they'd had a plan.

THE INCESSANT CHIRP of a million crickets kept Sierra awake. She tossed and turned on the hard ground, wishing she was back in her bed at the apartment. For the first time since she'd started her journey, she couldn't stop wondering what she'd find when she reached the cabin. If she got there and her family wasn't there, then what?

She sighed and rolled onto her back. At least the

Santa Ana winds were keeping her warm. If she'd been stuck out here in December or January, she'd be freezing her butt off.

A branch snapped.

She bolted up. Heart-pounding fear stole her breath.

What was that? An animal? Another human? Maybe it was Derek.

She crawled to the edge of the tent and peeked out into the darkness. Her eyes had adjusted to the lack of light hours ago, so she could see across to Derek's tent. His feet poked out of the end of the tent, but he wasn't moving. If he hadn't caused the noise, then who had?

Another crack fractured the stillness of the night. She flinched.

Her father had warned her over and over never to go hiking in the mountains alone. Mountain lions stalked and killed bicyclists. Attacks were very rare, but on foot, she wouldn't stand a chance. Was it a mountain lion? She strained to listen for the sound.

A branch snapped about twenty feet from the tent. She was a sitting duck. The tent wouldn't provide any protection. In fact, it might hinder her escape if the mountain lion leapt onto the tarp, tangling her up in it.

"Derek," she whispered.

He didn't move.

"Derek…are you awake?"

When he didn't respond, she slowly unzipped her backpack. She fished around until she found a multi-tool. She opened the knife and held it close to her chest with the blade pointing away. If the mountain lion attacked, she'd do what she could to protect herself. It might not work, but what choice did she have?

She sat in terrified silence for the next ten minutes.

When the crickets stopped chirping, her bottom lip trembled.

The slow crack of another branch sent chills down her spine. Was that a footstep? Maybe it wasn't an animal, maybe it was another person. They weren't *that* far from the road. She should have tried to walk farther into the mountains. They would have been safer.

"Sierra?" Derek whispered.

"Yeah." Relief poured through her.

"I thought I heard something," he said.

"Me too."

"A branch cracking?"

"Yes."

"Do you have a weapon?" he asked.

"A knife. But it's not very big."

"Better than nothing."

"Definitely," she said.

"Stay in the tent. I'll go check it out."

"No way. I'm going with you."

"Okay, but do everything I say as soon as I say it. Clear?"

"Yes."

He crawled out of the tent. A glint of light bounced off the steel of his gun. She let out a shaky breath. At least they had some protection.

"Stay behind me," he whispered.

She moved to stand directly behind him. Any closer and they'd be touching.

As he moved out from underneath the giant oak, she turned to check behind them. The faint glow of light from the city created twisted shadows. She squinted and strained, searching for movement.

She matched him step for step. After searching the immediate area, they continued out another thirty feet. He stopped so abruptly that she smacked into his back.

"Sorry."

"Shh."

Thirty seconds passed.

"Hear anything?" he whispered.

"No."

"Me either. I'm going to turn on my flashlight."

"But if it's another person they'll see us."

"If someone else is out there, they already know our location. They would have attacked by now."

"What if it's a mountain lion?"

"It would have pounced while we were sleeping," he said.

"I wasn't sleeping."

"Me either."

"Yes you were," she said. "I tried to wake you up, but you didn't respond."

"Maybe I slept a few minutes, but not much longer."

He flicked on the flashlight attached to the bottom of his gun. As the light swept over the area, she tensed, ready to run at the first sign of danger.

"There," he said, directing the light to a fresh pile of animal droppings. "Either coyote or mountain lion."

"Do you think it's going to come back?"

"If it's a coyote, probably not. They usually hunt in packs and I only see evidence of one."

"And if it's a mountain lion?" she asked.

"We should sleep in shifts. I'll take first shift."

"I don't think I'll be able to sleep."

"You need to get some rest. We've got a ten-mile hike ahead of us tomorrow. You won't be able to do it if you don't sleep," he said.

"I'll try."

When they returned to their campsite, she crawled back into the tent. She lay on her side, curled into a ball. He sat in the space between the tents. She closed her eyes. Every sound seemed amplified, as if she were listening through a stethoscope.

As the wind picked up, leaves fluttered against the tarp. In the distance, a coyote howled. When his pack joined the howl, the hair on the back of her neck prickled. Derek had said they'd be safe unless the coyotes were in a pack. They sounded far away, but she didn't have any experience judging distance. And how fast could they run? Maybe distance didn't matter.

"Do you hear them?" she asked.

"Yeah. They're not close. At least a mile or two away."

"My dad used to take me hiking out here when I was little," she said. "We saw coyotes in the distance, never up close."

"You're not sleeping," he said dryly.

"I'm trying."

"Talking isn't going to help."

"It will help me be less freaked out," she said. "Do you do a lot of camping?"

"My parents used to take me car camping at O'Neil Park," he said. "We'd go on holiday weekends and for a few days here and there during the summer. It's been a long time since our last trip. Probably a decade."

"Why so long?"

"Work. Life. Things get busy and you forget to maintain your most important relationships," he said.

"Don't you talk to them?" she asked.

"We used to talk a lot more, but life got in the way. Now I wish I'd made more time for them. I hope to God they're okay."

"I'm sorry I slowed us down."

"Don't be. It's actually kind of nice to have a traveling companion. I spend so much time alone that sometimes I forget what it's like to interact with another person. Maybe I'm turning feral." He laughed softly.

"What do you do for work?" she asked.

"I'm a firefighter."

"Seriously?"

She raked her gaze across his broad shoulders. No wonder he was ripped. He could pull off a hot "Men of Firefighting" calendar. Her cheeks burned. Thank God he probably couldn't see her well enough to catch it.

"Yep," he said.

"Why? It's a dangerous job."

"When I was in the Marines overseas, my best

friend's house burned down. Electrical fire. He was out of town on business. It killed his whole family." He paused as his voice gave out. "I was just drifting through life trying to figure out what to do after my tour was over. As soon as I heard the news, I knew. I didn't want anyone else to go through that kind of pain. Even though it wasn't his fault, he never forgave himself. Two years ago, he shot himself. He couldn't let go of the guilt."

"But it wasn't his fault."

"Doesn't matter," he said. "He'd convinced himself that he would have been able to save them if he'd been home. I doubt it. I saw the investigation reports. It started with a faulty heater. They'd died from carbon monoxide poisoning before the fire started."

"That's terrible," she said.

"Yeah."

Several minutes passed in silence. She couldn't imagine the hell his friend had been through. But was anything worth taking your own life?

She shook her head. No way.

"If you're not going to sleep," he said, "do you mind taking over while I do?"

"Sure."

As the night dragged on, she couldn't stop thinking about his friend and the fire. No matter how bad things got, she'd never kill herself. She couldn't imagine the pain it would cause her family. The world seemed to be falling apart, but she wouldn't let it destroy her. She wasn't a victim, she was a survivor. Now all she had to do was figure out how to survive a ten-mile hike after a sleepless night.

16

Luke slammed his foot onto the gas pedal and blasted past the prisoner in the orange jumpsuit. He glanced in the rearview mirror for a split second, and when he returned his attention forward, a gunshot blasted through the front window. It punched through the passenger seat's headrest before whizzing through the back window.

Four men in orange jumpsuits stood across the center of the road. They each leveled an AR-15 at him. Luke skidded onto the dirt shoulder, kicking up a barrage of gravel. He clipped the man on the far right, sending him flying into a field. The other three turned their weapons on him. They unleashed a firestorm of bullets, puncturing the tailgate and destroying what was left of the rear window.

Head down, breath heaving, Luke tried to feel the road under the tires. He couldn't risk looking up. One good shot would kill him. He'd never see his family again. But he'd walk through hell before he let that happen.

He flew down the road toward a large sign that read Pleasant Valley State Prison. A riot of orange jumpsuits blocked the road ahead. There was too many of them. The five men behind him ran toward him. The mob of escapees closed in from the front.

Move! Now!

As he fishtailed into a U-turn, the rear tire caught on the lip of the pavement. When it released, the truck lurched forward. His chest slammed against the steering wheel. Half-expecting an airbag to the face, he instinctively brought his hand up.

Pop-pop-pop-pop-pop.

Bullets blasted across the hood. He lifted his pistol and shot through the broken window. He took down two of the five men before driving straight into a third. The prisoner flew over the hood. He got caught on the jagged edges of the front window. His torso hung over the dashboard; his face landed on the passenger seat. Blood dripped down the glass onto the dashboard.

Luke shot him in the head. If the guy wasn't dead before, he sure as hell was now.

An AR-15 hung from the guy's shoulder. Luke shoved him to the side and yanked at the rifle. The man's body pinned the gun against the seat. Luke cursed and gave up on trying to get it.

After skidding onto the turnoff to Highway 33, Luke blew past another gaggle of prisoners. He had no idea what had happened at the prison, but it must have been due to the power outage. He didn't care and didn't have time to contemplate it. If he didn't get as far away from the prison as possible, he'd be toast. He'd already used up eight of his nine lives in the gunfight, so he wasn't about to tempt fate.

He didn't take a full breath for fifteen miles. The putrid scent of the prisoner's now-empty bowels mixed with the metallic scent of blood. He gagged and pulled over to the side of the road. As he stumbled into the empty dirt field, his stomach heaved, expelling its contents in an arc of mottled orange.

The retching continued for a full minute until his stomach cramped in protest. He spit and wiped the back of his hand across his mouth.

When he turned around, the dead man's vacant stare locked with his. A fresh wave of nausea consumed him. He bent forward, dry-heaving until blood pounded through his ears.

He forced himself to picture his kid's faces. They gave him the strength to fight like hell. He hadn't survived an impossible situation because he was a SEAL. He'd survived because he was a father.

The prisoner weighed a good two hundred and fifty pounds of solid muscle. It was like trying to move a water buffalo. But he couldn't keep driving around with a corpse. He considered getting his knife out and hacking away at the man's limbs to make him easier to move, but the gruesomeness of the task gave him pause.

He grabbed the man's legs and pulled. With the help of gravity, he was able to get the man to move a few inches. But the body was snagging on something.

Luke used the step rail on the side of the truck as leverage to push the man's torso up and over the glass shards in the window. Apparently he'd been caught on some of the intact pieces.

Once free from the window, the man slid down the side of the hood and crumpled to the ground like a broken marionette.

Satisfied, Luke yanked one of the man's tennis shoes off and used it to clear the glass out of the passenger side. He pounded the remaining glass out of the window seal. He couldn't risk having it fall and slice him up while he was driving. A chunk of glass to the face wouldn't do him any favors.

Blood spatter covered the interior. It soaked into the ragged upholstery, creating crimson stains. More blood seeped along the seams to pool on the floorboard.

He couldn't drive a homicide scene into Buttonwillow. The locals would have a shit-fit. After tearing a piece of the man's jumpsuit off, Luke did his best to clear off some of the blood. It smeared and spread with each wipe. He cursed and grabbed a small bottle of water from his food supply. He tore off more jumpsuit and used it along with the water to mop up the rest of the blood. It wasn't perfect, but it looked a lot better than it had ten minutes ago.

He also couldn't afford to have people asking questions. As far as he knew, he'd killed at least three prisoners. Maybe more. He'd been defending himself against eminent danger, but it would be a hard sell without witnesses. The truck looked like it had hit a deer. He could have used that as a cover story *if* there were deer in this part of California. Unfortunately, there weren't.

Luke picked up the AR-15 and ejected the magazine. It felt light, maybe five rounds left, but better than nothing. He slammed it back into the gun. He laid it on the passenger's seat for easy access.

He used the rest of the water bottle to wash the blood off of his hands and face. His shirt was saturated from carrying the man. Suffocated by the pungent odor of blood and sweat, he stripped off his shirt. He dug through his Get Home Bag and grabbed a spare camo-green T-shirt.

He'd smelled worse and had been through worse in Iraq. But he wasn't in the Middle East. He was in America. And in the span of three days, he'd been ambushed, shot at, wounded, and he'd only traveled two hundred miles so far. When he reached Buttonwillow, he'd have over one hundred and fifty miles to go, if he got lucky. If they didn't have the interstate closed.

After cracking open a fresh water bottle, he pulled a picture of his wife and kids out of his bag. He ran a thumb over their faces.

"I'm coming home," he whispered. "Stay safe until I get there."

He slid the picture back into a Ziploc bag and returned it to his pack.

The adrenaline had worn off, leaving him shaky and hungry. He tore into a Snickers and polished off a bag of beef jerky. According to his map, he was 72 miles away from Buttonwillow. He'd have to pass through the small towns of Avenal and Reef Station. He prayed he wouldn't run into any more trouble along the way.

LIZ STRUCK a match and lit the candle in the center of the table. Flickering light illuminated two bowls of chili. Kyle leaned over his bowl and shoveled steaming food into his mouth. She poked at her chili. As soon as they'd arrived at the cabin, the adrenaline of fleeing their home wore off, leaving her shaky and exhausted. But she couldn't sleep until they'd at least secured the house.

"After dinner, I'm going to set up trip wires in the forest," she said.

"Can I help?"

"No. I want you to stay in the house. Barricade the door after I leave. I won't be gone too long."

"Are we going to set up traps and stuff?" he asked.

"We'll do more to fortify the area tomorrow. We should be safe tonight as long as we weren't followed. It's highly unlikely anyone knows we're here. No one should even know the cabin exists."

"What if someone finds us?"

"You'll be safe inside," she said. "I'll take the shotgun with me. But I don't want you to worry. Everything's going to be fine."

She spoke with more conviction than she felt. They were out in the woods, miles away from anyone they knew. Sure, they had guns and ways of barricading the doors, but if someone was determined enough, would she be able to hold him off?

She swallowed and directed her attention to the chili. Spicy and warm, it helped keep the chill out of her heart. She missed Luke with every fiber of her being. If only he were here. Where was he? Was he safe? Did he miss her?

A ball of tension tightened her stomach. She couldn't take another bite, so she pushed the bowl away.

"Are you going to eat that?" Kyle asked.

"No. I'm full."

"Can I give it to Justice?"

"Only if you're willing to endure doggie farts all night," she said.

"Justice, come here, boy."

The dog scrambled down the stairs from the loft. He missed the last step and fell ass over teakettle onto his face. Unfazed, he jumped up and rushed to Kyle's side. He woofed as if to say, *You didn't see that happen.*

As Kyle lowered the bowl, Justice lapped at the chili, sloshing it over the edge. He licked every last drop up off the floor. He sat back on his haunches and looked at her expectantly.

"I don't have any more," she said.

Justice cocked his head to one side.

"You can have some kibble later."

He let out a satisfied woof. She'd adopted Justice from a kill shelter when he was just a puppy. She couldn't imagine life without him. Having him here was incredibly important. Not only would he provide fun companionship to Kyle, but he'd also be another layer of protection against unknown threats. She could leave him at the cabin while she set up the trip wires.

"I'm going to get the supplies," she said. "Want to help me tie bells onto fishing line?"

"Sure!"

She walked into the mudroom next to the kitchen and opened the first cabinet. After pulling out several cardboard boxes, she finally found the one labeled *Defensive Perimeter*.

The box jingled as she carried it back into the kitchen. She set it on the table and pulled the flaps open. A fishing box full of bells and several rolls of fishing line would do the trick. She'd laughed at Luke when he'd suggested they practice creating trip wires. Now she was glad they'd done a dry run.

"Do you remember how to do this?" she asked.

"Yep."

"Every foot add a butterfly loop knot with a bell to the fishing line."

"I know, Mom," he said, exasperated. "I've been tying them since I was ten."

"It's really important that it's done right."

He rolled his eyes as he picked up a spool of

fishing line. After he'd successfully tied the first bell to the line, she turned her attention to her own line.

"How long should I make them?" he asked.

"Ten feet. If I need them to be any longer, I'll tie them together outside."

"Okay."

They spent the next hour tying bells to multiple ten foot sections of line. She carefully placed each line into a plastic grocery bag so they wouldn't get tangled together. In total, they ended up with ten strings of bells. They jingled as she picked up the bags.

"After I leave, put the two-by-fours across the doors."

"Okay," Kyle said.

They'd installed brackets in three places across the front and back doors. Six two-by-fours were propped against the wall.

She grabbed the shotgun off the chair next to her and slung it over her shoulder. As she headed for the door, Justice trotted beside her.

"Make sure you keep him inside until I get back," she told Kyle.

"I will. Come here, boy."

Justice chuffed and ran to Kyle's side.

She affixed a headlamp to her forehead before heading out. Although she didn't want to have to use the light, she'd need to be able to see to tie knots. She waited on the porch until she heard the two-by-fours slide into place.

A warm breeze blew through the canyon. A thousand stars twinkled in the night sky. Even with light from the cities polluting the sky, she could easily see Sirius in the constellation Canis Major. Before the bombs, she'd spent many nights contemplating the nature of the universe. Were we really alone? If there were aliens out there, why hadn't they made contact?

She shook the thoughts away before she could fall down an existentialist path. Now wasn't the time. Later, when they were safe, she would be free to muse about the mysteries of the universe. Right now, she needed to focus on the task at hand.

An old, rusted gate hung from broken hinges near the front of the property. They'd been meaning to fix the gate for the last year, but hadn't gotten around to it. Since she couldn't secure it, she ran a line of trip wire from the gate to a small tree on the other side. At about a half a mile from the main road, no one would come across the gate unless they were heading toward the cabin.

Old oak trees and patches of coyote brush dotted the front of the property. It wasn't enough to keep potential trespassers out, so three years ago they'd planted blackberry bushes. In addition to growing dark, sweet berries, they formed a thick, thorny impenetrable barricade. No one in their right mind would try to get through it.

After checking for breaks in the bushes, she backtracked toward the cabin. She connected an octagon of trip wires around the house at a radius of about forty feet. Tomorrow they could create more trip wires. This would be good enough for the night. She doubted she'd be able to sleep anyway.

As she finished tying the last bowline to a tree, two beady eyes shimmered in the trees. She bit back a scream. She grabbed the shotgun and pointed it at the hidden animal. Mountain lions lived in the area. They'd been known to kill hikers, so she wasn't taking any chances.

She pumped a round into the chamber. Her finger dropped to the trigger. As she let out a breath and prepared to shoot, the door to the cabin burst open. Kyle ran out onto the porch.

"Justice!"

She took her finger off the trigger. What was the dog doing outside?

Justice jumped out of the forest, nearly knocking her over in the process. She pointed the gun down at the earth. Her heart pounded. Her damp hands clenched into fists. She'd almost killed him. She'd almost killed their dog.

17

Liz stomped toward the cabin, struggling to contain her explosive anger. When she reached the porch, Kyle was on his knees in front of the dog.

"I told you to keep the door shut," she snapped.

"It was shut."

"Then what was Justice doing outside?"

"He escaped out the back door when I wasn't looking," Kyle said.

"I almost—" She stopped short, unable to confess her nearly lethal mistake. "When I tell you to do something, you need to do it."

"Sorry." His tone wasn't as contrite as she would have wanted.

"I'm not kidding. Any little mistake could get us killed," she said.

"Okay. Jeez. I get it. But I think you're freaking out too much. Who's going to find us anyway? It's not like Jason lives out here."

"Jason who?"

"You know, the guy with the chainsaw from those old movies," he said.

Old? Ugh! Granted, she'd watched those slasher films in her youth, but was she actually getting old? Was forty really over the hill? Or was she just freaking out because of the dog?

She shooed them inside and jammed the two-by-fours into place. After repeating the process with the back door, she went into the kitchen and poured a glass of water. She headed into the living room and set the shotgun on the coffee table beside the couch. She plopped down and took a long swig of water.

"Are you okay, Mom?"

"I'm tired."

"You're freaking out," he said.

"No I'm not."

She didn't want to admit it to Kyle and freak him out, but she was beyond scared. Although she pretended like she had everything under control, she couldn't think of a time when she'd felt more out of control. Technically, the cabin was the safest place they could be right now. Their home wasn't safe anymore. Going to a hotel wouldn't help. They had to be here, in the forest, all alone.

After taking another swig, she stood and walked to the large window at the front of the cabin. She pushed back the curtain and stared into the darkness. Tomorrow she'd get the motion sensor lights up. They could also make more trip wires. Staying busy would keep the panic at bay.

She carried the box of perimeter defense equipment into the living room and set it on the coffee table. Kyle sat near the fireplace. Justice lay in his lap. Both boy and dog eyed her with suspicion, as if they weren't sure what to make of her silence.

"We should watch a movie," she said.

"Which one?"

"You pick."

Kyle rifled through a huge box of DVDs. They didn't have cable in the cabin, so they'd kept a large supply of movies on hand for entertainment.

He slid a shiny silver disc into the DVD player and hit Play. On screen, an atomic wasteland stretched out across a battlefield. Large humanoid machines stepped through the rubble. Their glowing red eyes scanned the rubble looking for survivors. A small group of men carrying laser guns shot at the machines, fighting a war they couldn't possibly win. She knew the movie by heart. *Terminator 2*.

"Can we watch something else?" she asked. "Something funny?"

"But this is my favorite movie."

"I know but…it's a little too close to the truth right now."

"Machines didn't bomb us, people did," he said.

"We don't know that for sure."

"That's what they said on the radio. Russia did it."

"So much for the Cold War," she said.

"The cold what?"

"Nothing," she mumbled. Getting into the intricacies of international politics wasn't at the top of her list of fun conversations to have in the middle of the apocalypse. "Never mind. Go ahead."

He shrugged and turned his attention back to the TV.

She dug through the defense box. She found six keychain alarms. Each held a little pin. She pulled one free and a high pitched chirping alarm filled the cabin. She jammed the pin back in to make it stop.

"Mom!"

"Guess they still work," she said.

She pulled a roll of 550 paracord. In the morning, she could go out and tie a few more trip wires farther out. At one hundred and twenty decibels, the keychain alarms would be loud enough that she could set them up a mile out and still hear them well enough.

As she reached into the box, a sharp spike bit into her finger. She pulled back with a yelp.

"What's wrong?" Kyle asked.

"There's something sharp under the extra paracord."

She gingerly removed several items before locating the source. She pulled the strange-looking metal out of the box.

"What on earth…"

"It's a caltrop," Kyle said.

"A what?"

"Cal-trop," he enunciated. "Dad and I made them."

She turned the caltrop, inspecting the four sharp spikes sticking out of it at various angles.

"When you throw them on the ground, they always land with a spike up," Kyle said. "So if we need to booby-trap the road, we can spread them all over."

"How did you make them?" she asked.

"With the soldering iron in the workshop out back."

"Please tell me Dad didn't let you solder any."

"Only a few. I had to wear really thick gloves. It

was kind of hard to hold the solder with the gloves, but it was badass," he said.

If Luke had been in the house, she might have strangled him with her bare hands. How could he have been so irresponsible? Kyle was way too young to be handling an eight hundred-degree soldering iron. She'd have to talk to Luke about it as soon as he arrived. If he arrived.

"How many did you make?" she asked.

"I only made a few, but Dad made about a hundred."

"Out of nails?"

"Yep. We got some three-quarter-inch nails and cut the heads off."

"How?" she asked, almost wishing she hadn't.

"He used a metal saw to cut the heads off."

"Did he let you use the saw?"

"No. He said it was too dangerous."

But apparently an eight hundred-degree metal rod wasn't too dangerous. She shook her head. She couldn't wait to hear Luke's explanation for why one was safer than the other. Both were terribly unsafe for a child.

"Where are the rest of the caltrops?" she asked.

"In the shed. He said we needed to keep them outside so they would get a little rusty."

"Glad we got our tetanus shots," she grumbled.

"Yeah. We can't step on them or we'll get a nail through the foot."

"That's the last thing we need."

"Dad said we needed to make as many combat multipliers as possible. He said it will give us a huge advantage against any tangos," he said as he puffed out his chest.

"Tangos?"

"Bad guys."

She arched a brow. It must be military slang left over from when Luke was stationed overseas. Every once in a while he'd slip back into military slang, usually when he spent time around fellow SEALs.

A loud screeching noise blared from the TV. She jumped as a chase scene unfolded. At least she wasn't fighting murderous cyborgs. The edges of her mouth quirked. Staying positive would go a long way toward keeping her sanity. She needed to maintain a good attitude. Luke and Sierra could show up any moment and they'd be a whole family again. She wouldn't let despair win. In a world gone mad, family was the only thing that really mattered.

LUKE HIT the outer limits of Buttonwillow in the early afternoon. The 5 freeway overpass was barricaded by three highway patrol units. Although he'd anticipated it being closed, he couldn't help but be disappointed. He continued under the freeway toward a strip of gas stations and fast food restaurants.

As he turned left onto the road, his eyes widened. Soldiers in full tactical gear patrolled a huge truck gas stop station. With twenty gas pumps and a large convenience store, it was easily the biggest gas station for a hundred miles.

Trucks and cars gridlocked the parking lot. Men and women in jeans and T-shirts formed a line along the sidewalk. Their animated faces and hand gestures left him cold. What in the heck was going on?

He rolled down the window.

"I don't give a shit who ordered it," a trucker yelled at a soldier. "If you've got gas, I want to buy it."

"This is America," a lady screamed. "You can't keep us from trying to get home."

As Luke continued past the growing mob, he spotted a huge, makeshift cardboard sign duct taped to one of the pumps.

"NO GAS!"

So were they out, or was something else going on? Trying to get through that mess would be impossible, so he drove past it toward the last gas station. The road dead-ended adjacent to the attached convenience store. A fallow field stretched out for several acres behind it.

Situated next to an empty strip of three stores, the gas station wasn't much to look at. Boxy without the usual frills, it seemed to be a mom and pop type operation. Several vacant cars were lined up near the back of the parking lot. He scanned the area but didn't see any people. How strange.

After parking next to a gas pump, he hopped out of the truck. A red plastic warning banner was wrapped around the nozzle. He frowned. Were they out of gas too?

He dropped and headed toward the store. Before he could reach the door, three men wearing a woodland camo uniform he couldn't identify stepped out. They each carried Bravo Company M4 Mod 2 Carbine rifles. He checked for nametag patches on their clothes. Nothing.

His chest tightened. Something wasn't right.

"I need to fill up," he said.

"Gas is being rationed," the tallest man said. "Military and law enforcement only."

"I just need a half a tank. Just enough to get home to my family."

"A lot of people are trying to get home," the shortest man said.

"I've got cash."

The three men looked at each other, barely containing sly grins.

"How much you got?" Tall Man asked.

"Forty dollars," he lied.

No point in letting them take anything more. He'd worry about how he was going to peel forty dollars off a wad of two hundred without them seeing later.

"Let's see the money," Shorty said.

"Okay. I'll be right back."

As Luke headed for his truck, the instinct to jump in and take off seized him. But he only had about twenty miles worth of gas left. He could try driving down the road to another station, but if he didn't have any luck there, he'd be stuck. At least these guys seemed like they might sell him some gas.

Halfway to the truck, he heard footsteps behind him. The men closed in quickly. As Luke spun to face them, Shorty slammed the butt of his rifle into Luke's back. He fell to the ground. A steel toe boot connected with his ribs. Every molecule of oxygen blasted from his lungs. He couldn't breathe as pain radiated down his side.

He tried to stand, only to be kicked again.

"Stay down," Shorty ordered.

"I don't have anything worth taking."

"Let's see what we've got," Tall Man said. "Food, water. Oh shit, he's got an AR-15."

"And a P938," Shorty said as he yanked the pistol out of the back of Luke's waistband.

"What the hell happened to your truck?" Third Man asked.

"Hit a deer." Might as well lie since the truth wouldn't matter.

"Must have been one hell of a deer," Third Man said.

"Where were you coming from?" Shorty asked.

"Up north," Luke said.

"Cuff him," Shorty said.

"Wait. You can't arrest me. I haven't done anything."

They laughed while Third Man slapped a pair of shiny new handcuffs around his wrists. The man hauled Luke into a sitting position and leaned him against the truck. "What should we do with him?"

"Throw him in with the other guy. Take his stuff and put it in the stockpile. We need to clear the lot before someone else comes," Shorty said.

"I demand an attorney. You can't arrest me without probable cause."

"You probably didn't hit a deer," Shorty said. He rummaged through the glove box and pulled out a piece of paper. "And I doubt this is even your truck, *Jose Fernandez*."

"My friend loaned it to me."

"Same friend who ended up in your grill?"

"I want a lawyer."

"And I want to fuck the president's daughter," Shorty said before spitting on the ground.

"That bitch is fuckin' hot," Third Man said.

Luke shook his head. Fucking assholes.

"I'm guessing you're not cops," Luke said.

"Jesus, we've got a fucking genius on our hands," Shorty said. "Take Einstein inside. Gag him if he keeps talking."

The two other men dragged Luke to his feet. They pulled him toward the empty row of stores adjacent to the gas station. Two of the three stores had boarded-up front windows. Tall Man used a key to unlock the door in the middle. They pushed him inside and slammed the door behind him. Before he could turn around, the key slid into the lock, trapping him for good.

"Fuck!"

"They got you too?"

The voice came from somewhere farther into the store. With the front window blocked, only a sliver of dim, hazy light sliced in to illuminate a parade of dust bunnies. As his eyes adjusted to the darkness, he picked his way through overturned tables. Toward the back of the store, a cash wrap counter blocked his view of the other person.

He cautiously stepped around the counter. A stocky man wearing jeans and a short sleeve red and black plaid shirt came into view. Large sweat stains darkened the fabric under his arms. His collar drooped under the weight of extra moisture.

"Name's Grady."

"Luke."

"How'd they get you?"

"Pulled up hoping to get gas. I should have turned around the minute I saw the warning tape," Luke said.

"Yeah. I figured they might sell me gas if I bribed them. It didn't end well."

"At least they only zip-tied you. Have you tried to get out of them yet?"

"No. These things are tight as hell." Grady held his hands up. The zip ties dug into his skin, leaving streaks of red in their wake. "Hurts like hell too."

"I know how to get out of them."

"How? I've already searched this place for anything sharp. Couldn't find a damn thing. It's picked clean."

"Stand up."

Grady rolled onto his knees then stood up.

"Pull the zip tie as tight as you can get it," Luke said.

"Any tighter and I'll lose circulation."

"Get it as tight as you can or this won't work."

Grady lifted his hands to his mouth. He gripped the end of the zip tie between his teeth and pulled.

"Make sure the locking bar is directly between your wrists. Now raise your hands over your head and come down hard against your stomach," Luke said.

Grady followed his instructions and brought his hands down hard. The zip tie snapped free.

"Holy shit!" Grady's eyes went wide. "I've been stuck in here for two days and you got me free in two minutes. Who the hell are you?"

"Just a man trying to get home to his family."

"Me too. I was almost home when they got me."

"Where's home?" Luke asked.

"Lancaster. I'm about a hundred miles out. All I needed was a half tank of gas and I would have been home."

"Where were you coming from?"

"Paso Robles. After the bombs dropped, I went up to check on my parents. Left the kids at home with their mom. I didn't expect to have problems getting gas. I tried the truck stop, but they said they're rationing to military and police only."

"So that part is true."

"Yeah. It's horseshit. What are the rest of us supposed to do?" Grady asked in an exasperated tone.

"I don't know, but we'll figure it out."

"How? You're in handcuffs."

"I don't know, but I'll think of something. How often do they come in here to check on you?"

"Twice a day. Lunch and dinner. Already had lunch today," Grady said.

"How long until dinner?"

"About two hours. See that streak of light?"

"Yeah?"

"Soon as it hits the first table, they'll come."

"They're consistent?"

"You could set a watch to it. If you had a watch," Grady said.

"Okay, so we've got two hours to figure a way out."

"Good luck with that. I've been in here two days and haven't been able to do a damn thing to get out. They punched me in the face the first time I tried. It didn't stop me though. I kept trying."

"We'll be out of here tonight," Luke said.

He had no idea how he'd manage it without tools, but he'd have to find a way. If he had to tear apart the walls to get out, he would. But with his hands cuffed behind his back, options were severely limited. As he stalked around the semi-dark room, he kicked furniture and looked under shelves. There had to be something in the room that could help him get free.

18

Liz dropped the frying pan into the sink and listened intently as bells jingled outside. She pushed back the curtains and spotted a man in his early fifties walking through the grass toward the front door.

"Did you hear that?" Kyle asked as he came barreling down the stairs. "The bells!"

"I heard. We've got company. Don't say anything. I'll handle this."

As the man stepped onto the porch, Justice growled at the door. He stood at attention. Back rigid. Teeth bared. He was in full protection mode. She grabbed his collar a second before the man knocked.

"Who is it?" she asked.

"Edwin Wright, your neighbor."

"What do you want?"

"I saw you folks come up the road last night. I wanted to see if you're doing okay."

She opened the door. Justice cocked his head to one side before sitting back on his haunches. His tongue hung out as he panted.

"There you are, Justice. I missed you the last few weeks." Edwin rustled the fur on Justice's head. "Oh, hey Kyle. How have you been?"

"Good! Did you catch anything in the lake after we left?" Kyle asked.

"You know him?" Liz asked.

"He goes fishing at the lake. Dad and I run into him all the time."

No wonder Justice had calmed down. He must have met the man while on a fishing trip.

"I caught a small one," Edwin said. "Had to throw it back."

"That sucks," Kyle said.

Edwin shrugged.

"I'm Liz."

"Nice to finally meet you."

"Likewise. Where do you live?" she asked.

"In the house on the next road over. Built it myself." Edwin looked around the cabin. "Where's Luke?"

"Out gathering wood," she lied.

She wasn't about to tell a man she didn't know that they were alone and vulnerable. Even though Kyle seemed to know him, she didn't. Until she could find out more about him, she wouldn't share any additional information.

"I can wait for him," Edwin said. "I damn near fell on my ass tripping over your alarm system. Pretty crafty to use bells and fishing line. You expecting trouble?"

"Haven't you heard the news?"

"Sure, but it doesn't mean the hills are going to fill up with the fleeing masses," he said. "People are more likely to hunker down and wait it out."

"Until they run out of food."

"Good point." He scratched his chin. "Maybe I should set some trip wires myself."

"It couldn't hurt."

"I haven't been able to get any signal on my satellite dish for the last two days. The radio works, but they haven't given out any new information since it started."

"Last we heard, eight cities had been bombed, including LA," she said.

"Same as I heard. Hell of a thing. We should have wiped the Russians off the map thirty years ago."

"I'll let Luke know you dropped by."

"I was hoping to see if I could borrow some waders from him."

"What happened to yours?"

"Soaked through," Edwin said. "Yesterday I fell out of the damn boat trying to reel a big one in. He pulled me clear over the edge. I thought they might be dry by today, but no such luck."

"I don't think Luke brought his waders with him."

"Uh…" Edwin raised a brow. "They're right over there." He pointed at a pair of large boots.

"Oh, right. Well, I would loan them to you, but I don't know if Luke will need them today."

"No problem. Just have him come over when he gets back. How long did he say he'd be out?" Edwin asked.

"He didn't say."

"What, probably an hour or so tops?"

"I don't know."

"I like you. You're not the kind of woman always needin' to know where her man's at. My wife would flip her lid if she couldn't account for my whereabouts for five minutes, let alone a couple of hours. Luke's a lucky man."

When his gaze swept up and down her body, she narrowed her gaze slightly.

"I've got to get breakfast started," she said.

"We already ate, Mom."

"Lunch. I meant lunch."

"Okay," Edwin said, clearly not believing her lie. "I'll come back later and see if Luke's around."

"He will be." She shot a glance at Kyle, hoping he'd keep his mouth shut. He did. "I'll send him over. No need to come back."

"I don't want him to waste a trip."

"It's no problem. I'm sure he'd be happy to head over to your place for a bit."

"Can I tell you a secret?" he asked.

Her hackles rose, but she nodded.

"I'll take any chance I can get to get away from Sandy," he said.

"Your…wife?"

"Yep. The old ball and chain drives me nuts. I thought moving up here for retirement would be a good thing. I could go fishing, hunting, be a man. But she's here too, so I've got to listen to her bitch and moan all day."

"I'm sorry to hear that," she said dryly.

"Now don't get me wrong, I love her. But when no one else's around, we can get on each other's nerves real quick." His eyes lit up. "Hey, I've got an idea. Why don't you come by later and meet Sandy? Maybe if we've got another woman around, she'll calm down. She's going stir crazy without the TV."

"Okay. I can do that," she said.

She'd definitely take the chance of heading over there. It would be a good reconnaissance mission. If people did start to flood the area, it would be good to have an ally down the road.

"Great," Edwin said. "Why don't you come by around three? I'll see if she can whip up some scones and honey. She may talk too much, but the woman can turn flour into the finest pastry you've ever seen. Her croissants are good enough to make a Frenchman cry. In a good way, mind you."

"Sounds like a plan," she said.

After he left, she breathed a sigh of relief. He seemed nice enough. Maybe after she met his wife she could tell them the truth. In the meantime, she didn't want anyone to know she was alone with Kyle.

"Can I go with you later?" Kyle asked.

"Sure. Have you been to their house before?"

"A couple of times. Sandy invites us over for cookies and milk."

"Hmm, maybe I should have come with you during all of your 'boys only' weekends," she said.

"You don't have anything to worry about, Mom."

"What do you mean?"

"Sandy's old. Dad wouldn't look twice at her."

"Why would you even…never mind."

"My friend Felix's dad used to take him on dates

with another woman." His voice dropped to a whisper. "It wasn't his mom."

"That's terrible."

"Yeah, his dad's a dick."

"Language!"

"Sorry. Anyway, his parents are divorced now and he lives with his mom. But don't worry. That will never happen with you and Dad."

"Of course not," she said. "I love your dad more than anything in the world. Except you."

She ruffled his hair. He scooted away and swatted his hair back into place.

"When we go later, are you going to tell them Dad's not here?" Kyle asked.

"Not yet. I think we should keep it quiet for now. They may be nice people, but we don't know who else they know. They could let it slip that we're all alone and end up telling the wrong people. We can't take that chance."

SIERRA YAWNED and stumbled behind Derek as they crested a hill. After being up all night, she was ready to fall asleep standing up. But she couldn't afford to slow them down. She definitely didn't want to spend another night outside. Although they never saw the coyotes or a mountain lion, she couldn't shake the feeling of being watched.

"We'll go another mile then take a break," Derek said. "How are you holding up?"

"Good," she said with forced enthusiasm.

"Okay. Let me know if you need to slow down. I'd rather take more breaks if it means getting farther today."

"I'm not stopping until I get to the cabin," she said.

They trudged up and down hills, but the hike wasn't too bad. At least they were on a hiking trail. She couldn't imagine trying to hike through the tall, dry wild grasses. They were probably teeming with snakes.

She eyed the edge of the trail and listened for rattling. So far they hadn't encountered anything other than a few scattering field mice and some persistent flies. She couldn't wait to take a shower. Her sticky, sweaty shirt clung to her. A ponytail full of grimy hair hung down her back. Dirt and dust covered her shoes. She'd probably have to burn everything by the time she got to the cabin.

The last time she'd been this filthy, she'd been rolling around in a mud pit while trying to rush a sorority. Stupid snobby bitches. She'd done everything they'd asked but they hadn't extended an invitation to her to join. Their loss.

Grasshoppers snapped their wings as they flew across the trail. Wind rustled the grass alongside the road. Her heavy breathing punctuated each step. She'd run out of water after the last rest stop and her tongue stuck to the roof of her mouth.

"How much farther is it to the stream?" she asked.

"It should be right around the bend up there. Do you want some of my water?"

"I don't want to take it from you."

"Go ahead." He pulled a canteen from his pack and handed it back to her. "We'll be able to refill everything soon."

"Do you come out here a lot?" she asked.

"Sometimes. I like to do practice runs through the canyons so I don't get lost on the trails."

"Have you ever fought any wildfires?"

"Yep. This area is extremely dry, especially in the summer and fall. When the Santa Ana winds are blowing, it's basically a pile of tinder ready to go up in flames. I've been on several calls out here. Anytime a fire starts to look like it might get out of control, they send out every available firefighter to battle the blaze. No one wants a repeat of the Santiago fire in 2007."

"I remember having to evacuate," she said. "I was

nine years old and thought the whole world was coming to an end."

"And now it is," he said.

"Do you really think the world's ending?"

"Maybe. I don't know. It's hard to know what's going on without a radio."

"My dad has one at the cabin. It's in a box in our storage shed out back. They're probably listening to it right now."

"At least we'll know more once we get there," he said.

"I thought we were splitting up when we got to Santiago Canyon."

"I want to make sure you get there safely. I'd hate to get you almost all the way there and find out you were hurt, captured, or killed."

"There's no one out here but us," she said.

"Right now there isn't, but we haven't hit the road yet. There's no telling what we'll find when we get there."

"I'm sure I can make it the rest of the way. It's only a mile or two."

In truth it was probably closer to four, but if she showed up with a stranger in tow, her dad would be pissed. He'd told her over and over again never to tell anyone about the cabin. She should have kept her mouth shut, but he'd rescued her, so he couldn't be a bad person, right? But what if he'd only rescued her so that he could get to the cabin, kill her whole family, and take it for himself?

She stared at his backpack as she wrestled with the decision. He hadn't known about the cabin until after he'd rescued her, so that wasn't his motivation. He hadn't tried anything since they'd been together, even though he'd had ample opportunity to take advantage of her if that was his intention. Maybe she was just overthinking everything, as usual.

Still, her dad wasn't going to be happy if she showed up with Derek. Maybe she could ditch him on the road that led to the cabin. She could lie and tell him one of the other cabins was theirs so at least he wouldn't know their exact location. Yeah, that could work.

Relieved, she picked up the pace. As they turned the bend, a stream appeared. They walked off the trail and stopped at the edge of the water. It wasn't much, not a raging river or anything, but it was better than nothing.

"Make sure you use a filter," he said.

She dug through her pack and found her blue Lifestraw water bottle with a built-in filter. According to her dad, she could fill it with the nastiest pond water around and not have to worry about getting a disgusting amoeba in her mouth, or her stomach, or her brain. She shuddered.

After removing the integrated filter, she skimmed the bottle along the stream, scooping up water as she went. Because the stream was so shallow, she couldn't get more than a quarter of the bottle filled at a time.

She screwed the filter back on. Inside the bottle, silt-riddled water churned. As it settled, large particles landed at the bottom of the bottle. She brought the straw to her lips but couldn't do it. Was it really safe? What if the filter was too old? What if she hadn't screwed it on tight enough?

Derek took an overly noisy swig from his bottle. The corners of his eyes crinkled as he smiled.

"Not thirsty?

"It's so gross."

"It's fine. These bottles are great at purifying 99.9999 percent of bacteria and protozoa out."

"What about the .00001 percent? You know, the part that will kill me?"

He laughed and shook his head.

"What?" she asked.

"It's not going to kill you."

"So you say."

"Either drink, or don't drink, but we're not stopping again until we hit Santiago Canyon Road."

"Fine." She scrunched her nose up as she took a tentative sip.

"Well?"

"It tastes like water."

"See, nothing to worry about," he said.

"For now. Ask me again in three days when I have microorganisms gnawing at my guts."

He shook his head again and sucked down the rest of his water. She finished the quarter bottle and refilled it twice more. Although the temperature was only about eighty degrees, all the walking had turned her body into a mini oven. She couldn't wait to get out of the blazing sun.

An hour later they crossed Santiago Canyon Road without any problems. They didn't see a single car on the road. Not too unusual, but she would have expected at least one car to pass while they were in hearing range of the road. The absolute silence was unnerving.

The closer they came to the cabin, the more she worried about showing him the location. She tried to shut off the endless barrage of "what if" questions, but her brain wouldn't stop coming up with new and terrifying scenarios.

As they passed other cabins, she felt unseen people watching them from the windows. The glare of the late afternoon sun reflected off the glass, making them opaque. But she could sense them anyway.

"Do you know your neighbors?" Derek asked.

"No. I hardly ever come up here. Dad and Kyle spend the weekends here sometimes, especially in the summer."

"Kyle?"

"My little brother."

"How old is he?"

"Thirteen."

"That's always a tough age for boys."

"Why?"

"They're on the cusp of adulthood, trying to figure out how to be men."

"Was it hard for you?" she asked.

"No," he said with a chuckle. "I was a man's man even from a very young age. I knew I wanted to join the military at seven. I started physical fitness training at ten. I've always been all man. It just took me a few years to grow into it."

She averted her gaze from the muscles in his shoulders. It felt somehow wrong to ogle him from behind. No wonder he was so ripped. He'd probably been lifting weights for years before most boys ever stepped into a gym. He wasn't a meat-head, but he seemed totally comfortable in his body. She envied his quiet confidence.

When they reached the small, unmarked road which led to the cabin, she stopped.

"Well, here we are. I can go the rest of the way," she said.

"I'll come with you."

"I can make it from here."

"I know, but I was hoping I could meet your dad. Tell him how brave you've been the last two days."

She chewed the edge of her lip before replying.

"He might be pissed that I brought you with me. It's supposed to be a secret location."

"I won't tell a soul. You have my word."

"Well… I guess it wouldn't hurt."

"If he gets mad, you can blame me."

"You've never seen him get mad. He might totally freak out."

"I can handle him if he does."

Which is exactly what she was afraid of. Handle him how?

As she reluctantly headed up the path toward the cabin, she prayed she wasn't making a huge mistake.

19

Luke kicked through every piece of furniture and tore the last bits of shelving from the walls. He couldn't find anything that would help get him out of the handcuffs. After knocking over the same desk for the second time, Grady cleared his throat. Luke glanced at him.

"I'm not sitting down until I find something I can use to get these off."

"There's not a damn thing in here," Grady said. "Trust me, I would have found it if there were."

"Dammit!" Luke plopped down on the floor next to him. "Okay, I have a new plan."

"What?"

"How many guys come when they bring dinner?"

"Usually just one."

"Have you tried fighting your way out?" Luke asked.

"Hell no! They've got me outmanned and outgunned. And until you got here, I was trapped in a zip tie."

"There's two of us now versus one of them. We've got the upper hand."

"How do you figure?" Grady's brow furrowed. "There are three guys out there."

"All we need to do is knock one guy out. We take his gun and the key to the cuffs."

"What if he doesn't have a key?"

"Well, then we run like hell and hope they're dumb enough to leave the keys in the car," Luke said.

"This isn't a TV show," Grady said. "The keys won't be in the visor. We won't be able to go Rambo on them, and we're going to get killed."

"We're dead either way. I don't know why we're still alive. They took our stuff, so keeping us around doesn't make sense."

"Maybe they don't have a way of getting rid of the bodies?"

"Maybe," Luke said. "But it doesn't matter. We're not staying long enough to let them kill us. Here's the plan. We break off a shelf and use it to hit the guy over the head. He'll be knocked out, we'll get the keys."

"You make it sound so easy."

"It is easy."

"I admire your confidence. Stupid, but confident," Grady said.

"I'm a Navy SEAL. Retired from the military a few years ago. But I can still kick some ass."

"No shit? You're a SEAL?"

"Was."

"Was…is…it doesn't matter. You've been trained in hand-to-hand combat, right?" Grady asked, a renewed hope shining in his eyes.

"Of course."

"Good. Then you get to be the one to knock the guy out."

"My hands are cuffed behind my back," Luke said wryly.

"Ugh!"

"Man up. If you want to get home to your family, you're going to have to bust out of here. No one's coming to rescue us. We need to rescue ourselves."

"Fine. You're right. Fuck!"

"Go get a shelf and get behind the door. As soon as the guy walks through, hit him as hard as you can."

"Okay," Grady said, but his pale complexion worried Luke.

"You can't fuck this up. We're only going to get one chance."

"I know." Grady grabbed a metal shelf off the wall and stood behind the door. "This better work."

They waited in silence for the better part of an hour before footsteps sounded outside the door. It swung open. A man holding two fast-food sacks stepped into the darkness. He squinted and took another step forward.

Grady heaved the shelf back and swung forward with all of his body weight behind the swing. He slammed the other man into the wall with the force of his hit. The man's head snapped back, striking the wall with a sickening thud. As he slid down the wall, a dark streak of blood marked his path.

"Shut the door," Luke whispered.

Grady closed the door. He grabbed a lanyard off of the dead man's neck and used the key to lock the door. He rolled the man over and felt around in his pockets.

"Found it!"

He ran over and unlocked the handcuffs.

With his hands free, Luke returned to the man and unbuckled his belt. He wouldn't be needing that anymore. He secured it around his waist. It was heavy as hell, but packed with equipment. He couldn't wait to look through it later.

"You know how to shoot?" Luke asked.

"Not very well."

"Then you get the Glock 22." He tossed it toward Grady who caught it. "I'll take the M4."

"Works for me."

"We need to find my truck. Let's keep a low profile until we find it. Stay behind me. And don't shoot me."

"Okay."

Grady ejected the magazine and locked the slide back. He checked the chamber and found it empty. He slammed the magazine back in and pulled back the slide to chamber a round. Luke nodded. At least the man had some experience.

Luke checked to make sure the M4 was hot. He set it to semi-auto. Either way he was sure to draw fire once he shot it, but at least he wouldn't draw a whole fleet of military down from the other gas station up the road. He unlocked the door, cracked it open, and peeked out. No movement.

"What were you driving?" Luke whispered.

"A maroon minivan."

Luke raised a brow.

"What? I've got three kids," Grady said.

"I think I saw it behind the building. There were some other cars back there too. I'm guessing that's where they're keeping everything they steal. Stay low."

"Got it."

They crouched low as they hurried around the

front corner of the building. No one was in sight. As they circled behind the building, one of their captors jumped off the front of Luke's pickup and spun to confront them. Luke put two in his chest and two in his head.

Footsteps pounded on the concrete between the building and the snack mart. He turned and put four bullets in the camo-covered man.

Although he'd only seen three men when they'd captured him, there could be more. He backed up toward the minivan.

"Shit!" Grady said.

"What?"

"They shot out the tires."

Luke headed toward his truck. All of the tires were flat.

"Dammit."

"Look! They've got a cop car over there. The tires still look good," Grady said.

Luke jogged over to check the patrol car. He cracked open the door and felt around. He found the keys in the ignition. Apparently they'd been keeping this ready in case they needed to get away fast. Lucky him.

"We're taking the cop car," Luke said. "Get any supplies you have out of the minivan. We need to leave in sixty seconds."

As Grady raced toward his van, Luke hurried back to the truck. He grabbed his Bug Out Bag and sacks filled with water and snacks. He popped open the cop car's trunk and when he saw what was inside, he went weak in the knees.

A duffel bag full of guns and ammo took up most of the space. Extra camo pants and shirts were stuffed in a clear plastic bag. Luke shoved the bag of guns forward for easy access in case he needed them. He crammed the rest of his supplies behind them.

Grady returned with a suitcase and some water bottles.

"What's in the suitcase?" Luke asked.

"Mostly clothes. Toothbrush. Toothpaste."

"Leave it."

"But—"

"We don't have enough room."

"But we have enough room for your stuff?" Grady asked in an angry tone.

"My stuff will keep us alive. A change of clothes and toothpaste isn't going to help us right now."

"Fine." Grady took his suitcase back to the minivan and locked it inside. "Now what?"

"The five is blocked, but we might be able to pose as cops."

"We don't have uniforms."

"Right, but check this out." Luke pulled the bag

of camo clothes out. "We can dress in these and pretend we're on patrol."

"There's no way it's going to work."

"It'll work. Just follow my lead."

After they'd changed into the camo, they got into the car. Luke drove while Grady sat in the passenger seat. They'd briefly contemplated pretending one of them was a criminal under arrest, but decided they'd have to field too many questions. Better to keep it simple.

As they passed the gas station near the main road, several camo-garbed military nodded their heads at them. Luke nodded back. Out of the corner of his eye, he watched Grady slink down slightly.

"Sit up straight. Remember, we're officers dispatched to LA for rescue operations. Let me do all the talking."

"This is so stupid."

"Have some faith. I did get you out of there."

"True."

When they reached the line of police cars at the onramp to the 5 south, Luke rolled down the window.

"Been pretty quiet?" he asked casually.

"Yeah. A couple of drunks tried to ram the barricade earlier, but we've got it under control. Where are you headed?" the officer asked.

"LA. We got orders to join the search and rescue effort," Luke said.

"The road's closed. You have to take 99 down."

"We'd have to backtrack too far. We were supposed to report to our assignment an hour ago. We got caught up in an accident near Bakersfield. If we don't get there as soon as possible, they're going to hand us our asses."

When the officer folded his arms over his chest, Luke's sphincter clenched. This didn't look good.

"I know," Luke said quickly. "We should have come straight here, but it was a minivan full of kids. We had to stop."

"Everyone make it? Any fatalities?"

"No. We were able to clear the scene without any further incidents," Grady said.

Luke held his breath as the officer continued to eye them. After ten seconds of silence, he thought for sure they'd end up in jail for impersonating an officer. Sweat beaded on his brow.

"All right," the cop finally said. "We'll let you through. There's another roadblock in the middle of the highway down near the 138 cutoff. If you're on the list, they'll let you right through. I wish they'd give us a list, because then I wouldn't have to stand here making judgment calls all day. Lucky bastards."

"Thank you," Luke said.

He quickly rolled up the window and waited for the cops to move one of the patrol cars out of the way. As he drove through the barricade, he nodded at the other officers. So far, so good.

Pulling onto a completely empty highway, it looked like every apocalypse movie he'd ever seen. Broken down cars and trucks with their hoods up littered the side of the road. Some looked as if they'd been pushed aside by tanks. And maybe they had been.

As they rolled south, the sun set. Twilight reclaimed the land. Up ahead, an enormous series of mountains separated the central valley from the LA basin. They were about one hundred miles from downtown LA.

"Can you drop me off in Lancaster before you try to head through LA?" Grady asked.

As much as Luke wanted to keep going, he couldn't drag Grady all the way to Orange County.

"How far is it to Lancaster?" Luke asked.

"About an hour or so. It's faster if you take 138 to 14."

"How would I get back to LA?" Luke asked.

"Take 14 back to San Fernando Valley."

"Or we could go through the valley first and see what it looks like. I need to know if I can even get through."

Luke hadn't wanted to voice his fear out loud, but they might not be letting anyone through LA at all.

"I guess we could try to go into the valley then backtrack on 14," Grady said.

"Okay."

They passed the exit to Gorman and continued up an increasingly steep grade. Two miles later, a lone streetlight illuminated a barricade.

"This doesn't look good," Grady said.

"Yeah."

As he pulled to a stop in front of the barricade, he rolled down the window. A soldier ran over to meet him.

"Road's closed to LA," he said.

"I heard it was still open. We have orders to join the recovery effort."

"Orders from who?"

"Uh, the command post in Bakersfield."

"We radioed and told them to hold off sending more troops until tomorrow."

"Why, what's going on?" Luke asked. It was a risk to push them, but he needed more information.

"They bombed LA again a few hours ago. We think they might have been dirty. We're getting reports of what looks like chemical burns."

"Are they sure they're not radiation burns?"

"No. But they don't want to send in more men

until they know for sure. We've got a base camp set up in Gorman. You can turn around and go wait there until we get the all clear."

"Thank you," Luke said.

He made a U-turn and backtracked to the 138 turnoff. Fortunately it wasn't blocked. He'd been lucky so far, but every time he had to talk his way through another roadblock, he'd be risking their freedom. It was too dangerous to keep using the same ploy.

"I want to try to stay off the highway as much as possible," Luke said. "Are there any alternate routes into Bakersfield?"

"There's a shitty, winding road that cuts through the mountains," Grady said.

"Sounds like fun."

"You have a pretty messed-up idea of what fun is."

"After everything I've been through, I'm looking forward to a leisurely drive up a dangerous mountain road. At least I'll know the dangers."

"Maybe. Or maybe we'll run into a militia or something," Grady said.

"A militia?"

"I don't know. Just trying to think of everything that could possibly go wrong."

"Been there, done that. About the militia I mean."

"No shit?"

"Lost my truck to them."

"Then whose truck were you driving in Buttonwillow?" Grady asked, twisting in the seat to eye him warily.

"Some guy I killed. It's a long story."

"You're not planning on killing me when we get to my house, are you?" Grady asked.

"No. Why would I do that?"

"So you could steal my stuff too."

"I didn't steal anything. I was defending myself. I don't kill unless provoked."

"I'll be sure not to provoke you." Grady slid farther away from him.

Luke didn't blame him for being scared. They'd only known each other a few hours, and he was right. A less honorable man would drive him to his house, kill his family, and steal everything. He just hoped his family wasn't suffering a similar fate.

20

Late afternoon brought reprieve from the heat. As Liz walked the perimeter of her property, she tried to memorize as much as she could about its current state. The more she could remember about the lay of the land, the easier it would be to see if anyone had trespassed onto her property. Later she'd string up more trip wire alerts. She'd found two more boxes of bells in the storage along with several spools of fishing line.

As she stepped out of the woods into the clearing in front of the cabin, a perimeter bell rang. She grabbed up the shotgun which was hanging in a two point sling across her chest. The moment she leveled it, two people walked up the road from the gate. She lined up the sight, ready to shoot.

"Stop!" she commanded. "You're trespassing on private property. Turn around immediately or we'll shoot."

"Don't shoot Mom, it's me!"

Liz lowered the shotgun an inch and peered over the sight.

"Sierra!"

Liz let the shotgun drop back against her chest. She raced across the field and pulled her daughter into a hug worthy of a momma bear. Tears ran down her face as she clung to her daughter. She hadn't wanted to admit it, but she'd been terrified that she'd never see her daughter or husband again. Now at least one of them was home.

"How did you get here?" Liz asked.

"We walked," the man answered.

Liz released Sierra and took a step back. Her hands rested lightly on the shotgun.

"Who are you?"

"Mom, this is Derek. I was attacked by some men on the trail and he saved me."

"What?" Liz's stomach dropped. "What trail? Which men?"

"I used the trail Dad told me to use to walk to the cabin. But there were a bunch of men blocking the way. I tried to get around them but they attacked me. If Derek hadn't come along…"

Sierra turned and flung herself into Derek's arms. He took a half a step back. Wide-eyed, he patted her back as if he wasn't used to this level of affection. So he couldn't be her boyfriend.

"How do you know each other?" Liz asked.

"We don't," Derek said. "I happened to be on the same trail."

"Why did you help her?" Liz's eyes narrowed. Altruism was a rare trait these days. He had to have some kind of ulterior motive.

"Mom!"

"It's okay," Derek said as he gently pushed Sierra away. "She was a woman in trouble. Of course I was going to help her. After I rescued her, she mentioned that her father was Navy. I was in the Marines. We were heading the same way, so I asked if she wanted to travel with me."

"I wouldn't have made it without him."

"Well, thank you," Liz said.

As much as she wanted to believe he'd taken care of Sierra out of the goodness of his heart, she wasn't naïve enough to take his word at face value. Sierra shouldn't have brought him to the cabin. Now their location was compromised. Was that his real motive? Was he scoping out their supplies so he could come back and take them?

"Where are you headed?" Liz asked.

"My parents live in the next canyon over. They bought a cabin out here when they retired. I wanted to check on them."

"Where's your car?"

"Some thugs stole it."

"That's unfortunate," she said, still suspicious of his motives.

"You can stop the interrogation now," Sierra said. "He's a good person and he kept me safe. You should be thanking him, not grilling him."

"It's okay," Derek said. "I can understand your concern. If I were a father, I'd be extremely suspicious if a stranger walked up with my daughter in tow. Is her dad here? I'd like to meet him."

"Why?" Liz asked.

"Mom!"

"I just want to shake his hand and tell him what a good kid he's got here. She's brave. She walked twenty miles without whining and complaining."

"I complained a little."

"Not enough to be annoying," he countered.

Sierra laughed and smiled at him.

"Luke's busy at the moment," Liz said. "He probably won't have time to sit and chat."

"I should be getting on my way." Derek turned to Sierra. "I'm glad you're safe. I hope you don't run into any more problems."

"Thank you," Sierra said. "I hope your parents are doing well. Thanks again for rescuing me."

He nodded and smiled before turning and heading back up the road. As soon as he was safely out of earshot, Liz put her hands on her hips.

"What were you thinking bringing him here?" she demanded.

"Why are you so paranoid? He saved me. He wasn't going to hurt us."

"How do you know that for sure? He could have been lying the whole time. How do we know he isn't going to come back with his friends and kill us all?" Liz asked.

"I don't think he has any friends."

"Everyone has friends."

"Not everyone. Some people prefer to be alone," Sierra said. "Why are you being so paranoid? Where's Dad?"

"He's not here."

"What? But you told—"

"I lied."

"If Dad's not here, where is he?" Sierra asked.

"I don't know," Liz snapped. "Which is why we need to be careful. We can't let anyone know we're here alone."

"What about Kyle? Is he here?"

"He's inside the cabin. I told him not to come out

unless I tell him it's safe." Liz sighed and adjusted the position of the shotgun on her chest. "I don't know if you understand how serious this situation is."

"I understand completely," Sierra snapped. "I'm not a dumb kid. We're getting nuked by God-knows-who and we might not live through the week. I get it. But you didn't have to be such a bitch to Derek."

"I'm just trying to keep us safe. I don't know where your dad's at. I don't know when or if he's coming home. I don't know anything right now, so I think I'm allowed to be extra vigilant."

When Sierra burst into tears, Liz sighed. Maybe she was being too hard on her, but fear for her family's safety had taken over. She would fight like hell to keep them safe, but she'd rather not have to fight at all. If other people found out about their large cache of survival rations and preps, they could easily come and take them. With only three people to defend the cabin, they could be outnumbered and outgunned with very little effort on the part of another group. She didn't want to scare Sierra, but her daughter needed to understand the importance of keeping their location secret.

"Now that you're home, I don't want you wandering off."

"I won't. Trust me, I never want to leave the

cabin. Not until Dad gets home. Do you think he's okay?"

"I hope so. He's a strong man. He knows how to fight. I'm sure he's on his way here right now," Liz said, praying he really was alive and heading home.

"I'm tired. I didn't really sleep last night," Sierra said sheepishly.

"Go inside and get some sleep."

The front door of the cabin opened and Kyle stuck his head out.

"Sierra!"

Justice pushed open the door and bounded down the porch steps. Sierra bent over to hug the dog, but Justice's momentum pushed her back on the ground. Justice licked her face and chuffed with joy. She laughed and hugged the furball.

"I missed you, doggie."

"Woof!"

Kyle joined them a second later. He dropped to his knees and tried to wrap his arms around Sierra and Justice. To see her family partially reunited renewed her strength and conviction that everything would be okay. But until Luke came home, she couldn't truly celebrate.

Liz slowed her pace as she approached Edwin and Sandy Wright's modest log cabin. She scanned the ground, checking for trip wires or other traps. Since he'd mentioned he might set some up, she wanted to be extra careful in her approach. Sierra and Kyle followed behind like ducklings.

She reached the front porch without incident. After knocking on the door, she waited. A grandmotherly woman opened the door and smiled.

"Well hello," she said. "I'm Sandy. It's so nice to meet you."

"Hello. I'm Liz, and this is Sierra and Kyle."

"Come on in. Edwin told me you'd be coming so I whipped up some biscuits and honey butter. I hope you're hungry."

They headed into the log cabin. A large stone fireplace dominated one wall. Several tan leather sofas formed a U-shape in the center of the room. A small hallway led to a bathroom and two closed doors, presumably bedrooms.

The large open-concept living room opened to the kitchen. Sandy had already set the knotted pine table with red and white checkered placemats as well as plates, mugs, cups, and various utensils.

"Please make yourself comfortable. Edwin's just getting up from his afternoon nap."

As she bustled around the kitchen, she set a

teapot on the stove and pulled fresh baked biscuits out of the oven. Steam curled up from the biscuits along with the yeasty aroma of fresh bread.

Liz's mouth watered. She hadn't had real homemade biscuits in… well, not since she and Luke had visited his parents two years earlier. Had it really been two years? They'd planned on visiting them for Christmas this year, but who knew where they'd be in two months. With the whole world falling apart, their Christmas plans were probably going to be postponed at the very least.

Her heart dropped. She should have taken the kids to see their grandparents during the summer. She'd taken for granted she'd be able to fly to Tennessee to see them. But since the attacks, she hadn't seen a single plane in the sky. It would easily take three days of driving to get there, and who knew if the roads were passable. Probably not.

"This is my great-great-great grandmother's recipe," Sandy said with pride. "I learned to make them as soon as I could reach the table. My mom used to say I started kneading dough when I was still in a booster seat. That might explain my arthritis."

"Thank you for cooking for us," Liz said. "You didn't have to do that."

"Nonsense. I'm not going to let my guests go hungry."

"Thank you," Sierra said before taking a bite from the biscuit. "Oh my God, Mom. This is so good. Why don't you cook like this?"

Liz flushed. The closest she ever got to baking involved driving to the store for a premade cake. If there was a black thumb of cooking, she had it. She'd never met a meatloaf she couldn't burn, and even frozen pizza was a gamble.

"Yeah, Mom," Kyle said with his mouth full. "Why don't you make these?"

"I'm sure your mom's a very busy woman," Sandy said. "What do you do for work?"

"I'm a stay-at-home mom."

"How nice. Not many women get to stay at home to raise their children anymore. That's why this world has gone straight to hell."

Liz tried to cover her surprise at Sandy's comment by biting into the biscuit. Flaky layers of perfection melted in her mouth. Somehow she'd managed to infuse butter in every nook and cranny. It didn't even need honey butter, but why not try a little?

As Liz slathered the biscuit, Sandy opened a cupboard and pulled out a box of teabags.

"I have chamomile, mint, raspberry, orange pekoe, ginger, blackberry—"

"Blackberry," Sierra said. "It's my favorite."

"I like mint," Kyle said.

"Ginger, please," Liz said. "My stomach's been acting up."

"It's probably all the stress of having to leave home. What made you finally decide to come up here?" Sandy asked.

"Things were falling apart in our neighborhood."

"What happened?" Sierra asked.

"People were running around with guns at night and the police couldn't come to help anyone. The phone lines were down. Cell service was gone. It seemed like the right time to leave."

"It's good you got out while you could," Sandy said. "I heard there's a group down on El Toro Road blocking traffic up into the canyons."

"I ran into that on my way up here," Liz said.

"There's a church in the next canyon over. Pastor's crazy as a loon, but there are enough *sheeple* in this world to follow him around. I think they're the ones setting up all the roadblocks, but I'm not about to go investigate."

"Have you seen the roadblocks?" Liz asked.

"No. Edwin was on the HAM earlier today. We've got some friends a few canyons over. They had to loop around through Rancho Santa Margarita and come in through the fire roads to get to their cabin."

"Sounds familiar," Liz said. "Have you heard any other news?"

"Nothing new. How's Luke doing? Will he be coming over too?" Sandy asked.

"He's working on some stuff back at the house," Liz said. A twinge of guilt pulled at her gut. Sandy seemed like a nice, sincere woman, but she wasn't ready to bet her life on it.

Edwin strolled in from the hall.

"I thought I smelled biscuits," he said with a grin. "How're you doing, Liz?"

"Great. Your wife is an incredible cook."

"She can cook a mean pie too. Maybe we'll crack open some peaches and make a peach pie later."

"We?" Sandy raised a brow. "Since when do you ever do anything in the kitchen?"

"I eat in the kitchen."

"Mm-hmm."

"I do dishes…sometimes," he added.

"Only when they're piled so high I refuse to cook."

Liz kept her head down while the two bickered. They were an old married couple in every way that mattered. People who didn't love each other didn't argue like that. Although they probably wouldn't admit it, they were clearly meant to be together. Just like her and Luke. God, every time she thought about Luke her stomach churned with fear. Where was he?

After spending another hour chit-chatting with the couple, Liz stood.

"It's been so nice spending time with you," she said. "I'll be sure to give Luke the biscuits as soon as I get home."

"Don't forget to tell him to put the honey butter on them," Sandy said.

"I won't."

"You kids be good to your mom," Edwin said. "Right now we need to be good to each other. No one else will be."

Liz nodded in agreement. The world at war could become a cruel, dark place. Fortunately she felt like they'd formed an unspoken alliance while sharing tea and biscuits. She might not be able to count on them to come in guns blazing if they encountered trouble, but they'd at least try to warn her. Maybe in time they could strengthen their relationship so that they could each provide an extra measure of protection for the other family.

As Liz and the kids walked back to the cabin, she watched the golden light of sunset blanket the canyon. The occasional tweet of a songbird and the rush of wind through the trees helped relax every muscle in her body. For now, they were safe. And with any luck, Luke would be coming home.

21

As night fell, Luke navigated the winding mountain road toward Lancaster. Forty miles later, they drove through the darkened city streets. The occasional bark of restless dogs punctuated the eerie silence. Several groups of men roamed the shadows, clearly up to no good. As the car's headlights hit the gangs, the men and their guns melted back into the night.

"Somehow I don't think the cop car will keep us safe," Luke said.

"Yeah. Where are the other cops? I would have thought they would have checkpoints all over the city," Grady said.

"I don't know. Maybe they were sent to LA."

"They wouldn't leave a city of one hundred fifty thousand people to fend for themselves, would they?"

"I hope not," Luke said. "But we don't know much about what's going on."

"Let me see if I can get the radio working."

As Grady fiddled with the radio, static filled the air. He flipped through various frequencies, but they were all silent.

"Nothing," Grady said. "Turn left at the next light."

"How much farther is it?"

"Three blocks. I don't like the look of things out there."

"Me either," Luke admitted.

When they turned onto a residential street, a man raced out of the bushes. He swung a baseball bat at the front windshield. The bat bounced off the reinforced glass, hitting the man in the face. He stumbled backward, falling into the bushes and out of sight.

"It didn't take long for people to stop trusting cops," Grady said.

"It may not have anything to do with the bombs," Luke said. "Some people stopped trusting cops after seeing beatings livestreamed."

"Maybe I'm a fool, but I still trust them. Right at the next street."

"At the moment I don't trust anyone. Well, except

you," Luke said. "I would probably still be back in that store if you hadn't been there too."

"You would have found a way out."

"Maybe, but thanks for taking out that guy."

"I hope I never have to do it again," Grady said. "That's my house on the left. No, the next one. The driveway runs around back. I don't like parking my car out front."

As Luke pulled back behind the house, a light flicked on.

"Motion sensored," Grady said.

"Good. Do you have any other preps?"

"Nothing fancy. We've got a shotgun and a house alarm system."

"That's better than most people have," Luke said.

"Not sure what good an alarm is going to do when there aren't any cops around to respond to it."

"It will at least give you enough warning so you can grab the shotgun. And maybe it'll scare a potential intruder away."

"Maybe," Grady said.

The sliding glass door at the rear of the house cracked open. A woman poked her head out.

"Baby is that you?" she asked tentatively.

"I'm home, honey." Grady pushed the car door open and strode toward his wife.

She flung open the door and raced into his arms.

They hugged and kissed with abandon until Luke walked over and cleared his throat.

"This man saved my life," Grady said.

"Thank you," she said.

"I don't know about that," Luke said with a chuckle. "Let's call it even."

"Where are the kids?" Grady asked.

"Asleep."

"Are they all okay?"

"Fine," she said softly.

"Good." Grady turned back to Luke. "You should stay the night. I know you want to get back to your family, but it's not safe to travel at night."

"Please, you can stay on the couch. It folds out," she said.

"Thank you, but I need to keep moving. I still have a long way to go," Luke said.

"How far?" she asked.

"At least a hundred miles. Probably more. Depends on how I can get there. I'm planning on taking Highway 14 across to the 5, then heading south."

"The 14's closed. You can't get through," she said.

Luke's heart dropped.

"What about Bouquet Canyon Road? He could take that. It's a few miles out of the way, but parallel to 14," Grady said.

"That could work," she said.

"How do I get there?"

As Grady's wife drew directions on a paper map of the LA area, Grady helped Luke refill his water bottles. He insisted on giving Luke a bag full of snacks. After politely turning him down twice, Luke relented and took the extra food. He probably wouldn't need it, but it wouldn't hurt to have more than enough.

After packing the food and water in the police car, Luke took the map.

"Thanks again for the offer to stay," he said. "Be sure to lock up and set that alarm. Keep the shotgun ready."

"We keep it by the bed but not loaded because of the kids," she said.

"How old are they?"

"Youngest is five, oldest is fifteen," Grady said. "So some are old enough to know better than to pick up a loaded gun, but not everyone. Don't worry though, I can load it in under ten seconds. I nailed a shotgun shell carrier to the top of the doorframe inside our closet. That way the kids can't reach it, but it's still close enough to get to."

"You might want to get a gun safe instead," Luke said. "I have one on my nightstand. I can get into it in three seconds."

"See honey, I told you we should have gotten that safe," she said.

"You're right, honey." Grady said. "As soon as they open up the stores again, I'll grab one."

"Thank you, baby."

"I need to get on the road," Luke said.

"I hope your trip isn't as eventful as ours was," Grady said.

"As long as I get to keep the car, I'll be fine."

An hour later, he was as far from fine as he could possibly be. He hadn't been able to find an open gas station, so he'd run out of gas in the middle of the mountains. He coasted into a dirt pullout next to the Bouquet reservoir just as the car died.

"Shit!" He pounded the steering wheel. "Can't I get one damn break?"

He flung the door open and got out to check the trunk. Although he'd packed it earlier, he hoped he'd missed seeing a five-gallon gas can.

After checking the trunk, he slammed it shut. Twice.

The duty belt he'd been wearing for the last few hours dug into his waist. He unbuckled it and set it down on the trunk. In all the chaos since fleeing Buttonwillow, he hadn't stopped long enough to take stock of what he had. And since he couldn't go anywhere, he might as well do it now.

In addition to a Glock 22, he unclipped a can of pepper spray which was attached to the belt with a black lanyard. He was also the proud new owner of a Taser. That would have come in handy back in Buttonwillow.

He flicked on a Streamlight SL20XP-LED flashlight. Not too bad. Useful if he needed to light up a whole room. There was also a smaller secondary flashlight, a Blackhawk Nite-Ops Gladius.

After unclipping the magazine pouch, he checked the contents. Two more full mags of 9mm for the Glock. Awesome. At least he had some extra firepower.

He found a small first aid kit with disposable gloves, a CPR mask, antiseptic wipes, an UZI Responder knife, and a multi tool. He put everything back on the belt and set it on the passenger seat.

As he searched the trunk, he found a portable defibrillator, bolt cutters, a bulletproof vest, and another fully equipped first aid kit. But best of all, a recharger for a cell phone.

He almost couldn't believe it. His cell had died on the way to Buttonwillow and he hadn't thought to charge it back at Grady's house. He immediately plugged the adapter into his phone, then into the car. When the charging light blinked on his phone, he whooped. It worked!

Now he had everything he could possibly need to get home, except gas.

He would have stopped back in the city if he'd known there weren't any gas stations on the road. He figured with his uniform and car, he would have been able to fill up without a problem. California was covered in gas stations. They were as ubiquitous as cockroaches in a fifty-year-old motel. Except here.

After kicking the tire in frustration, he pulled out the map Grady's wife had given him. He located the reservoir and traced a line back to Lancaster. As he ran his finger over a dotted line, he squinted to make out the minuscule text. *Pacific Crest Trail.*

He eyed his Get Home Bag. Trying to get anywhere near LA had been a fool's errand. But what if he hiked over the mountains? He could take the Pacific Crest Trail to the Cajon Pass and then he'd only be sixty miles from home. The trail wasn't straight, so it could be eighty miles or more to get to Cajon, but if he walked twenty miles a day, he could make it in a few days.

And what difference did a few days make at this point? He could walk the last sixty miles in another three days. So he'd be home in a week, tops. As long as nothing went wrong.

He laughed out loud at the absurdity of the situation. With a running car, he could be home in a few hours. But stuck on a mountain road without any other options, was it really stupid to consider hiking the rest of the way? It wasn't his first choice. Maybe he could flag down a motorist instead. But if that didn't work, then he'd have to hike for the rest of the trip.

LUKE PACED around the police car. Several hours had passed since he'd run out of gas, but no one had come up the road. Fatigue and hunger pulled him back into the car. He dug through his food supply. A bag of beef jerky and a granola bar would do the trick. He washed both down with a liter of water.

He had three more gallons of water in the car. It was probably enough, but he never wanted to be without water, so he hiked over to the reservoir and refilled the bottle he'd just emptied. He found a water purification tablet in his pack and dropped it into the water.

Back at the car, he sat in the passenger seat and closed his eyes. Every muscle in his body ached. He hadn't slept since he'd left the farmer's house. His eyes flew open. Had it only been a day? So much had happened in that time.

Hours later, he woke with a start. A truck roared

by, heading toward Lancaster. He jumped to his feet and raced out. His attempt to run after the driver and flag him down ended in failure.

Encouraged by the sighting, he watched the sunrise as he waited. A fresh new day lightened his spirits a bit. It couldn't be any worse than the last few days. As long as he wasn't shot at or captured, he'd have a great day. He laughed and grabbed a granola bar for breakfast.

Midmorning brought the end of hope. Not one single car had passed since the truck. Maybe he would end up on the Pacific Crest Trail after all.

He opened the map and studied the trail. It seemed like a straight shot over the mountains toward Interstate 15. He'd have to trek through miles and miles of mountainous terrain, but maybe being alone in the woods would be safer than trying to hitch a ride into town. Even if he did get a ride, what would he do then? Steal a car?

He'd been on plenty of long-range hikes as a SEAL. He could easily do twenty miles a day. The more he considered his options, the more he was convinced this would be the best route to take. Sure, it would take longer to walk over the mountains, but at least he wouldn't be battling people along the way.

With his mind made up, he assessed his gear. He couldn't carry everything on the trail. He'd only be able to bring basic necessities. Anything more than what he had in his Get Home Bag would be overkill. However, he'd need all the food he could carry. From what he could remember, there were plenty of water sources available along the trail. But food was another matter. He wouldn't have time to stop and hunt.

He unpacked and repacked his bag. Since he wouldn't need an armory full of guns, he settled on keeping the P938, and the Glock 22. The shotgun weighed too much to be hauling all over the woods. He stuffed the bag full of food and used an extra shirt to make a hobo-style bag. He took three bottles of water. As much as he wanted to carry all of the jugs with him, he wouldn't be able to drag that much weight around.

Overhead, a hawk squawked. Luke looked up, shielding his eyes from the sun. The bird dove toward a sparse patch of sagebrush, probably after a mouse. He eyed the landscape. Most of the vegetation was coastal sage, barely waist height. Trees were few and far between. The sooner he could get moving, the better.

After packing as much gear as he could reasonably carry, he sealed the map in a Ziploc bag. It wasn't the best topographic map available, but it was all that he had.

As he headed back to the Pacific Crest Trail

marker, he listened intently for the sound of any approaching cars. Nothing. It was silent but for the screech of the hawk.

The clearly marked trail wound up into the hills. He glanced back at the police cruiser one last time before starting up the trail.

Hours later, sweat dripped into his eyes. He'd hiked up and down two ridgelines as he headed toward Highway 14. Before crossing the empty road, he stopped to take a swig of water and eat a granola bar. He estimated he'd walked about fifteen miles so far. The sun had finally dropped lower on the horizon, but he had a couple of hours left before he'd have to make camp.

After crossing the highway, he continued along the switchbacking trail into the hills. An endless sagebrush landscape stretched from one hill to the next. He gained elevation along the way, but not enough to get into a tree line. He walked several more miles until he finally reached the Santa Clara River. Surrounded by tall, gnarled oaks on every side, it was the perfect place to rest for the night.

He searched for a relatively flat, dry patch of earth. After pulling out his tarp, he strung it up with a length of paracord. He gathered broken branches and other debris from the surrounding area and set it in a tepee-style pile. A second pile of dry grasses and leaves would serve as a nest to capture the initial sparks.

He pulled a piece of flint out of his bag. As he scratched shards of magnesium off the side, they formed a small pile in the center of the nest. Satisfied with the pile, he turned the steel around and scraped his knife along the ridged length until sparks flew.

The dry tinder smoldered before bursting into a single flame. He quickly moved the nest into the tepee of small sticks. As he fed the fire more wood, it grew until he had a reasonably good blaze going.

Night fell. The temperature plummeted. Clouds rolled in to filter the moonlight, giving the sky an ominous tinge. He gazed up at the shadowy moon. Was Liz looking up at it too? Did she wonder where he was? If he was dead or alive? Did she have the kids with her? Were they okay?

He tortured himself with unanswerable questions until the fire burned low and hot. He got up and refilled his water bottles from the river. Only one had a filter cap, but he could easily change it as needed. He drank as much water as he could stand. Since he didn't have a good trail map, he didn't know when he'd encounter the next water source.

For years Liz had been begging him to move out of the state, to go to a place where they could buy a ranch and live off the land. They could have sold their house for almost a million dollars. At least that was one good thing about living in one of the most expensive states in the country: you could sell your modest home and buy a mansion in another state, and have money left over to live off for years.

He loved his job, but was the weekly commute worth it? Was he trying to live a lifestyle predicated on expensive houses and fast cars at the expense of his family?

The weight of regret rested heavy on his chest. He couldn't change anything now, but he wished he'd listened to her years ago. They'd probably be living blissfully on an almost completely self-sufficient homestead somewhere in Wyoming, far away from nuclear bombs and unsustainable cities.

But what good were regrets when time only marched forward, not backward? If given the chance, he might have made different choices, but it didn't matter now. He could live in a torturous state of what-if, or he could fight like hell to get home to his family. He always chose action over inaction. And as such, he spent the rest of the night mentally preparing himself for the long journey ahead.

22

Luke rose before sunrise and hiked approximately five miles before he had to stop to tend to his feet. He hadn't walked this many miles since SEAL training. Although he kept himself in great shape, he'd let long-distance endurance runs fall by the wayside, something he vowed to rectify in the future.

As he searched for a place to sit, he spotted the North Fork Ranger Station. As far as he could tell, it was deserted. Several empty picnic benches sat under several sparse pine trees. He welcomed the shade and a chance to tend to his feet.

After setting his pack down, he pulled out his medical kit. It contained a blister pack with everything he'd need to treat his aching feet. He pulled off his socks. Although they were specifically made for hiking, they were damp with sweat. Hiking through a desert environment on an increasingly hot day hadn't helped things. He gave his feet a minute to cool off.

He opened a tube of antibiotic ointment and applied it to several hot spots before covering the areas with Band-Aids. Duct tape came next. He used it to cover the Band-Aids. This would allow his foot to slide in the shoe without causing more friction burns.

A sign attached to a fire grill pointed toward a water cache. He gathered his bottles and headed toward a large propane tank. His back ached as he bent to fill the bottles, but he was grateful for the cache. Finding water on the trail might be more difficult than he'd considered. He'd taken water availability for granted at home, but on the trail, it took on an almost mystical importance. Without it, he'd die.

Sweat dripped into his eyes. With the sun directly overhead, heat blazed down to fry everything in the path of its rays. He returned to the picnic table in the shade. He hadn't planned on resting this early in the day, but maybe it made sense to stay out of the heat.

He didn't realize he'd dozed off until he heard footsteps coming up the trail. He bolted upright in time to see a young man and woman wearing full through-hiker gear enter the clearing. They were probably in their early twenties. Both extremely fit and smiling.

"Hey," the guy said. "Are you headed north or south?"

"South," Luke said.

"Cool. We're going north."

"How long have you been on the trail?"

"A couple of months," the woman responded. "You?"

"A couple of days."

"I'm Peter and this is Mandy."

"Nice to meet you."

"So you're not a through-hiker?" Mandy asked.

"No. My car ran out of gas on the other side of Highway 14."

"I bet a lot of people are out of gas now," Peter said. "You know, with the restrictions and all."

"Restrictions?"

"Yeah, you know about the bombs, right?" Mandy asked.

"Yes. I was up north when it happened."

"Everyone's going nuts. We got off the trail a few days ago at the Cajon pass. People are losing their minds," she said.

"How so?"

"They're shooting each other," Peter said. "Lots of looting and riots going on."

"But you two got back on the trail?"

"Heck yeah," Mandy said. "It's probably the safest place in California right now. I'll take snakes and bears over humans any day."

"Have you run into other people?"

"No. You?"

"No. But I've only been on the trail maybe thirty miles or so. I'm not really sure. I don't have a map."

"There's a map on the ranger station. It's on the side wall," Peter said.

"Thanks. I'll check it out in a bit. How far is it to Cajon Pass?"

"You cross it at mile 342, so you're about ninety-four miles away," Mandy said.

"Wow, I thought I was a lot closer."

"No. And it's mostly uphill," Peter said. "And I hope this doesn't crush your soul, but it snowed a couple of nights ago."

"Snow?"

"There's a pretty big elevation gain between here and Cajon. You're up over six thousand feet for a lot of the hike. It gets up to nine thousand feet in some places. I hope you have a jacket and some long underwear."

"I've got a space blanket," Luke said.

"Where are you headed? Cajon Pass can't be your final destination," Mandy said.

"I'm going home. Orange County."

"Good luck. Getting through the valley on foot will be a total nightmare."

"Peter!" Mandy smacked his arm before turning back toward Luke. "I'm sure you'll make it home."

"How's the water situation on the trail?" Luke asked.

"There's no water until the Mill Creek Fire Station. It's about seventeen and a half miles away," she said. "You'd better take all you can carry now."

"Already stocked up."

"Good. We're going to fill up and keep going. We want to make it to the Santa Clara River today."

"You're not too far away, maybe five miles," Luke said.

"Good luck," Peter said. "And watch out for bears. With an early snow, they might be looking to fatten up sooner than later."

"And snakes," Mandy said. "I almost stepped on a Western Diamondback. He coiled up so fast I almost didn't get out of the way in time. You should have seen the fangs on it, a good two inches long."

"She also catches fifty-foot-long fish from lakes," Peter said sarcastically.

"I do not. Twenty feet maybe, but not fifty." She

flashed a teasing smile at Peter who rolled his eyes. "Come on. Let's fill up and get going."

"Have a good hike," Luke said. "Watch out for humans."

The couple laughed as they headed toward the water cache. A few minutes later they returned to the trail and waved as they headed down the way he'd come.

He lay in the shade for another hour until the air cooled slightly. It was still probably over ninety degrees, but the sooner he could get up into the mountains, the better. Snow actually didn't sound too bad right now.

After hiking another six miles, his feet refused to take another step. They throbbed as he walked into Messenger Flats campground. Since he had his pick of campsites, he chose one under a pine tree with a picnic table. It would be nice to sleep up off the ground tonight. At least he wouldn't have to worry about snakes curling up next to him in the middle of the night.

ANOTHER LONG DAY of hiking led to an hours-long meditation on his failings as a father. Running into the two kids near his daughter's age the previous day had affected him more than he wanted to admit. He should have gone to visit her on the weekend. She'd claimed that she needed her space so that she could get settled at school, but she was his daughter. What daughter didn't need her father hanging around to protect her from frat boys?

As he continued toward the Mill Creek Fire Station, the sparse landscape finally gave way to a forest of burnt trees. Their skeletal remains stretched toward a sky darkening with heavy rainclouds. Although he wanted to press on for as many miles as possible today, he decided to make camp before the rain.

He found an area of high ground and set up his makeshift tent. After wrapping himself in his space blanket, he settled in for the night. Within hours, lightning sliced through the night sky. Deafening cracks of thunder vibrated his bones. Freezing air whipped against his tarp, rattling it until he was sure it would rip.

Hail joined the foray. Under attack from every direction, he had no choice but to weather the storm. His teeth chattered. His muscles ached from overuse and cold. Without any illusions that he'd be sleeping the night away, he prayed he'd survive the night. If he didn't get struck by lightning it would be a miracle.

Minutes passed like hours, giving him plenty of

time to obsess about the safety of his family. His daughter was old enough to take care of herself and she'd had some survival training, and so had his son. But were they together? He could only hope they'd found each other amidst the chaos.

When he woke the next morning, he poked his head out to find a landscape blanketed with snow. He quickly packed his bag and searched for signs of the trail. A depression in the snow marked the path. It was enough to guide him to the Mill Creek Fire Station.

He used the water spigot at the station to refill his water. After using the outhouse, he spotted a plastic-covered hiking register. He flipped open the pages and read several entries from recent hikers. Mandy and Peter had left detailed accounts of their encounters with rattlesnakes. Before them, several other hikers noted nuclear strikes on America. He used a Sharpie marker from his pack to add his own entry.

"Luke Anderson, father to Sierra and Kyle, and beloved husband to Liz, passed through on—" He stopped. Unable to guess the exact date, he simply added, "October, 2017. He was heading home to Orange County, California." He held the pen poised over the paper for a second before completing his entry, "If you find this, if the world survives, tell my family I loved them."

An epitaph to his time on the trail. Maybe his actual epitaph if he kept standing around feeling sorry for himself. He stuffed the pen back in his pack and shook out his body. Now wasn't the time to fall into despair. He'd already made it hundreds of miles, so another couple of hundred were absolutely doable. As long as he pulled his head out of his ass.

He set out at a fast clip. Although he battled against an increasing elevation, he refused to slow his pace. The forest would help shield him from the biting wind. He could handle snow, but wind chill would be deadly.

An hour later he crested a hill. Miles of forest spread out before him. Finally he'd be protected from the wind. He took long strides up the trail into the forest. The visible change in landscape lifted his spirits. He hiked with his head up and a smile on his face until he heard a strange sound up ahead.

He slowed his pace and peered into the forest. Something large and black moved in the shadow of the huge pines. Luke cocked his head to one side. What on earth?

The ball of black suddenly turned and barreled straight for him.

Bear!

Luke raised his hands overhead and started frantically waving and screaming.

"Go away, bear!"

The bear stopped and cocked its head to one side.

"Go on, get lost!"

His heart beat a staccato against the walls of his chest. The tightness in his lungs intensified as the bear rose up on its hind legs. The black bear roared once before dropping down and charging. Every instinct in his body screamed that he should run, but he knew that would only enrage the bear further.

As the bear closed the twenty-yard distance between them, she ran past two cubs which he hadn't noticed until now. Shit! An enraged momma bear would tear him apart.

He yelled and swung his arms overhead in a last-ditch attempt to ward off the bear. When she pounced on him, all of the air in his lungs exploded as a shrill shriek. He fought back, punching the bear anywhere he could make contact. With one swipe of her huge paw, she knocked him to the ground. He rolled onto his back and kicked at the bear. She clawed a long slit in the side of his shirt, breaking through the top layer of skin, and leaving a bloody trail in her wake.

Determined not to die, he fought back. Kicking, screaming, and clawing at her face, he managed to get a solid hit in on her nose. She jerked back and scrambled toward her cubs. He rolled onto all fours and forced himself to get to his feet.

"Go away!"

The bear and her cubs scrambled back into the forest. As soon as they were out of sight, he collapsed in a heap on the ground. Blood poured from a gash on his arm. If he didn't stop the bleeding, he'd be a dead man.

He used a bottle of water to wash out the puncture wound. Either her teeth or one of her claws had left a deep laceration in his arm. He quickly opened his medical supply kit and grabbed the antibacterial ointment.

After slathering it over the wound, he grabbed a trauma pad. He wound a strip of sterile, heavy gauze around the pad as tightly as he could. Knowing that he didn't have much time to spare, he grabbed an Ace bandage and tied it. He used his teeth to pull one end until he was ready to black out from the pain.

He couldn't stay in the area any longer. The bear could come barreling back onto the trail and finish him off. He groaned as he hoisted his pack over his mangled arm. Sharp bolts of pain grated down his arm. With every step, agony intensified until sweat poured down his back.

He listened intently for any sign of the bear. He didn't stop hiking for another two miles. When he finally couldn't take another step, he collapsed at the base of a tree.

Blood soaked the bandages. He gingerly peeled them away to check the flow of blood. It had reduced to a steady trickle. He squeezed the opening of the deepest gash. At over two inches long, it would require stitches.

After grabbing the medical kit, he pulled out a suture kit. In the Navy, he'd been trained to sew stitches on practice dummies. He'd never had to actually use his knowledge in the field. Hopefully he could do it without passing out from blood loss or pain.

He held the threaded needle up to his skin and took a deep breath. It stung worse than a pack of hornets, but he was already drowning in enough pain that a little more didn't make much difference.

It took ten stitches to close it. He slathered more antibiotic cream over the stitches before digging around for his supply of antibiotics. He'd told his doctor that he wanted to keep a full dose of antibiotics at his cabin in case he wasn't able to get back to the city. Although his doctor had tried to argue against it, Luke persisted until he finally got a prescription.

He popped one pill and washed it down with a bottle of water. Hungry from the extra exertion of fighting the bear, then fleeing, he dug into his food stash. He found a Snickers bar. The first bite of sugary goodness melted in his mouth.

After devouring it, he followed it with a pack of beef jerky. He'd lost enough blood to be concerning. Without iron from the meat, he'd have a harder time manufacturing red blood cells to replace what he'd lost. The additional salt would help balance his electrolytes.

Beaten and weak, he forced himself to walk another mile before giving up for the day. He couldn't go farther. He had to be at least three miles away from the bear now. Bears weren't known for stalking humans. If it had been a mountain lion, he'd be more concerned. But he was probably safe for the night.

After setting up his tarp-tent, he lay on his back. Sleep quickly sucked him into darkness. When he woke up in the middle of the pitch-black night, the sound of heavy panting sent shivers of dread down his spine. He wasn't alone.

23

Sierra stacked the final pile of firewood behind the shed. She'd been chopping wood for hours and couldn't wait to be done with her chores. The day-to-day monotony of living without TV, a phone, or internet were wearing on her. She'd been watching the same movies over and over since the day she arrived. There were a few paperback books in the cabin, but nothing she hadn't already read. Today, she had to do something new or she'd lose her mind.

Although her mom had warned her not to wander off of their property, Sierra ignored the ridiculous rule and headed into the forest. She crossed the stream and scampered up one steep hill before sliding down the next. The shrill squawk of a raven disturbed the quiet peacefulness of the oak forest. A flock of gray doves took flight, beating their wings furiously.

Sierra was so entranced by the birds that she didn't notice the man standing near a tree about ten yards away.

"Hey there," he called. "How's it going?"

As she walked closer, she realized he wasn't much older than her. Maybe a year or two older.

"Hi," she said. "What are you doing out here?"

"Gathering acorns."

He lifted the lid on the picnic basket he carried. A huge pile of acorns shifted under the sudden movement.

"What are you doing with those?"

"Making acorn flour."

"That's a thing?"

"Yep. My mom said we can make bread with it."

"So you've done this before?"

"No, but she's got a book about cooking wild food, so we're going to try it."

She plucked an acorn out of the basket and held it up. How was his mom going to turn this into flour? Didn't flour come from some other kind of plant or something?

"Do you live around here?" he asked.

"Over the hill. You?"

"Down in the canyon."

"Which one?"

"Silverado."

"Over by that church?"

"Yeah."

"Mom says they're weird over there," she said.

"A little fire and brimstoney, but the people are nice."

"Did you always live up here or did you move after the bombs?"

"After the bombs. We lived in Coto De Caza. This is one of our cabins. We've got one at Big Bear and another one in Colorado. But my mom says this is the safest option right now since travel is so dangerous."

"We lived in Foothill Ranch," she said.

"Nice."

"Not as nice as Coto."

He shrugged. "A house is a house. The bigger the house, the more you have to clean it."

"Your mom made you clean the house?"

"No. We had a live-in housekeeper," he said. "But she was always cleaning. I kinda felt bad for her."

"Why? It was her job."

"I don't know. Anyway, I should be heading back."

"Wait!" She stepped forward and put her hand on

his forearm. "Don't go yet. I haven't talked to anyone but my family in days."

"You should come to the church with me. There are a lot of people you can talk to over there."

"How many people?"

"I don't know. Thirty maybe? Forty? I haven't really counted."

"I probably shouldn't," she said. "No one's supposed to know we're at the cabin."

"Where is your cabin?"

She hesitated. He seemed nice, but her mom would kill her if he randomly showed up one day.

"I should get going. Maybe I'll see you here again one day," she said.

"We could meet here tomorrow."

"That would be fun."

She smiled for the first time in days. Finally, she'd have someone her age she could talk to, and he was kinda cute too. Shaggy brown surfer hair, a deep tan, and bright blue eyes. Not bad. He had some muscles too, especially in his arms. Maybe he'd gotten them from carrying a bunch of acorns around every day.

"See ya," she said as she turned to walk away.

"Hey, what's your name?"

"Sierra. Yours?"

"Adam."

"Nice to meet you. Good luck with the acorn flour."

"Mom says we can make it into cookies too. I'll see if she'll make some and then I'll bring you one tomorrow," he said.

"Wow, that sounds awesome. We've been eating rice and beans almost every day. I'd be willing to try anything at this point."

"Hey, do you want to come back to my house with me? Maybe my mom can teach you how to make acorn cookies."

"I can't," she said. "I really should be getting back."

"Getting back to where?" a deep voice asked.

She jumped and spun around to find a man wearing jeans, a tan, long-sleeved shirt, and cowboy boots standing right behind her.

"I'm sorry," the man said. "I didn't mean to startle you. I'm Elijah."

He held out his hand. She shook it quickly before releasing it. He studied her with sharp, steel-gray eyes. Although he had a smile on his face, the expression didn't seep into his gaze. It stayed steady, cold. Almost lifeless. A chill shimmied down her spine.

"I should be going," she said.

As she turned to leave, Elijah grabbed her upper arm.

"Hold on. I didn't realize anyone else was living out here," he said. "What's your name?"

"Sierra." She jerked her arm free.

"I hope I didn't scare you."

"I'm not scared." Her wobbly voice betrayed her, so she paused before continuing to speak. "I just need to get home."

"Where do you live?" Elijah asked.

"Over the hill."

"Across the stream?"

She nodded. Although she hadn't wanted to give him any information, she didn't want to be rude. She was probably overreacting to him because he towered over her by at least a foot. At only five feet two, everyone towered over her, but not everyone made her feel so small.

"Do you live with your family?" Elijah asked.

She nodded.

"I'd love to have them join us at church. We have a big potluck every night about an hour before sundown. Please bring your family tonight. I'd love to meet them."

"I'll ask if we can come."

"Good." He turned to Adam. "How's the acorn collection coming?"

"Basket's almost full," Adam said.

"Excellent."

"I'll, uh… I'll see you later," she said.

She hurried away from them, knowing full well that she wouldn't tell her mom about the encounter. Her mom would be furious and would probably ground her for a week. Which was ridiculous anyway, because what could she possibly ground her from? Watching the same movies? Reading the same books?

As she crossed the stream, she laughed softly. She was still thinking like she was back in high school. She was an adult now. Her mom couldn't ground her, but she could give her the silent treatment, which was even worse. She hated it when her mom refused to speak to her. The lack of conversation and interaction drove her nuts. Of course her mom had to know that or she wouldn't use that technique on her.

Maybe going to visit the preacher and Adam wouldn't be such a bad thing. Having a secret all to herself gave her a delicious little thrill. She skipped the rest of the way to the cabin. She couldn't wait to eat a delicious acorn cookie tomorrow. Maybe it would taste like sawdust, but at least it would be something different. And she'd get to see Adam again. He was cute. And in a post-apocalyptic world, meeting up with a cute guy was worth any potential punishment.

The next day, Sierra flew through her chores so fast that her mom added the extra task of checking the trip wires around the property. She grumbled as she moved from tree to tree checking the wires and testing the bells. Everything was still in place.

When she finally finished and reported back that everything was intact, she was free to leave. She ran through the stream, then up and down several hills before reaching the place she'd met Adam the day before. A small triangle of three oaks formed a recognizable meeting point. She sat on a tree stump and waited for him to appear.

An hour later, she wasn't sure if he was going to show up. Maybe he'd been forced to do extra chores too?

Footsteps crunched through the forest. The preacher strolled up to where she sat.

"Good afternoon," he said. "Adam said you'd be here."

"Where is he?"

"The cookies are taking longer than expected, so he's still at home with his mom. He mentioned that you'd be waiting for him, so I offered to come up and get you." He held out his hand.

She eyed it warily before getting to her feet without his help.

"I could come back tomorrow," she said.

"Well, you could, but honestly, I don't think there will be any cookies left. Once word gets out that Melinda's baked anything, pandemonium breaks out." He smiled. Again, the movement didn't reach his eyes. "If you'd rather take your chances and wait until tomorrow, no worries."

He turned to leave.

"Wait." The temptation of a mouthwatering cookie overrode her hesitation. "I'll go with you."

"Excellent."

She followed him through the woods, carefully noting landmarks so she could try to find her way back. Next time she'd remember to bring some string so she could tie markers on the trees. They'd been walking for almost thirty minutes and she was so turned around she wasn't sure which way would lead her home. She might have to look for the main road and follow it home.

When they finally emerged onto a paved road, she breathed a bit easier. She recognized the church's spire. It rose up over the hills as if to lay claim to the entire canyon. Outside the church, small gatherings of three to eight people stood together talking and laughing. The tension in her gut relaxed. She wasn't even sure why she'd been so scared to begin with. They all seemed like perfectly normal people.

As the preacher weaved his way through his flock,

they turned to greet him. Several women seemed to bat their eyelashes at him. Weird. Weren't preachers celibate?

She followed him to a large grill where a woman in a yellow apron stirred a pot of stew.

"I'd like you to meet my wife, Patrice."

The woman turned around. She was about the same age as the preacher, somewhere in her forties. Her pale complexion and ruddy cheeks made every line on her face stand out. She had the worn look of someone who'd been sick for months.

"Hello." Patrice forced a smile.

"This is Sierra," Elijah said. "She's come from over the hill to partake in our hospitality."

"I'm just here for the cookies," Sierra said.

"Patrice has been simmering the stew all day. I must insist you stay for dinner," he said.

"Oh, I definitely can't stay that long. My mom will be wondering where I went."

"You didn't tell her you were coming here?"

"No."

"Thou shalt honor thy father and thy mother," he said.

"I'm not dishonoring them. I don't feel the need to tell them everything I'm doing all the time," she snapped.

"Fair enough," he said.

"Leave the poor girl alone," Patrice whispered.

Elijah shot her a withering look. She turned back to stir the stew.

"If you can only stay for a cookie, so be it."

"Where's Adam?" Sierra asked.

"With his mom in the church kitchen."

She followed him into the church. With its wooden pews and simple podium, it had the classic look of a country church. She'd seen several replicas of this type of church when she'd gone to visit her dad's parents in Tennessee.

"Are you Baptist?" she asked.

"No. Fundamentalist Christian."

"So also not Catholic."

"No. We believe in the literal word of the Lord."

"So you literally believe that women shouldn't teach or have authority over men?" she asked.

"The sexes have their place in God's world. Women should be in charge of the household and children while men take care of providing for them."

She rolled her eyes behind his back. Take away the modern lighting and they could have stepped back a hundred years into the time when women were property and men ruled with iron fists. Based on the way his wife didn't argue with him, she suspected he firmly executed his archaic beliefs in his own life.

As they entered a back hallway, the smell of sugar

and nuts filled the air. Saliva flooded her mouth. Cray-cray preacher or not, these people had sugar. She wanted to do a cartwheel in the middle of the hall. Praise the Lord indeed.

"Melinda, I have a guest with me," Elijah said as he entered the kitchen.

"Hello honey," Melinda said. "I've been so excited to meet you."

"Really?"

"Yes. Adam said you're a lovely young woman and he's right. Isn't she beautiful, Elijah?"

"Stunning."

Sierra resisted the urge to throw up in her mouth. As soon as Elijah left the room, she made a face. Melinda's smile dropped.

"You shouldn't do that," she whispered.

"What?"

"Make faces behind people's backs."

"He'll never know," Sierra said.

"He knows everything."

"Uh… okay." These people were weird. She couldn't wait to grab a cookie and get out of there.

"Anyway…" Melinda flashed a huge smile. "The acorn cookies are cooling on the racks. They should be ready soon. Adam told me a little bit about you, but we didn't realize people were living up on the other side of the river."

Although Melinda seemed nice enough, she heeded her warning about Elijah somehow knowing everything. Maybe the place was bugged or something, so she decided not to tell them anything else about her house or her family.

"Is Adam around?" Sierra asked.

"He's out collecting more acorns."

"Really? I didn't see him in the forest."

"Maybe they went to a different part today," Melinda said. "Here, try a cookie. They're cool enough now."

"Thank you."

Sierra took the cookie from her hand. It was slightly thicker than the cookies she was used to, but it smelled sweet, like maple syrup. As she bit into it, sweetness sparked across her tongue. It tasted like warm chestnuts and had to be packed with sugar. She resisted the urge to moan. It was one of the best cookies she'd ever tasted.

"These are so good. I need to teach my mom how to make these."

"I could teach you how to make them," Melinda said.

"Really?"

"Of course. I would need you to help collect more acorns, but I'd be happy to have another pair of hands in the kitchen with me."

"Oh, I wouldn't be able to make this a regular thing. I can't be gone for hours every day," Sierra said.

"She doesn't know you're here?"

"No."

"Why not?"

"She doesn't trust strangers."

"Understandable considering the state of the world." Melinda lowered her voice. "Sometimes I think it's best not to join new groups. But what do I know."

"Don't you like it here?"

"Of course." Melinda smiled again as her gaze shifted to the door. "What's not to like about a great congregation filled with God-fearing people?"

Sierra turned toward the door, half-expecting someone to be lurking in the shadows. No one was there.

"Thank you for the cookie," she said. "I should be getting home."

As Sierra headed toward the door, Melinda hurried over and grabbed her wrist to stop her.

"Things aren't always what they seem. Be careful."

After delivering the chilling warning, Melinda returned to kneading a pile of dough. Sierra opened her mouth to ask her what she meant but was cut off by Adam.

"Hey! You made it."

"She just tried one of the cookies," his mom said.

"It was great," Sierra said.

"Are you staying for dinner?" Adam asked.

"No. I have to get home."

"Let me walk you back. Is that okay, mom?"

"Ask Elijah."

"Okay."

As they entered the hall, Sierra stopped him. "Why do you need to ask Elijah?"

"He likes to know where everyone is, so no one goes missing."

"That seems a bit controlling," she said.

"It's for our safety. Come on, we need to hurry so I can be back in time for dinner."

She stood silent while he asked permission from Elijah. The sooner she could get home the better. The entire trip had left her uneasy. She couldn't quite put her finger on why. After all, they'd been very nice to her… but something wasn't right, and she didn't want to stick around to figure it out.

24

Elijah walked several paces away from the barbecue before motioning to Turner. As chief of the security team, Turner had access to the resources Elijah needed to keep his flock safe. Turner joined him underneath a large oak.

"I need you to do something for me," Elijah began. "There's a girl running around in the woods. You may have seen her here today."

"The blonde?"

"Yes. Adam found her wandering around the acorn trees. She lives somewhere over the hills."

"Any intel on who she's living with?" Turner asked.

"No. But she can't be alone. How would she survive?"

"She's probably with her family." Turner scratched his beard. "We should scout her location. See what she's got in terms of resources."

"My thoughts exactly."

"I can send a couple of guys after dinner to do some recon."

"Please be discreet," Elijah said. "I don't want to raise an alarm until we know what we're dealing with."

"True. It might just be a normal family living in the woods."

"She was clean, well fed. I think they have a cabin somewhere."

"We'll find it," Turner said.

"Good. Report back to me directly."

"Of course."

"And be careful. I don't want to lose any men. We're a strong force to be reckoned with right now, and we must keep our numbers," Elijah said. "It's the Lord's will."

"Amen."

"Good. Good. Be sure to eat well. I want you out there tracking that girl until you find her. I don't care if it takes all night."

"We have flashlight mounts on most of the shotguns. We'll be able to see just fine."

"But don't let her see you," Elijah warned. "For now, I simply want to gather information. I don't want to engage until we know whether or not it will be to our advantage. Most people without groups will die within the next few months. People typically don't stockpile enough food or water to last longer than a few weeks, if that."

"We could wait them out," Turner said.

"Maybe. I prefer not to speculate. Let's get some real intelligence."

"Yes, sir." Turner saluted before turning on his heel and marching back to his picnic table full of men assigned to security.

Elijah stood back and watched his flock. Forty-three people relied on him to run a tight ship. He had no doubt he'd been called by God to fight the final battle of Armageddon. He'd recognized President Grayson as the antichrist the moment he'd come to power through a rigged election. He'd only had six months to prepare for the end times, and here they were, ready to face the final battle of good versus evil.

He slipped away from the gathering and headed toward the arsenal in the shed behind the church. He carried the key to it around his neck at all times. Turner carried a duplicate. He was the only man Elijah would trust with the weapons.

Over the years, Turner had proven to be a great leader within the congregation. He'd fought for America in the Gulf War. A soldier through and through, Turner viewed any attack on the congregation as a direct attack on God's chosen ones. Because make no mistake, they were chosen, and Elijah intended to fulfill his sacred pact with the Lord.

He unlocked the large padlock on the shed and opened the doors. Turner had rounded up all the weapons within two days after the bombs dropped. They had twenty-eight shotguns, fifteen rifles, twenty pistols, fourteen revolvers, and one, beautiful .50 caliber M2 Browning machine gun someone had stored in his garage.

Elijah didn't ask how the man had purchased the gun. California's excessively restrictive gun laws didn't apply now. Although they'd searched all the houses in the valley, he suspected some people still hid guns in their homes. On the one hand, he didn't blame them for being wary, but on the other, he wanted all the guns, especially the large-caliber guns.

On day three, they'd had to fire the M2 at a group of insurgents coming up from El Toro Road. They'd fired one warning shot as the trucks had breached the barricade. When the insurgents didn't stop, they'd burned through half a belt of ammo. Unfortunately all that firepower had destroyed the other men's trucks, rendering them completely useless. They'd been able to siphon some gas out of one tank that hadn't been punctured, but the rest was a total loss.

Elijah didn't mind though. Let the carnage stand as a warning to others, and as a reminder to his flock to stay in line.

He locked the gun shed. As he turned to leave, Patrice came around the corner.

"What are you doing?" he demanded.

"I overheard Turner talking to some men. Did you tell them to go after that girl?"

"What were you doing listening in on conversations that don't involve you?"

"You should leave her and her family alone," she said. "They've done nothing to us."

"They may be an asset to the family."

"These people aren't your family. I'm your family."

"You're my wife, but you sure as hell don't act like one." He snarled and grabbed her upper arm. "If you really cared about me, you'd do as I say and stop asking so many questions all the time. A woman's place isn't to ask questions, it's to obey. And right now you're disobeying me."

When she cowered, he smiled. *Much better.*

"I'm sorry," she stammered. "I was just worried about your intentions."

"Never mind my intentions. Are you done serving the stew?"

"Yes."

"Then you should be processing acorns with Melinda. She knows how to behave like an obedient wife."

"Her husband's dead."

"Yes, but she's got a new allegiance now. She's part of our family, and unlike you, she actually listens to what I say."

"She's afraid of you."

"Why would she be afraid?" he yelled before lowering his voice. "She's not afraid. Stop projecting your insecurities onto her."

"I know what you do at night. I know where you go," she whispered.

Her sniveling, simpering tone grated on his nerves. What he'd ever seen in her was such a distant memory that he couldn't call to mind even the smallest list of her positive qualities. If he hadn't preached so vehemently against divorce, he would have dropped her years ago. But every man of true faith had been forced to carry an albatross of one kind or another.

"Go fetch Melinda," he said.

"No."

He reeled back and slapped her hard across the face. An angry red blotch instantly formed on her cheek. Tears sprang into her eyes and her bottom lip trembled.

"You disgust me," she whispered.

He grabbed her by her hair and slammed her into the shed. With her face pressed against the wood, he whispered into her ear.

"One day I'll be rid of you," he growled. "Tomorrow maybe. Or the day after. Or maybe in a week. Keep trying my patience, woman. It may be the last thing you do."

When he released her, she crumpled to the ground.

"Go get Melinda. Don't make me ask again."

She crawled away from him.

"Get to your feet and clean yourself up. I don't want to hear a single complaint from the flock. They already whisper about your clumsiness. Needless speculation will only hurt the family."

As she rose to her feet, all light had faded from her eyes. He recognized the slack-jawed look of defeat. Good. She needed to learn her place in the new world order.

Several minutes later, Melinda appeared.

"You called for me, sir?"

"Yes…yes I did."

He wrapped an arm around her shoulders and led her into the forest.

Liz sat in the blind she'd created part way up the hill behind the cabin. Constructed with natural materials from the forest, she'd situated it next to a large oak tree. Using infrared goggles, she scanned the forest around her house. The only sign of movement came from the occasional ground squirrel. They were ubiquitous in the area due to a lack of predators.

She'd been on watch for three hours when she decided to take a break to use the bathroom. As she hiked down the hill, her foot landed on a pile of loose rock and slipped out from under her. She landed hard on her butt.

"Dammit."

As she climbed to her feet, she heard the loud snap of a branch somewhere in the distance.

She froze.

A squirrel wouldn't make that much noise. It could be a coyote or a mountain lion. Although those animals were stealthy enough that they wouldn't step directly on a branch. That left only one possibility.

She seated her goggles over her eyes and scanned

the tree line at the edge of the clearing around the cabin. When she spotted movement, she dropped to the ground and lay on her belly. She pulled the rifle sling off and pointed the rifle toward the movement.

The green landscape offered little contrast, making it hard for her to see what was causing the branches to snap.

The sudden jingle of the bell traps sent a bolt of fear down her spine. Whoever was out there now knew that someone was living in the cabin. The kids were both asleep inside and it was her job to protect them.

She raised the rifle and adjusted the sight as much as she could. It wasn't the perfect setup; thermal imaging would have been better, but she had to work with what she had.

As she scanned the area of trees, the outline of a man appeared. He stepped into the clearing and cautiously stalked toward the porch.

She aimed the gun at his chest and let out a soft breath before pulling the trigger. The man went down with a shout.

Inside the house, a light snapped on. She cursed under her breath. She'd told the kids a thousand times never to turn the lights on, especially at night. She just prayed they'd stay inside the cabin.

Two more silhouettes raced into the clearing.

They stopped where the other man writhed on the ground. Loud moans rolled up the hill, becoming shrill and sharp when the other men tried to help the fallen man to his feet.

From a distance, she wasn't able to make out any identifying features. But there were definitely three of them, and they were all big enough to be men.

As they carried off their fallen comrade, she considered following them. Letting them leave could be a huge mistake. They knew where she lived, knew she was armed, and they might return with reinforcements.

She waited until they were out of sight before sneaking down the hill. She stayed within the tree line, circling around until she'd reached their breach point. As she paused, she listened for the sound of cracking branches. It was easy to identify her prey. They weren't doing anything to try to mask their retreat.

Although they'd gotten a head start, she was able to stay on their trail all the way to the stream. The open area around the stream wouldn't offer much protection, so she proceeded with caution.

As she stepped out toward the stream, the bright flash of a gunshot registered a split second before the sound. She dropped down and ran back into the tree line where she hid behind a thick oak.

Six additional shots hacked away bark from the trees surrounding her location. Completely pinned down, her only option was to wait. She considered firing return shots, but they were likely to chip away at trees instead of hit their target. It would be a complete waste of ammo.

The shots stopped.

She cautiously raised her head and peered around the edge of the tree. Silence suffocated the forest. Nothing moved. Not a single squirrel. Not a single bird. Nothing.

Crouched behind the tree, she finally registered the distant crack of a branch. They'd used their gunshots as cover to beat a retreat.

Without information on their location, she couldn't risk moving forward. For all she knew, one of them could have left the others and circled back to the cabin. She couldn't leave the kids unprotected, so she turned and picked a silent path through the forest.

When she reached the cabin, Sierra cracked open the front door.

"Mom, is that you?"

"Yes. Get inside."

Liz pushed the door open just enough to slip through. She closed it and set the two-by-four lock into place.

"I heard gunshots. What's going on?" Sierra asked.

"Men came out of the forest toward the house."

"Men? What men?" Sierra paled.

"I don't know. I couldn't see much because it's pitch black out there and these goggles aren't much good for details."

"Did you see anything? How tall were they? Did any of them have anything special, like a beard?" Sierra asked.

"A beard?" That seemed oddly specific. "Why would you ask about a beard?"

"I don't know. It seemed like something that might be easy to see."

"I couldn't see shit out there. We need to get our perimeter lighting installed. Just enough to light up the area around the house. We'll use motion sensors to do it."

"Dad has all of that stuff in the shed," Kyle said as he poked his head over the edge of the loft.

Justice scrambled down the steps and ran to her side. She petted the dog. Maybe she should let him roam around at night. But how much warning could he really give? He probably would have been shot had he been outside when the men arrived.

"Where did they go?" Sierra asked.

"Past the stream. I lost them there."

"So they were headed over the hills toward the west?"

"Yeah."

Sierra bit the edge of her lip. She wrapped her arms across her belly.

"I know it's scary," Liz said, not wanting to see her daughter so terrified. "But we knew this might happen. That's why we have the trip wires with bells set up. We just need to work on the perimeter more."

"I wish Dad were here."

"I do too, but he's not. No amount of wishing is going to change that, so we need to do what we can to fortify this place until he gets here."

"How do we know he's not dead?" Sierra asked.

"We don't. We don't know anything."

"We should assume he's dead," Kyle said softly.

The grim expression on his face tore at her heart. If he gave up hope, how long would it take for Sierra to follow suit? How long before *she* lost hope herself?

"He's not dead," Liz said. "He's out there fighting his way home. We don't know what he's going through, but I'd know if he were dead."

"How?" Sierra asked.

"I'd just know."

Liz walked into the kitchen to pour a glass of water. Although she tried to maintain a strong façade with the kids, inside, she was breaking. Even if she could handle this alone, she didn't want to. Luke had to come home, and soon. The stress chipped away at her body every day, and eventually she'd be so worn down, she wasn't sure she'd be able to defend the cabin. And then what would happen to her family?

25

Three minutes after midnight, Elijah jolted awake at the sound of pounding on his front door. He slipped out of bed.

"What's going on?" his wife asked.

"Nothing. Go to sleep."

She rolled over.

He slipped into a robe and headed to the door. As he opened it, Turner and Ivan stood outside. They carried a limp, lifeless Paul between them.

"He's been shot," Turner said.

"Get him inside," Elijah said. "Ivan, get Kat. Don't tell her why. Don't tell anyone else.

"Yes, sir."

After Ivan left, Elijah helped Turner carry Paul to

the kitchen table. He moved everything off the table except for the tablecloth and laid Paul on top of it.

"What happened?" Elijah demanded.

"We tracked the girl's trail back to a cabin a few hills over. We didn't see any sign of life, but as we got closer, Paul tripped over a trip wire. They'd strung bells across it. Not a bad trick for an amateur."

"Then they opened fire?"

"No," Turner said. "We didn't see any movement, so we continued toward the cabin. Paul got about three yards out from the forest when a sniper opened fire."

"A sniper?"

"Yep. They had him positioned on a hill overlooking the cabin."

"Smart."

"I would have done the same," Turner said.

"How many were there?"

"I'm not sure. Other than the sniper, I didn't see anyone else. I didn't even get a good look at him."

"Could it have been a girl?" Elijah asked.

Turner frowned as if insulted by the question.

"No way. I don't know any female who could shoot like that. It had to be the girl's father. Or maybe her brother. Regardless, the guy's a great shot. He would have taken us all down if we hadn't returned fire."

Paul groaned.

"Stay still," Elijah said. "We're getting help. Where the hell's Kat?"

The front door burst open and Kat walked in followed by Ivan.

"Status?" she said in a clipped tone. Probably habit from her days as an ER nurse.

"Bleeding from a gunshot wound."

"Who shot him?" she asked as she slapped her medical bag down on the table.

"We don't know." Elijah shot a warning look to Turner and Ivan behind Kat's back. "Is he going to make it?"

"He's lost a lot of blood. Get me some clean towels, water, and I need more light. A lamp or a flashlight would help me see."

As Ivan ran to gather the items, Elijah held Paul's hand. He knew there'd be casualties in a holy war, but Paul was a good man. A good father too. His family would be devastated if they lost him. His wife was three months pregnant. A terrible time to lose a husband, not that any time would be good.

Ivan returned with a lamp and clean towels. As he went into the kitchen to boil water, Kat cut off Paul's shirt. She spread the fabric and used a washcloth to clean the wound area. She rolled him onto his side and checked his back.

"You'd better start praying," she said. "Looks like the bullet didn't exit."

"Can you operate?" Elijah asked.

"I'm not a surgeon."

"You're the closest thing we've got to one."

"I'll do what I can, but I'm not going to lie to you. He's probably not going to make it."

Elijah stepped back and prayed with every ounce of righteous conviction he could muster. Ultimately it would be the Lord's will, but as His faithful servant, he liked to think he had God's ear.

As Kat dug around to try to get the bullet, Ivan turned and ran toward the kitchen sink. He threw up, then washed his mouth out with water. He leaned over the sink with his hands braced on either side for several seconds. When he turned to glare at Elijah, the preacher responded with an equally cold stare. How dare he set his accusatory gaze on him? Who did he think he was?

Ivan pushed away from the sink and walked toward the table.

"This is your fault."

"Mine?" Elijah balked. "It's the shooter's fault."

"We shouldn't go on recon missions at night. Who knows what kind of traps we could be walking into," Ivan said.

"Are you not a member of the security team?" Elijah asked.

"I am."

"Are you not sworn to protect the family until the end of days?"

"I am, and I will. But I'm not taking any crazy chances anymore. That girl Adam found is not what she seems. We don't know anything about her. She could be holed up with an army of men waiting to protect her," Ivan said.

"She's just a girl." Elijah sniffed. "And as far as when and where you'll be sent, I will determine that. You will do as you're told."

Ivan's fists clenched at his sides. His jaw twitched. Shadows from the flashlight jerked across his face. For a moment, Elijah wasn't sure the other man would back down. Then he finally relented.

"What can I do to help you, Kat?"

"I can't get the bullet. I'm going to need more light."

As he held the light for Kat, Elijah surveyed the team. Eventually he'd need a real doctor on his team. Maybe he should sent scouts back to the city to try to find one.

A sudden gush of blood spurted from Paul's chest. His entire body convulsed before falling limp.

"Shit, we're losing him," Kat yelled.

The bedroom door opened and Patrice walked out.

"What's going on?" When she spotted Paul, she let out a sharp cry. "What happened?"

"Go back to bed," Elijah snapped. He didn't need to deal with her sniveling on top of everything else.

"What happened to your face?" Kat asked Patrice.

"Nothing," Elijah answered. "You know how clumsy she can be."

Kat narrowed her eyes before returning her attention to her patient. Patrice went back into the bedroom and slammed the door.

Several minutes later, Kat backed away from the table. A grim expression marred her face.

"He's gone. There's nothing else we can do. He lost too much blood."

Elijah's stomach clenched. To lose one of his flock was a blow not just to his ego, but to his numbers. Paul was one of his strongest men. Without him, they were weaker. He'd have to be replaced as soon as possible.

"Please notify his wife," Elijah said.

Kat nodded. She washed up in the kitchen before gathering her medical equipment. She left without a backward glance.

"This means war," Elijah said to Ivan and Turner, who stood in the shadows. "At first light, I want another team out there. Survey, but don't engage. I can't afford to lose any more men."

"*We* can't," Ivan corrected.

"Yes, we. Of course." Elijah dismissed him with a wave. "Bury him away from town. Get a wheelbarrow if you need help carrying him."

"What should we tell people when they ask what happened?" Turner asked.

"Tell them..." Elijah paused as he formulated a plan. "Tell them the holy war has begun. Insurgents are circling the camp and we must be ready to fight. I will address the flock at the morning meal. We will use this to our advantage. It will bring us closer together."

"Yes, sir," Turner said. "I'll get the wheelbarrow."

After he left, Elijah turned to Ivan, who'd been silent during the last exchange.

"If you have anything to say, son, now's the time to do it," Elijah said.

Ivan pressed his lips together and shook his head no.

"Good. I want all traces of his blood cleaned up by morning." Elijah walked toward his bedroom door. Before going inside, he turned back to Ivan. "Make no mistake, there will be more casualties. More violence. More death. If you want to leave, you're free to go. But if you're here come morning, I'll expect you to follow my orders without question. Are we clear?"

"Yes, sir."

"Good."

Elijah closed the door behind him. As he slipped into bed beside his frigid wife, he laced his fingers behind his head. Eventually he'd do something about her too, but for now, he'd have to maintain the charade of being a doting, loving husband. Just one more sacrifice he'd have to make as the chosen leader of God's children.

SIERRA COULDN'T SLEEP for the rest of the night. She paced back and forth from window to window peering out into the darkness. As she searched for any sign of the men who'd snuck up to the cabin, she couldn't help but think that it was all her fault. She shouldn't have gone past the stream. She should have run as soon as she saw Adam. But why would they sneak over in the middle of the night instead of during the day? Was it really someone from the church, or was it a different group?

Determined to find out the truth, she waited until after breakfast before venturing out into the forest. As she followed the landmarks back toward the church, she stopped to tie green string around a branch every few feet. If someone wasn't looking for the string, they'd never notice it. But she could use them to navigate home.

When she reached the road that led to the church, she considered her options. She could stay in the trees and try to spy on them, or she could march right down there and demand answers.

The scent of beef wafted up from a plume of smoke near the front of the church. They were probably eating lunch. If she went to confront them now, she'd have to do it in front of the entire congregation. And maybe that was the right way to approach them. At least she'd be safe. They wouldn't all band together and try to kill her, right? What kind of people would they be if they did?

It probably didn't matter since she'd be dead, but she highly doubted they were all psychopathic killers. She would have seen it in their eyes when she'd been there the previous day.

As she walked toward the gathering, the scent of barbecue invaded her nostrils. Her stomach clenched. Other than the cookie, she hadn't eaten any meat in days. Her mom had insisted on rationing it.

The closer she came to the grill, the more her stomach churned. No one noticed her approaching until she reached the first picnic table. There were ten picnic tables situated in two rows. Several men turned to stare at her as she strode toward the preacher. He had his back to her.

"Hey," she said when she reached him.

"Sierra, what a pleasant surprise," Elijah said.

"I need to talk to you."

"Of course. I'd be happy to talk, but we're about to serve lunch. Would you like to join us?"

Her traitorous stomach rumbled.

"As our guest, you will be served first," he declared without waiting for her answer.

"I guess I could wait."

"Come, sit with me and my friend Turner," Elijah said, indicating a seat at the picnic bench next to an older man.

Sierra sat. A woman she didn't know placed a paper plate in front of her. Steam curled up from grilled chicken. Several stems of broccoli and half of an apple accompanied the meat.

"Go ahead," Elijah said. "Eat up."

She dug into the food, savoring the partially burnt chicken skin. Before the bombs, she wouldn't have touched broccoli with a ten-foot pole, but now it had risen to the level of exotic delicacy.

"Does your family have a garden?" Elijah asked casually.

She wasn't fooled. The coldness in his gaze sent a shiver down her spine.

"No." They'd actually planted seeds two days earlier, but she didn't see the point in revealing this information. "Were you at my house last night?"

Conversation halted around them. Several people turned to watch Elijah, who immediately plastered a smile on his face.

"Of course not; I don't even know where you live. Why, did you have company?" he asked.

"Three men. My mom shot one of them," she said.

"Really?" Elijah glanced at the man sitting to the other side of her. A look she couldn't identify passed between them. "Is your mom okay?"

"She wasn't hit. The men who came were shitty shots."

At the next table over, someone whispered to the person sitting next to them. Elijah glanced their way, effectively silencing them with one look.

"We don't use foul language here," he said.

"Good thing I don't live here." She chomped into the apple and chewed obnoxiously.

"Why wasn't your father outside?" he asked.

"How did you know she was shot at outside?"

"I just assumed it was outside or she would have been hit. It's not hard to hit someone inside a house."

"And you know this from experience?" Sierra asked.

The corners of his mouth turned down slightly.

"No, not directly. But I can assure you, whoever attacked your home last night wasn't from our church. We're a peaceful community as long as no one attacks us."

Several people mumbled in agreement.

"Have you heard of any other groups lurking around?" she asked.

"No. Although we did have a group attack us several days ago. We had to kill them or they were going to kill us."

She tried not to show her shock, but she was sitting amongst killers. And they had guns. Although she didn't see any, they had to have guns, otherwise they wouldn't have been able to kill off another group.

"I've been thinking…maybe you'd be safer if you moved in with us," Elijah said. "You and your family would be more than welcome to stay in one of the empty houses in the canyon. We have more than enough food to go around. Of course, we'd ask that you bring any supplies and weapons with you."

"I'd have to ask my mo—dad," she said. She had to make sure they still thought her dad was with them. "I should go."

"I'd love to meet your father," he said. "Bring him for dinner tonight. Maybe if he sees how our group operates, he'll be more inclined to join us."

"Maybe," she said noncommittally. "Thanks for lunch."

After leaving the church, she walked into the woods for about a quarter of a mile. She stopped and turned to make sure no one was following her. The forest remained silent but for the chirp of a bird and the scamper of a squirrel.

She slowly made her way back to the cabin, checking every quarter mile to make sure they weren't following her. She didn't believe the preacher. As far as she could tell, there weren't any other groups in this part of the forest. They had to be the ones who'd attacked them last night.

Her mom was going to kill her when she found out. Not only had she broken the rule about leaving the property, but she'd led a band of murderers right to their door.

26

Several days after the confrontation with the preacher, Liz returned from perimeter patrol to make dinner. She turned on the gas stove which had an electronic ignition switch. It didn't light. She glanced at the clock on the stove. Instead of the usual blue numbers, it was completely black.

"That's weird," she said.

"What?" Kyle called from the living room.

"The clock isn't working on the stove and I can't get it to light."

"Yeah the DVD player won't work either," he said.

"When did that happen?"

"I don't know, a few hours ago."

"What about the lights?" she asked.

"We're not supposed to turn them on, remember?"

"Right. I'll make an exception so I can check the power." She flicked on the light switch in the kitchen. "It looks like the power went out."

"Maybe it'll come back on later. Can't you light the stove with a match? Dad does that sometimes."

"Yeah."

Liz opened the junk drawer and pulled out a box of long matches. She struck one and turned on the gas. She held the match to the burner. Flames flickered to life. She blew out the match and tossed it into a bowl by the sink. After grabbing a cast iron skillet from the cabinet, she turned around just in time to watch the flame flicker out and die.

"What on earth?"

Bells jingled outside. She dropped the pan onto the stove and raced to grab her rifle by the front door. She checked to make sure a round was in the chamber before opening the front door. She looked down the sight and spotted Edwin and Sandy Wright, the neighbors, walking up from the road.

"Hey," Edwin called. "You guys have any power?"

"No." Liz lowered the gun. "You?"

"Lost it an hour ago or so," Sandy said. "Gas is out too."

"That's weird," Liz said.

"I think we've been hit again," Edwin said.

"With what?"

"An EMP."

"An EMP?" Liz couldn't help but crack a smile. "Isn't that science fiction?"

"No," Sandy said. "We knew something like this could happen, especially if we're under nuclear attack. The enemy only needs to detonate a nuke three hundred miles up over the center of America. Nebraska, Kansas, any of those corn states would do. Then poof, everything's gone. No electrical grid. Very few cars will still work. Computers will be fried."

"What makes you think we had an EMP strike?" Liz asked.

"Anything with a battery still works. No battery and it's not working. We tried hooking my laptop up via our battery backup and it's not working. Circuits are probably fried," Edwin said. "I got on the HAM and everyone's saying the same thing."

"How did your radio survive?"

"It's got a vacuum-tube which isn't affected when an EMP strikes," Edwin said.

"And other people also have these kinds of radios?"

"Yup," he said. "A lot of HAM operators run their radios for exactly these types of situations. We want to be prepared."

"An EMP strike seems highly unlikely," Liz said. "Are you sure?"

"There's no way to know for sure because it's hard to get any information these days," Edwin said. "But I'm sure. What else could it be?"

"The power plants could have gone offline because of the computer problems."

"Maybe," Sandy said. "But that doesn't explain the gas lines."

"Maybe they are rationing it," Liz said.

"No," Edwin said. "My guess is that the pumps are down. Natural gas is kept under pressure. They use electrical pumps to maintain that pressure."

"Which makes my point," Liz said. "It could just be a power plant issue."

"Well, either way, we're out of electricity and power for now. We've got some gas stored up to run our backup generator, but it'll only last us a few weeks if we're careful," Edwin said.

"I guess it's back to the creek to do laundry," Sandy said. "I'd better get the old washboard off the wall."

"You have one?"

"Yeah. We were using it as a decoration," Sandy said. "Ironic that we need it now."

"I guess we're going to have to do a lot of things the old way," Edwin said.

"At least until the power comes back on," Liz said.

"Let us know if that happens," Sandy said. "I don't know what I'm going to do with myself all day now that I can't watch my movies."

"Was your cable working?"

"No, but I have over one hundred DVDs," Sandy said proudly.

"Don't let the kids hear you or they're going to be over there three times a day borrowing new ones," Liz said.

"How can they watch them if the power's out?" Edwin asked.

"Oh, right." Liz flushed slightly. "I forgot."

"No worries. If you need anything, just holler," Sandy said.

"I've been thinking, we've got an extra pair of walkie talkies," Liz said. "Maybe we should use them to stay in touch."

"Do you have a lot of batteries?" Edwin asked.

"Enough to power them."

"Sounds like a plan then," he said.

"Hang on. I'll go get them." When Liz returned, she handed one to Edwin. "Keep it on channel two. These are short range so I don't expect we'll run into any interference."

"Sounds good. Take care. If you need anything,

give us a holler. Are you set up okay on food?" Edwin asked.

"We're good for now. You?"

"We've got enough to last a while," Sandy said.

"Good. With any luck we won't have to go too long without power," Liz said. "At least it's finally starting to cool off."

"Yep."

After making small talk about the weather, the Wrights headed back toward their house. Liz switched on her walkie-talkie and stuffed it into her waistband. Back inside the house, she found Kyle rolling around on the floor with Justice. The dog woofed and wagged his tail furiously.

Liz smiled and let them play while she went out back to set up the grill. She wasn't totally convinced they'd been hit with an EMP yet, but with the gas and electricity out, she'd have to cook dinner as if they were out camping.

After putting a pot of beans on the grill, she headed back in to get a cup of rice. She grabbed the salt and pepper shakers as well as dried garlic flakes for added flavor. They'd been eating beans and rice every day since they'd arrived. They did have a stockpile of canned food out in the shed, but she was trying to save those for when Luke arrived. She planned on creating a massive feast to celebrate his return.

Until then, they'd have to enjoy what meager changes in seasoning she could manage. She'd found some seed packets for herbs out in the shed. She didn't know much about gardening, but she figured she could try to plant them and see what happened. Worst case scenario the seeds wouldn't work. But if they did, she'd be able to add mint or basil to the mix. Something as simple as that would go a long way in lifting morale at the house.

SIERRA SWUNG the hammer one last time to complete the wooden platform for the solar panels. She stepped back and admired her handiwork. She'd used her brother's protractor to create the angle she'd calculated on a notepad. Who knew she'd actually use geometry for something useful?

According to the directions, she needed to use the latitude, times 0.76, plus 3.1 degrees. She found the latitude on one of her dad's maps: 33-45'23" N. So the angle needed to be 28 degrees. She did some rounding so she wouldn't lose her mind trying to calculate an overly specific angle. Hopefully the possibility of being off by a degree would be okay. She'd know whether or not it was working after they plugged it in.

Her mom sat in the dirt a few feet away, studying the wires and connectors. The solar panels were laid out side by side. Although they'd unpacked the brand-new panels and battery right after breakfast, it had taken hours to try to understand it all. Fortunately Liz had a basic understanding of electrical wiring because she'd helped Luke rewire one of the rooms a couple of years earlier.

"The platform's done," Sierra said.

"Okay. I think I have this figured out, but I guess we won't know until we plug it in."

"We'll see."

"Help me lift the panels onto the platform," Liz said.

As Sierra helped her lift the panels, Liz maneuvered them into place. They made sure that they were in the right position before they moved on to the next step.

"Hand me the silicone sealant," Liz said.

Sierra grabbed the tube and passed it across the solar cells. As Liz glued the cells into place, Sierra walked over to get the wires.

"Don't move those," Liz said.

"Why not?"

"I have them all laid out according to how we're

going to connect them. Also, we need to wait for the sealant to dry before we try to attach the wires."

"How long will that take?" Sierra asked.

"Twenty-four hours."

"I'm sure we can solder the wires without moving the solar cells."

"I don't want to take any chances."

"I'm sure it will be fine." Sierra couldn't keep the impatience out of her tone. After taking three ice-cold showers in a row, she was ready to get the hot water heater back up and running.

"If we screw this up, we don't get a second chance," her mom snapped.

"I know."

"We won't have any way to cook and you can forget hot water."

"What about the grill?" Sierra asked. She'd skip a shower if it only meant waiting twenty-four hours.

"I don't want to advertise to anyone who might be out there that we're cooking. We'll have to use it again tonight, but I don't want to have to use it after we get the solar battery running. Go get your brother and get him to help you with laundry. I'm going to take the wiring back into the shed and lay it out so that it's ready for tomorrow."

Sierra headed into the house to gather the laundry. Their neighbors had found a second washboard in their old barn and had given it to her mom. On one hand she was thankful they'd have clean clothes, but on the other, she hated having to do even more chores. Not having electricity sucked.

After gathering the clothes, she walked past Kyle, who was sitting on the couch reading a book. She didn't want to ask him to help her because she didn't want to deal with his endless questions about when the power would come back on. If she knew the answer to that, she wouldn't have spent all day putting together the platform.

She carried the basket of clothes out to the old red wagon they used to play with when they were kids. Sometimes Kyle still played with it when they were spending a weekend at the cabin, but even he was getting too old for it.

As she dragged the wagon behind her, she scanned the woods. Ever since she'd gone to confront the preacher, she'd felt like she was being watched. She never spotted anyone, but it was as if the trees had eyes. It totally creeped her out.

When she reached the stream, she took one more look around before beginning to do the laundry. She laid out the washboard and grabbed a bar of soap. After dipping the clothes in the stream to get them wet, she scrubbed away until everything was clean.

As she wrung water out of the last pair of pants, a

rustling in the trees caught her attention. She looked up to find Adam walking toward the stream. She stood and eyed him warily. Although he hadn't done anything to make her think he was a bad person, he didn't hang out with nice people.

"Hey," she said.

"Hey." He dropped his gaze to the basket. "Doing laundry?"

"Yeah."

"Did you lose power too?"

She nodded. "A couple of days ago."

"Us too. It sucks."

"Tell me about it. How's everything in cray-cray land?"

"Cray-cray? Huh?"

"Church." Maybe he wasn't as smart as he looked. "Anything weird going on over there?"

"It's okay. Well… except… a few nights ago I saw something strange. It was the night before you came and yelled at the preacher."

"I bet he loved that. Did he say anything about it?" she asked.

"No."

"What was the weird thing that happened?"

"I was out in the woods, just walking around," he said. "Sometimes I can't stand being around other people so I walk."

"You sound like me. I'd rather do laundry than have to listen to my brother talk nonstop."

"You have a brother."

Shit! Way to reveal even more information.

"Yeah," she said. "You?"

"Only child."

"So what happened?" she asked impatiently.

"I think someone got shot."

"What?" Her breath caught.

"I saw Turner and Ivan carrying someone. I think it was Paul Olmen."

"Who's that?"

"One of the other guys in the congregation. He's got two kids, Ingrid and Oliver."

"Why do you think someone shot him?" she asked.

"Because I went back the next morning and there was blood in the forest. There was a trail and—" He chewed on the edge of his lip.

"And what?"

"It led me back to your house."

She flinched. Her mom had told her she'd thought she'd shot someone.

"Is he okay?" she asked.

"He's gone.

"Dead?"

"No, he just… I don't know. Vanished. Elijah told

everyone that he and his family decided to move away, but I found a fresh grave in the cemetery later that same day."

"Oh God." Sierra covered her mouth with her hand. She tamped down the urge to barf. Her mom killed him. She'd actually shot and killed a man to protect them.

"I'm sorry, I shouldn't have said anything," he said.

"Did you tell Elijah anything?"

"No."

"Don't. I don't trust him," she said.

"I thought I did, but now…"

"I have to go. Please don't tell him you met me again. I'm afraid of what might happen."

"Did your dad shoot Paul?" he asked.

"No. I don't know exactly what happened, but no one can know." She grabbed his arm. "You can't say a word."

"I won't. I promise."

She released his arm and he took a step back. He took two more steps before turning and running into the forest. She prayed he wouldn't tell anyone that he knew the truth about what had happened to Paul.

"Who was that?"

Her brother's voice came from directly behind her. She spun to confront him.

"No one. Mind your own business. What are you doing out here?"

"Mom said I was supposed to help you. You are so busted. I'm telling on you."

Sierra lunged forward and grabbed his arm.

"If you say a word about this, I will put a pillow over your face and smother you in your sleep," she snarled.

"You can't kill me. Mom won't let you," he yelled.

He took off running into the forest. She raced after him. If she didn't catch him before he got back to the cabin, her mom was going to find out her secret.

27

Luke froze at the sound of panting just outside his makeshift tent. He'd been careful to dispose of the candy and beef jerky wrappers in a plastic Ziploc bag. How had the damn bear found him again? Was it the same one? Was she out for vengeance? He wanted to peek out to see if it was the same bear, but futilely hoped she wouldn't realize he was in the tent.

He didn't dare move a muscle. Still weak, he wouldn't be able to fight as hard as he had the previous day. His arm still throbbed where she'd clawed him. He wouldn't survive another fight. Even if he miraculously managed to live, he didn't have enough additional medical supplies to patch himself back up.

As he waited, he pictured what he'd say and do when he finally reached his home. He'd pull Liz into his arms and kiss her until his lips ached. He'd hug the kids until they squealed in protest, and then he'd fire up the barbecue and cook a feast. Juicy hamburgers, plump steaks, fire-grilled corn on the cob, potato salad, and all the fixings. Leafy lettuce, ripe red tomatoes, grilled onions, and salty pickles. His mouth watered as he surveyed his imaginary table.

If only he were there already.

It took over an hour before the animal left. He packed up as quickly as possible and headed down the trail. He could change his bandages later. Right now he wanted to put as much distance between himself and the bear as possible. Maybe it wasn't the same bear, but he wasn't willing to stick around and find out.

One long mile bled into the next on his endless trek through the mountains. Occasionally, he'd be rewarded with an expansive view of even more mountains. Deep within the wilderness, he was completely cut off from civilization. If things were really bad back home, they'd have to stay in the cabin for as long as possible. But if the cabin was overrun with refugees from the cities, then maybe he'd have to lead them back to the mountains to take refuge.

Not knowing anything about what was

happening back in the world was killing him. He hadn't encountered anyone on the trail since the two hikers he'd run into miles ago. Maybe no one else was crazy enough to attempt what he was doing. Completely unprepared for a week-long hike, every day brought with it a new fight for survival.

Had he made the right choice by taking the mountain path instead of waiting for a car to pick him up? He'd never know, but torturing himself with the possibilities helped pass the time.

The sky clouded over in the early afternoon. Small patches of snow hid beneath shadows at the base of trees. Probably dropped by the storm from a few days earlier.

Wind howled up the mountainside. He kept walking. According to the map he'd seen back at the North Fork Ranger Station, Camp Glenwood should be coming up somewhere in the next few miles. Unless it started raining or snowing, he had no intention of stopping until he reached the camp.

When he spotted the old red cabin, he wanted to fall to his knees. Sharp pellets of snow being driven by wind pelted him in the face.

As he approached the cabin's wide porch, he sighed with relief. This would be the perfect place to set up camp for the night.

He knocked on the door to see if anyone was

inside. When no one answered, he tried the door. It was unlocked. He couldn't believe his luck.

Inside he found a wood-burning stove. A stack of firewood and some newspaper were piled up beside it. He dropped his pack. He sorted out smaller pieces of kindling which he used to form a tepee in the center of the stove. After lighting it with his flint, he carefully added wood until the blaze warmed the room. He stripped out of his wet clothes and hung them over a couple of wooden chairs.

He found a sink with running water. Since he wasn't sure if the water was potable or not, he filled a cast iron pot and set it over the fire. He let the water boil for five minutes to be sure any bacteria had been killed.

After removing the pot, he set about washing himself. He soaked a bandana from his pack in the hot water, then used it to wipe a week's worth of sweat, dirt, and blood from his skin. He dumped then refilled the water several times until it finally ran clear.

He set a fresh pot on to boil. While he waited, he unwrapped the bandage on his arm. Caked blood held it in place. As he tore it away, he gritted his teeth against the pain. It wasn't nearly as bad as the day he'd been attacked, but it still hurt.

There were no signs of infection. The skin was

pink and slightly swollen around the stitches, but that was to be expected. He checked for any red streaks which might indicate a blood infection. Nothing. Thank God for small miracles.

After cleaning and redressing his wound, he set about washing his clothes. The stench wafting from them curled his nose hairs. No wonder the bear had followed him. He'd been marinating for days. She probably thought he would make a tasty snack.

"Too bad, bear."

He set his clean clothes back over the chairs to dry. He dragged them closer to the fire to make sure they'd be ready by morning.

Fatigue set in. Feeling safe for the first time in a week, he could hardly drag himself over to the raised wooden sleeping bench before his eyes closed. He slept like the dead, completely oblivious to the raging storm.

When the fire died down, he woke long enough to add as many logs as he could fit into the stove. As he walked back toward the bed, the distinct sound of a rattle stopped him. His shoes were on the other side of the room. Other than the dim light cast by the stove, it was as black as a witch's cauldron in the room.

Alone in the room with a snake in the dark could

easily rank in his top five most terrifying nightmares. Maybe he was dreaming?

He literally pinched himself. Nope. Awake. Dammit.

He considered his options. Running willy-nilly across the floor would be a recipe for disaster. He'd probably step on the damn thing before he made it to the platform.

If he retreated toward the stove, he could run into a snake who was simply looking for a warm place to curl up. His flashlight was in his pack, also on the other side of the room. Why he hadn't thought to take it to bed with him was beyond him. What a stupid move.

Unable to decide on the best plan, he waited until the rattler shook its tail. It came from the direction of the stove. Good enough for him. He ran across the room and leapt onto the wooden platform he'd been using as a bed. He'd expected to find a snake out on the trail, not holed up in a cabin.

Wide-eyed and unable to sleep, he sat with his back to the wall. When morning finally came, orange light from the sunrise filtered in to illuminate a three-foot-long Diamondback. It sat between him and his pack.

Awesome.

Until it moved, he was trapped in the cabin. He wanted to laugh at the absurdity of it, but he didn't have any way of counteracting snake venom. One bite would finish him. Even if he could walk to some semblance of civilization, could they treat him? Were hospitals still running? Ambulances? Fire departments?

The lack of information drove him nuts. He was so used to being able to pick up his phone, type any question into it, and be given a nearly instantaneous answer. He'd been spoiled by the information age. One week without the internet and he was already jonesing for the good ol' days. Oh what a glorious day it would be if he could hop online and watch cat videos all day. He'd never make fun of Liz for enjoying such simple pleasures ever again.

Snakezilla didn't slither away until sometime in the midafternoon. The second it was out of range, Luck snapped up his clothes and grabbed his pack. He went running outside, naked as the day he was born. No one was around, so what difference did it make?

He quickly dressed and headed toward the Pacific Crest Trail. He'd had just about enough of these close encounters with nature. Even the prospect of fighting his way through a rioting city was starting to hold more appeal.

AROUND NOON, Luke passed Eagle's Roost Picnic Area. He stopped to grab a granola bar. For the last three days, he'd been rationing food. With only five more bars left in his pack, he didn't have enough to get him to Cajon. He'd checked his map and tried to guess where he was, but wasn't sure.

The small mountain town of Wrightwood seemed to be about thirty miles away. It wasn't directly on the trail, so trying to get to town could cause more problems than it was worth, but he figured he had to try. If he could replenish his supplies in town, he'd be able to get to the Cajon Pass.

He made great time, getting from Eagle's Nest to a small, unmarked campsite in a little over two hours. He still had several hours before dark, so if he could knock out a few more miles, he'd be that much closer to home.

Several miles down the trail, he stopped at an overlook. Stunned by the beauty of the mountains, he didn't hear the other men approaching until they were right behind him. The hairs on the back of his neck stood on end. When that had happened in Afghanistan, he'd paid attention to the primal warning. He didn't have to understand how his sixth sense worked to be able to use it.

He turned to face two men. Clad in camo pants, plain olive green T-shirts, and carrying rifles over their shoulders, they would never pass as friendly hikers.

"Hello," Luke said. "How's your hike going?"

"Good. You?" the man with sandy brown hair asked.

"Pretty good." Luke took a few steps away from the edge of the mountain as he spoke. "I was heading south. Are you through-hikers?"

"Yeah." The man with blond hair's lips curled into a sneer. "Just out for a Sunday hike."

"Is today Sunday?" If so, he'd been on the trail for longer than a week.

"No. It's Friday," Sandy said.

"Have you been on the trail long?" Blondie asked.

"A few weeks," he lied. "I need to get into town to get some new supplies."

"Wrightwood?"

"Yeah."

"It's up ahead a few miles. You'll see a fork in the trail," Sandy said.

"Are you traveling alone?" Blondie asked.

"No. I've been hiking ahead of my group. They're a lot slower than me so I get to camp first and set up."

"So you're camp bitch?" Sandy asked.

"I'm the camp coordinator."

"Camp bitch," Blondie said before spitting on the ground.

"Whatever you say. I don't mind helping out. I'm sure the other guys would take over if I asked them to," Luke lied.

"How many of you are there?" Sandy asked.

"Eleven plus me, so twelve."

"Any women?" Blondie asked.

"No. We left them at home. It's all men."

"You guys have cell phones?" Sandy asked.

"No. Why, did you need to make a call?"

"Did you hear about the nukes? Hit LA twice. Blew it right off the map," Blondie said.

"What nukes? Like, nuclear weapons?" Luke decided to play dumb. If he could get them to think he was just another hiker with a big group, they might leave him alone.

"Yeah. North Korea or China or Russia, they're saying, but nobody knows shit," Sandy said.

"You're kidding." Luke widened his eyes as if stunned by the news. "Are you guys pulling my leg?"

"Man, you really haven't heard?" Blondie asked.

"No. We don't have our phones. We're roughing it in the wild." Luke flashed his most idiotic grin. So far they seemed to be buying his line of complete bullshit.

"Shit hit the fan, old man," Sandy said. "It's a new world order now."

"What do you mean?"

"No law. No order. It's every man for himself," Blondie said.

"Gosh, I guess we should head into town," Luke said.

"Go back and tell your people," Sandy said.

"They'll catch up. I should get going. Have a good hike."

Luke had to pass the men to get back onto the trail. He half expected them to jump him, so when they didn't, he breathed a sigh of relief. But as he picked up his pace, the crunch of their combat boots trailed behind him.

"Hey, mister," Blondie called. "What do you have in your backpack?"

Luke continued walking, pretending not to hear him. When the men broke into a run, Luke sprinted down the trail. He raced past small boulders, sending lizards skittering back into their hiding places.

Although he ran as fast as he could, the younger men caught up to him. One grabbed Luke's pack and swung him toward the ground. Luke went down hard. Dirt and rocks smashed into the soft skin covering his knees. After landing face-first, he scrambled to his feet. Blondie ripped the backpack from his back.

"Let's see what we have here."

As they rummaged through his pack, he formulated a plan. The second they brandished his pistol, he'd jump them and take it back. Unfortunately his plan failed spectacularly. Instead of grabbing the gun, the man pistol-whipped him across the face. Pain burst along his jaw. He reeled back, stumbling over a large rock before crashing back to the ground.

When his hand landed on a sharp rock, he grabbed it. He jumped to his feet and hurled the rock at the man holding the gun. Blondie dropped the weapon and howled. His friend moved to raise his rifle. Luke sprang at him, toppling him over before using the man's own gun to knock him out.

Sandy lunged for the pistol that had flown out of Blondie's hand. He'd almost reached it when Luke kicked it out of the way. He dove for it, grabbed the gun, then spun and put a bullet in Sandy's chest. The man's eyes went wide before his gaze dropped to his chest. He grabbed the gaping wound with his hand before crumpling to his knees. He fell over. To be sure he'd stay down, Luke put a bullet in his head.

Luke looked up in time to catch Blondie grab a rifle and go running into the trees. Instead of giving pursuit, Luke grabbed the other rifle, his pack, and his pistol. He'd never walk around again without his gun within easy reach.

To avoid being a target, he walked ten paces off the trail and continued south. He trekked through underbrush, aware that with every step he could potentially land on a rattlesnake. But if he stopped, Blondie might be able to track him through the woods. Maybe he should have stayed on the trail.

Unable to decide, Luke hurried around a bramble of bushes. Dried overripe and rotting berries clung to thorny stems. Stopping to eat his fill was out of the question. He wasn't even sure if they were poisonous or not. And since he didn't know Blondie's precise location, Luke definitely couldn't afford to take any chances.

An hour passed with no sign of the other man. The sun dropped behind the trees, taking its heat and light with it. He wouldn't make it to the cutoff tonight. He'd have to spend another night in the forest.

Staying on the trail would be a death sentence. About fifty feet off the trail, he found a spot of dense, fallen and rotting logs to camp behind. Instead of setting up his tent, he used the tarp to cover himself. If Blondie somehow decided to venture off the trail at this exact spot, Luke was screwed. To get this far only to be killed by an idiot would be a fate worse than being eaten alive by a bear. He actually wished the bear would find them. At least then he'd have a 50/50 chance of making it out alive.

28

Liz used a meter to test the voltage and current output of the solar cells. Satisfied with the setup, she wiped the back of her hand across her brow. Standing in direct sunlight for an hour fiddling with the solar cells had taken a toll on her hydration level. She needed water before she could do anything else.

As she headed down the slope behind the house, Kyle ran out of the forest at breakneck speed. Concerned, she picked up her pace, nearly twisting her ankle as she hit the flat area.

"What's wrong?" she called.

"Sierra's been meeting with people." His bright pink cheeks puffed as he sucked in several deep breaths. "I saw her."

"Where? What people?"

"Way over the hill. She keeps running away without me and when I finally followed her, I saw her with a guy."

"Young, old? Just one? I thought you said people."

"One young guy, but they were talking about when she went to the church to meet the preacher."

"What preacher?" Liz asked, exasperated.

"I don't know. I only saw the one guy, but there has to be more and she's seen them." Kyle turned as Sierra walked out of the forest. "I already told her."

"You're such a little brat," Sierra snapped. "You need to learn to keep your damn mouth shut."

"Sierra!" Liz put her hands on her hips. "Don't talk to your brother like that. What's this about other people?"

After giving her brother a withering look, she folded her arms over her chest.

"I ran into this guy, Adam."

"When?" Liz asked.

"A few days ago."

"Days ago? Before the attack?"

"Yeah. The day before."

"And you didn't think this might be important information to share?" Liz snapped.

"I didn't know it was them. Not until a few minutes ago. I thought it was a different group."

"What were you thinking? You could have gotten us all killed!"

"I know," Sierra said, finally contrite. "How was I supposed to know they'd try to attack us?"

"You can't know. The world isn't the same anymore. You can't trust anyone. You got lucky with that guy who helped you get to the cabin."

"Derek."

"Right. You're lucky he wasn't a rapist," Liz said.

"Trust me, he had the chance," Sierra said while rolling her eyes. "Not everyone's a psycho killer. I just happened to get unlucky."

"So who are these people?"

"There's a church a few hills over in one of the canyons. I think we went there once a long time ago for a chili cook-off."

"How many people are over there?" Liz asked.

"Maybe forty? I had lunch with them once but didn't get a good count. I wasn't really counting, I was trying to figure out if they'd come to the house the night before."

"Oh my God."

"What?"

"They could have killed you and we never would have known what happened. Do you know what that would do to me?!" Liz screamed.

"No."

"I swear to God, if I didn't love you I would strangle you with my bare hands right now."

"Wow, so you've lost your mind too?" Sierra eyed her.

"No. I think I'm the only sane one around here."

"What about me?" Kyle asked.

"Shut up!"

"Sierra!"

"I was coming back to tell you. I just wanted to be sure that the church people were the ones who came to the house. I think the guy you shot died."

"He did?"

Liz brought her hand to her heart. Although she'd suspected she'd hit him with a fatal shot, she wasn't sure. She'd killed him. Justifiable or not, he was dead. And she'd killed him.

She dropped to her knees and dry heaved.

"Mom, are you okay?" Sierra asked.

"Go away," Liz said. "I need…I need a minute."

"They were going to kill us. You had to stop them."

Tears burned in Liz's eyes. The full force of her choice rained down like nuclear fallout, poisoning everything that was good inside her. Numb and unable to reconcile who she was becoming, she got to her feet and headed toward the stream.

She dropped down, not caring that she was

getting mud all over her pants. She scooped up several handfuls of water and splashed it across her face. It wasn't enough. Horrified that she'd killed someone, she let out a primal scream.

When it finally dissipated, she plopped back onto her butt and cried until her throat was so swollen she could hardly swallow. Pain radiated out from her chest, as if she'd been the one who'd been shot.

If Luke had been home, none of this would have happened. Where was he? Was he doing everything he could to get back to them? Was he dead? How many more men would she have to kill to protect her family?

She wallowed in self-pity until the sun hung low on the horizon. After endless internal arguments and rationalizations, she finally pulled her head out of her ass. She'd been defending her home. It was a fundamental right. They had no business being on her property, and if they came back, she'd pick them off one by one. Anything to keep her family safe.

But she didn't want to kill anyone else. What the church group needed was a warning. If they knew she was prepared to kill them all, maybe they'd back off. Maybe they'd leave her and the kids alone.

She got to her feet and used several more handfuls of water to wash the salt-caked tears from her cheeks.

Was she a meek, whiny, fading violet, or was she a

warrior? A momma bear! A vicious defender of her family!

She could almost hear Luke yelling in her ear. She may have been losing her mind, but she didn't care. Nothing was more important than her family, and it was time that preacher and his flock of sheep found out how far she was willing to go.

LIZ ADJUSTED the grip on the rifle as she followed Sierra across the stream. Her daughter wasn't a complete fool. She'd actually taken the time to mark the path back to the church group. Wonders never ceased. She tried to remember what she was like when she was nineteen years old. Had she ever been so careless and flippant?

Maybe.

As they reached the edge of the forest, Sierra came to a sudden stop.

"They're down there eating dinner."

"Good," Liz said. "Perfect timing then."

"What are you going to do?"

"I don't know."

She hadn't stopped to formulate a plan, but maybe that was a good thing. If she'd sat around trying to come up with a diplomatic way of approaching the group, it would have been much less effective than just barging in, guns blazing.

She strode out of the forest at a fast clip, not waiting for Sierra. She could hear her daughter jogging to catch up, which was good considering Sierra had the pistol with her.

When they reached the picnic area, Liz raised the rifle toward the sky and fired one shot. People screamed and several ducked under the tables.

"Listen up, assholes," she barked. "I don't know which one of you came onto my property, but I swear to God, if I catch any of you anywhere near my house, I'll kill you too."

A man near the barbecue stood. Wearing jeans, a tan, long-sleeved shirt, and cowboy boots, he looked as if he'd just jumped off a train from Texas.

"Hello, I'm Elijah." He smiled, but she didn't believe it for a second. "Welcome to our church. I'm not sure what you're referring to, but you're welcome to stay for dinner."

"You know damn well what I'm talking about. I killed one of your own a few nights ago."

Several people gasped and a cluster of whispered conversations broke out.

"Silence." The preacher spoke and they all immediately obeyed. "We should speak in private."

"No," Liz said. "Whatever you have to say can

be said right here. I want to be perfectly clear. If I catch any of you even remotely close to my kids, my land, or my house, I'll shoot you on sight."

"I can assure you we've never been to your house. We're not even aware of other people living in the nearby canyons. Or, at least we weren't until your daughter ran into Adam."

"I don't believe you," she said.

"That's okay. We're not all chosen."

"Chosen? Chosen for what?"

"For the final battle," he said.

Several people nodded.

"What battle?"

"The one foretold millennia ago by the apostle John in the Book of Revelation," he said.

"Armageddon?"

"Yes."

"You think we're in the middle of Armageddon?" She arched a brow.

"If it hasn't already started, then it's coming. The bombs were just the beginning," he said.

"Wow. I can't even…Wow."

How do you try to rationalize with crazy people? Where can you even start?

"I see you're a non-believer," he said.

"I believe in God and the Bible, but I don't think

four horsemen are literally going to ride down El Toro Road with flaming spears."

"Maybe not, but we may already be in the final battle between good and evil."

"Okay. Well, enjoy your battle and leave my family alone. Got it?"

"You're always welcome to join us," he said.

She laughed until the glares from multiple people silenced her.

"We have no intention of ever joining your flock of crazy," she said. "Stay on your side of the mountain and we'll stay on ours."

"If you change your mind, we're here," he said. "I have a very forgiving nature."

"Well I don't, so I hope you take my warning seriously. I will shoot, and I will kill. I've done it once, and I'll do it again."

She turned on her heel and marched back toward the forest. She didn't let out a full breath until they'd crossed the steam.

"Mom?" Sierra called from a few feet behind her.

"What?"

"That was pretty badass."

"I just hope they don't come back."

"They won't," Sierra said. "They'd be stupid to do it now that we've shown them we mean business."

"People like that aren't rational. You can't take them at their word."

"Because they're religious?"

"No. That's irrelevant. That guy's running a cult. Did you see the way they all hung on his every word? He silenced them with a look. It was creepy."

"He kinda creeped me out too when I met him," Sierra said.

Liz stopped and turned to face her.

"We can't keep secrets from each other."

"I know, Mom. I'm sorry. I won't leave the property again. Trust me."

"I wish I could."

"You can. I didn't know people could be so dangerous."

"We don't even know what they're capable of," Liz said. "They came onto our property, but we still don't know why. Were they coming to ask us to join them?"

"At midnight? Probably not."

"Then were they coming to kill us?"

"I don't know," Sierra said.

"Exactly. We don't know. So unless proven otherwise, we need to assume that everyone is out to get us, that everyone we encounter is trying to kill us, and that we're not safe unless we're at the cabin. We need one person on watch at all times. It's going to be hard with just three people, but we don't have any other options. Once your dad gets home, he can take up the slack."

"So I've been thinking, did we ever hook up the satellite phone?" Sierra asked.

"What satellite phone?"

"The one in the shed. I saw it in a box and figured you knew it was there. It's not like it was hidden."

"Show me."

Liz followed Sierra to the shed. She waited outside while Sierra grabbed the box. It looked almost brand-new.

"Dad and Kyle take it on camping trips."

"He never mentioned it."

"He probably thought you'd freak out about the price," Sierra said.

"How much was it?"

"A lot? I don't know. I wasn't with them when he bought it. Kyle told me about it."

"Go get your brother."

While she waited for them to come back, she opened the box. A packet of instructions fell out. She flipped to the section written in English and began reading. It seemed simple enough, charge the battery, point it toward the sky, and wait for it to connect.

"Hey, Mom," Kyle said. "I thought you knew about the phone."

"Nope. It makes me wonder what else I don't

know. If you guys think of anything that might help us, please tell me. Even if you think I already know, I might not. Okay?"

"Okay," they responded in unison.

"Show me how it works." She handed it to Kyle. Within seconds he had it live and connected to a satellite signal.

"Dad has the number," Kyle said.

"What if he's tried to call us? Does it have voicemail?" Liz asked.

"I don't think so. Dad said it was mostly for emergencies for calling out."

"But he could try calling us too. Someone needs to keep the phone on them at all times."

"You can only use it outside, and you have to have a clear view of the sky," Kyle said. "And you can't use it if it's raining, or if there's smoke or fog."

"Good to know."

"See, I pay attention. I know things," he said triumphantly.

Sierra rolled her eyes.

"New rule," Liz said. "Whoever's on watch needs to carry the phone with them and make sure it's charged. We don't want to miss a call."

"Do you really think Dad's going to call?" Sierra asked.

"I don't know, but if he's able to, he will. He loves

you guys. I love you guys. I know I might come off as a hard-ass sometimes, but it's only because I love you, okay?"

They nodded.

"Family hug," Liz said.

"Eww, do we have to?" Kyle asked.

"Yes. I need a reminder of how much I love you so that I don't throttle your sister for giving away our location."

"Twice," Kyle said.

"Shut up!" Sierra said.

Liz shook her head and pulled her kids in for a hug. Although she still wanted to strangle Sierra for putting them in danger, it was too late to change things. From now on they'd have to rely on each other to stay safe. Hopefully they had enough guns and ammo to last until order was restored in the city. Until then, she planned on keeping a gun on her at all times.

29

Elijah plastered a smile on his face as he finished dinner. He could hardly swallow each bite of chicken. Bile born of simmering rage rose up in his throat to choke him. No woman had ever dared to challenge him in front of his flock. The gall. He glanced at Turner, who seemed equally perturbed.

After scraping the last morsel of food from his plate, he caught Turner's eye and jerked his head to the side. Turner rose and carried his paper plate to the trash. Elijah tossed his plate too. The men walked to Elijah's office in the back of the church. Turner closed the door behind them.

"We have to do something about the woman and the girl," he said.

"What do you recommend?" Elijah asked, curious

to see where the other man stood. How much vengeance was he willing to seek? His response would help formulate their level of retaliation going forward.

"They're not willing to join the group," Turner said. "And if they're not with us, they need to be eliminated."

"My thoughts exactly." Elijah smiled. "What do you propose?"

"We need to see what we're dealing with. So far we only have confirmation of the woman and the girl, but there could be men too. We need another reconnaissance mission. Once we know how many people they have to defend the cabin, we'll design a foolproof capture or kill mission."

"Capture?" Elijah raised a brow.

"Why not? We need more manual labor around here. The horses and chickens need to be fed. Stalls need to be mucked. And I'm sure Patrice wouldn't mind a day off from cooking."

"Perhaps." Elijah preferred to keep Patrice busy so she'd stay out of his business. "We can decide their duties once we capture them—*if* we capture them. If they put up too much of a fight and we're unable to take them, then we'll have to kill them."

"Agreed."

Elijah smiled. He gestured toward the chair in front of his desk. The men sat across from each other.

"I haven't told you this," Elijah began. "But you're my right-hand man."

"I don't need accolades."

"Even so, I want you to know that you have a special place in the church. If you need anything, please let me know and I'll see what I can do to get it."

"That's not necessary," Turner said. "To know I'm doing the Lord's work is all I need."

"Excellent." Elijah pulled open the bottom drawer of his desk and pulled out a bottle of brandy. He poured two glasses and pushed one across the table. "Join me in a toast."

Turner raised his glass.

"To a stronger community," Elijah said.

"To a stronger community."

They clicked their glasses together before draining them.

"Another?" Elijah asked.

"Not for me. I need to gather my men and get them ready for a recon mission. We'll head out at first light. I don't want to lose another man. At night they have an advantage. But come sunrise, we'll be staked out, ready for a head count."

"Don't engage yet. I want to watch them for a while. They may have supplies hidden at another location. We need to take everything they have," Elijah said.

"Yes, sir."

"There's something else I need you to do before you round up your team. I didn't see Paul's wife or kids at breakfast or lunch."

"I'll check their house."

"I'll come with you," Elijah said. "They may need to pray."

The men left the church and traveled a mile farther into the valley. They reached a small mobile home. Paul's pickup truck was still parked outside. Elijah walked up the rickety porch steps. As he knocked on the door, the cheap sheet metal reverberated against his hand, causing a terrible racket.

"Should I check around back?" Turner asked.

"Look in the windows. See if you can see anything."

As Turner circled around behind the house, Elijah tried peeking in through a window next to the door. He used his sleeve to brush dust off of the glass.

An empty living room appeared hazy though gray curtains. Elijah walked to the other side of the porch and peered into the kitchen. Also empty.

When he tried the front door, it opened. He poked his head inside.

"Emily?" he called Paul's wife's name.

No response.

"Ingrid? Oliver?" he called the kid's names.

Again, no response.

He walked through the house. Although the living room and kitchen seemed intact, the bedrooms told a different story. Dresser drawers hung open, their contents strewn across the floor. In the bathroom, an empty toothbrush holder and the lack of any medication confirmed his suspicion. They'd left in a huge hurry.

"You in here?" Turner called.

"Back here."

"Looks like they took off in the middle of the night."

"Or at first light."

"Patrol didn't see anything."

"They could have hiked over any of the hills to get out," Elijah said. "We need fencing. We need to contain our people."

"Why would they run?"

"They're non-believers," Elijah said. "They didn't understand that Paul gave his life in service to the Lord."

Turner nodded solemnly.

"I doubt they'll come back," Elijah said. "We should inventory the contents of the house. We can use all the extra supplies and rations for the church.

Everyone will benefit from their faithless cowardice."

"We'll get this inventoried and distributed to the various supply homes."

"Good."

"If anyone asks about them—"

"—faithless non-believers. You tell anyone who asks that the whole family left. No one needs to know that we buried Paul in the cemetery."

"Yes, sir."

As they walked back toward the church, Nadine strolled toward them. At five foot ten, she stood almost eye-level with Elijah. Blonde hair tumbled down her back. A red and white halter top dress clung to every curve, and her blue eyes sparkled with mischief. As usual, she was up to no good, and damned if he didn't get hard just thinking about her filthy mouth.

"I brought you a piece of cherry pie," she murmured.

She always spoke in a sultry tone, low enough to make Elijah strain to hear what she was saying. Somehow he suspected the twenty-five-year-old knew exactly what she was doing.

"I'll give you an update tomorrow," Turner said as he frowned at Nadine.

"Thank you," Elijah said.

After Turner excused himself, Elijah gently grabbed Nadine's elbow and guided her toward his office.

"We can share it," he said.

"I was hoping you'd say that."

After she brushed past him into the office, he closed the door. Before he could turn around, he heard the telltale click of her zipper. He slowly turned the lock on the door—and smiled.

30

After a night filled with the terrifying crack of branches and the chill of fresh snowfall, Luke set out before daybreak. Leaving the protection of the fallen trees behind, he stood and waited. In the predawn darkness, the occasional scamper of a small animal and the whisper of a breeze through the pines were enough to send electric sparks of adrenaline into his legs. Blondie, the man who'd attacked him the previous night, could be out there. Watching. Waiting.

Luke shoved his pistol into the front of his waistband. He carried the rifle at the ready and marched forward, as if on a mission in enemy territory. And make no mistake, anything stopping him from getting home was an enemy.

While trudging down the muddy trail, he swept his gaze from side to side. He scanned every silhouette, looking for a human outline. On high alert, he traveled several miles before reaching a fork in the trail. A small sign nailed to a leaning post indicated the path to Wrightwood.

He'd had just about enough of the damn trail and couldn't wait to get into town. It took another exhausting five miles to get to the outskirts of town. With better visibility, he was able to relax slightly.

A paved road arced toward the small mountain town. As he walked along the road, he passed abandoned cars. Some doors had been left wide open, fast food wrappers strewn about their floors. A gust of wind blew through, carrying with it a French fry box. It cartwheeled into a nearby pasture.

Several log cabins were set back twenty or more feet from the road. He studied them for any sign of occupation. What he wouldn't give for another night of peace and protection, preferably without snakes.

As he passed a single-story log cabin, the curtain on the front window moved to the side. A man peered out from behind a sticker depicting the Pacific Crest Trail logo. He swung open the door and called to him.

"Hey, are you a through-hiker?" the man yelled.

"Yeah."

"Come on up here. I've got water and food."

The man stepped onto the front porch. His hands hung at his sides, weaponless. He grinned at Luke and seemed to be friendly. But so had the men on the trail. Granted, they'd been carrying rifles, so he'd had no illusions as to the potential danger there. And he'd been proven right.

Could he trust another stranger?

"You look like shit, man," the guy said.

"It's been a tough journey."

"Which way were you headed?"

"South."

"Killer. Way to buck the trend. Most people head north. Although I guess it makes sense since it's October now. When did you get on the trail?"

"A week ago."

"Are you an ultra-marathon runner or something?" the man laughed. "Don't tell me you started in Canada because I know that's bullshit. The trail record is around sixty days. No way you did it in a week."

"I didn't get on in Canada, I was over by LA."

"When the bombs hit?" the man's eyes went wide.

"No. After. I was in San Jose when they hit."

"Good thing you weren't in San Francisco."

"I saw that one hit…well, I saw the explosion."

"Crazy. How'd you get down here from Nor Cal?"

"Driving. Hiking."

"Killer. Where are you headed?"

"Orange County. I need to get home to my family."

"I get you. Look, I'm a trail angel. I help out PCT hikers during the season. I wasn't expecting to see a hiker outside this time of year, or after the bombs. But I still have a lot of food, so I'm happy to share."

"You should preserve all you can," Luke said. "Who knows when food shipments will start again."

"Oh man. Dude…you haven't heard about it…"

"About what?"

"They hit us with an EMP."

"What?" Luke set his pack down on the porch rail.

"Yeah. It happened yesterday. I was waxing my snowboard, you know, getting it ready for winter, and bam! The lights go out. I'm like, what the hell? So I go out and some guy's parked down the road a bit. He walks up and tells me his car just died. I mean, I thought they might get us with an EMP, but it's so sci-fi, man. Can you believe that shit?"

"Are you sure?"

"Yeah. I went into town. Some of the older cars still work, but all the power's out. Anything with a circuit is fried. We figured it out when some people tried to run computers with their generators. Everything was cooked. But at least my generator still works. It's old as shit, but I guess my old man was good for something. He did maintenance on it every year until he died last year. Now I maintain it."

Luke couldn't even begin to formulate a response. Numbness seeped into his bones. In the back of his mind, he'd been holding onto a fantasy about getting to the Cajon Pass and hitching a ride to Orange County. It wasn't realistic, even before the news of an EMP, but the extra hurdle an EMP posed literally sucked up the rest of his energy.

He followed his host into the cabin.

"I'm Brock, by the way."

"Luke."

"It's short for Broccoli. It's my trail name. I'm also vegan, so there's that. I hope you like freeze-dried tofu."

"Sounds amazing."

"Ha! You'll change your mind after you've had my Kung Pao broccoli tofu."

"I'm honestly looking forward to it. Anything other than food in bar form sounds good to me."

"Sweet."

"Can I do anything to help?"

"Nah, I got this. Just kick back in a hammock and chill."

Luke headed into the living room area of the

cabin and selected one of two hammocks hanging from hooks in the wall. He selected the one that looked less worn, assuming the other belonged to Brock.

As he crawled into the hammock, the cloth contraption spun, spitting him out the other side.

"You okay?" Brock asked.

"Yeah. Tricky sucker."

"It takes some getting used to."

On his second attempt, Luke managed to get into it without flipping. He lay back. Every ache and pain flared as the hammock cradled his sore muscles. It took several minutes for his nerves to calm down enough for his muscles to relax.

"You live alone?" Luke asked.

"Yeah. My girlfriend took off with a through-hiker last year. Didn't see that coming. I was pretty cut up for a while until I realized how many hot females come through town. Now I'm a trail angel and I get more pus—girls than I ever dreamed of. It's a sweet gig."

"What's a trail angel?"

"I pass out food and water. I let people ship re-supplies to my house. It's pretty cool. I meet maybe thirty to fifty people every season."

"How can you afford to host so many people?" Luke asked.

"I sell wood art to tourists in town. Everybody seems to want bears these days. Personally I prefer wolves or fish, but I've got to make what sells. It helps to own the land. I grow everything I need in the summer and can for the winter."

"Sounds like you have it all figured out."

"It can get lonely in the off season, but overall, I love my life. I do have one regret though. I've been saving up to get off-grid. I guess I should have saved faster or bought more solar panels. I've got a couple out back, but it's not enough to run much more than the water heater. A hot shower is something I'm not willing to compromise on.

"I don't care if my food's cold or if I need to fire up the wood-burning stove to keep warm because I'm free. I'm not tied down to a greedy, materialistic society. I don't have to tie a noose around my neck and drive an hour to an office job I hate with coworkers I'd love to strangle with my bare hands. Don't worry, I'm not gonna strangle you."

Luke laughed. The guy wasn't small, but he wasn't big enough to get the jump on Luke either.

"Anyway, a few more years and I would have been off-grid. I guess an EMP's one way to speed up your timeline. What's your deal? You mentioned a family?"

"Wife, kids, noose. I guess I'm a typical American. My wife talked about moving to the country and living off the land. I was so caught up in saving for a bigger house, a faster car, a better 401k. I lost sight of what's most important."

"Family?"

"Yeah."

"Mine's dead."

"I'm sorry. What happened?" Luke asked.

"Dad had a heart attack. Mom died from cancer. I don't smoke, drink, or eat meat. I don't want the same fate."

"I hear you. I spend a lot of time in airports eating airport food."

"That stuff will kill you," Brock said.

"Probably."

"Dinner's ready. I hope you don't mind, but I only eat at the table."

"No problem."

Luke rolled out and landed on his feet. He joined Brock at a small, polished redwood table.

"Did you finish this yourself?" Luke asked.

"Yep. I got the piece from someone who was going to throw it out. All it needed was some sanding and polishing. No one wants to do any work anymore. They think everything's disposable when all it really needs is some elbow grease."

"Now you sound like *my* dad," Luke said.

"Smart man."

"He's got a farm in Tennessee. He keeps everything. You should see his scrap metal pile. You'd think he was building a stairway to heaven."

"Great, now I'm going to have that song stuck in my head," Brock grumbled.

"It's a great song."

"You know they were accused of stealing it, right?"

"Really?"

"Some of the chords, anyway. The original song was Taurus by the band Spirit. They actually went to court over it last year."

"No shit."

"Zeppelin won. It was a crazy trial though. The jury didn't even get to hear the artist's recordings. They had an expert play the sheet music and had to render a verdict on that alone."

"A lot of music is influenced by other music," Luke said. "Doesn't mean it was copyright infringement."

"True. I forgot to ask, are you allergic to peanuts?"

"No."

"Good. I added some."

As Luke dug into a bowl of brown rice, rehydrated tofu, fresh broccoli, and spicy Kung Pao sauce, his stomach clenched. He wasn't used to eating so much food, or so much roughage. It had only taken his stomach a week to shrink down to the size of a granola bar.

After dinner, Luke helped clean up.

"I was thinking about your family," Brock said. "Have you talked to them since the attack?"

"No. I tried calling and texting but the lines were down. Then my phone died."

"I've got a satellite phone you could use."

"It's still working?" Luke couldn't keep the surprise from his voice.

"I think so. It's in my Faraday cage. I built it myself."

"How?"

"I took a shoebox and wrapped it in foil about ten times. Then I stuck it inside a cardboard box and wrapped that another ten times. I made it a habit to keep my satellite phone in it."

"How do you run the battery?"

"I have an adapter for my solar panels. We could hook it up and see what happens," Brock said.

"Okay."

Luke tried to tamp down his excitement as Brock retrieved a tinfoil-wrapped box from a closet. He opened the box and pulled out a shoebox, also covered in multiple layers of tinfoil.

"I'll go get the adapter and battery," Brock said.

As Luke waited for him to return, he eyed the phone. This was it. If he could just hear his wife's voice, if he could hear his kids, it would make the hellish journey all worth it. If the phone didn't work, he'd be devastated. Not knowing the fate of his family was a cancer eating away at his soul.

He needed to hear their voices. The prospect of battling through another hundred miles of unknown dangers wouldn't be bearable unless he knew he was returning home to his family. If they were all dead, he'd have nothing to live for anymore. Nothing.

Brock brought in the adapter and battery. He hooked everything up before handing the phone to Luke.

"Good luck, man."

Luke headed outside into the open space behind the home. With a clear view of the sky, there was nothing to block the call. He opened the antenna, pointed it up, and turned on the phone. The display flashed for a second.

Searching for Network...

Registering with Network...

It beeped.

Ready for Service...

His heart raced as he dialed his country code, area code, and finally his home number. Then he waited.

Dialing...

He waited and waited, but it didn't connect. They were probably at the cabin. He disconnected and then reconnected to get service. After punching in the number to the satellite phone at the cabin, he waited.

Dialing…

31

Luke paced back and forth in Brock's backyard. The line rang so long that he almost couldn't believe it when Kyle finally answered the phone. His son's voice cracked as he spoke.

"Hello?"

"Kyle?"

"Dad, oh my God! Dad, is that really you?"

"Yes." Luke fought the sudden deluge of tears. He couldn't speak for several seconds. "How are you doing, son?"

"Where are you?"

"Wrightwood. It's a small town near the Pacific Crest Trail."

"What's the Pacific Crest Trail?" Kyle asked.

"You pass over it on the way to Hodge, that place we go to shoot guns… in the desert."

"Uh…"

"Remember when we shot up the old TV?"

"Oh yeah, that place! It's really far from here," Kyle said.

"Are you at the cabin?"

"Yep. We've been here since a few days after the bombs dropped."

"Is your mom there? How about Sierra?" he asked before Kyle had a chance to respond.

"Yeah, Mom and Sierra are here but they are pissed at each other right now."

"Why?"

"All I know is that they were yelling at each other about some insane preacher guy that I think Mom shot and—"

"Wait! What did you say? She shot someone?" Luke scrubbed his hand across his face.

"The guys were sneaking up to the house. She had to."

"What guys?"

"The guys from the church. Oh, hang on a second… Mom! Dad's on the phone!"

Luke's stomach plunged as he processed what his son was telling him. They weren't safe. His family wasn't safe, and he was still over one hundred miles from home.

"Babe, is that you?" Liz choked out.

"It's me, honey."

"Thank God. Thank God." She burst into tears. "I knew you were alive."

"Of course I'm alive, hon. I missed you so much." If he could have crawled through the phone to kiss her, he would have. "Are you okay? Kyle said something about a shooting?"

"We're okay," she said. "It's…I'll tell you about it when you get home. We're at the cabin. The power's out, but we've got solar hooked up."

"The EMP must have hit everyone," he said.

"It's really an EMP? I thought maybe the neighbors were wrong."

"Which neighbors?"

"The Wrights."

"Edwin and Sandy are good people."

"We've gotten to know each other a bit more over the last few days," Liz said. "Where are you?"

"I'm almost at the Cajon Pass."

"But… that's nowhere near San Jose. How did you get there?" she asked.

"It's a long story. But baby, I'm coming home."

"I love you so much," she whispered. "I don't think I can do this without you. I need you."

"You're smart and strong and powerful. You can do anything. I'm coming home, but I don't have a car. I've been on foot the last week. I hiked the Pacific Crest Trail from Highway 14 to a small town called Wrightwood."

Luke looked up to find Brock watching him from the back porch. Luke gave him a thumbs up before turning away to hide his tears. Joy, frustration, and love expanded in his chest until he couldn't hold it anymore. He choked back a sob and fought to get his emotions under control. After everything he'd braved to make it this far, he wasn't going to fall apart now.

"How far away are you?" she asked.

"I'm guessing about a hundred miles."

"How are you going to get here if you don't have a car?"

"I'll walk."

"Through Riverside? Please tell me you're armed."

"I've still got the P938 and I'm now the proud owner of a rifle," he said wryly.

"How did you end up with a rifle?"

"Someone tried to use it on me. They lost."

"You killed someone?" she whispered.

"Self-defense." He lowered his voice. "Kyle told me you shot someone. Are there people trying to get onto the property?"

"I-I had to. It…they were coming toward the

house. I had to. I didn't think I killed the guy. I saw the others carry him off."

"Oh honey," he murmured.

"I'm sorry."

"No. Don't be sorry," he said more gruffly than he'd intended. "Never be sorry about defending yourself or the kids. I'll get home as soon as I can. If I have to walk night and day to get there, I will."

"Even if you cover twenty miles a day, that's still five days," she said.

"If I don't run into any problems."

"Have you had a lot of problems so far? Other than losing your car. Also, where'd you get a car?"

"Rented one. Stole another. Although technically I guess it wasn't stolen since the owner was dead."

"What happened?" she asked.

"I had to kill the owner. I caught him trying to murder a family on their ranch. I couldn't abide by that, so I took him out. His friends too."

The line was silent for several seconds. Maybe he should have waited to tell her everything once he got home. But he needed her to understand the severity of the situation. If he was lucky he'd get home in five days. So far he'd been anything but, so he needed her to stay strong.

"I love you," she said. "I don't care what you have to do. Get home."

"I will. I swear to you, I'll get home. Be careful. Set up a perimeter—"

"Already did. Caltrops too."

"I didn't even think it was possible, but I love you even more now," he said. "You can do this. You can keep everyone safe until I get home. Lie low. Don't do anything to draw attention to the cabin. We should be far enough back in the canyon that people won't stumble onto our property."

"We would have been fine, but Sierra befriended the wrong people."

"Some preacher?"

"From the next canyon over. But I told him I'd shoot his men on sight if they ever step foot on our property again. And I meant it."

"I wish you didn't have to go through this," he said. "I wish I'd been there."

"You will be. You're coming home, and that's all I could ever want right now. Well, that and a mocha Frappuccino."

He laughed despite the pain in his heart. That was Liz, always looking for a way to lighten his mood. He loved her with the ferocity of a hundred lions. If he had to literally rip people apart to get home, he would. Nothing would stop him from getting back to his family. Nothing.

"I can't keep the phone," he said. "But I'll try to

call again when I get to Riverside. That's about half-way. I can't make any promises..."

"You don't have to. I know you'll make it. You're a SEAL at heart. You lived through Afghanistan and Iraq. This is America; it can't be worse than that," she said.

"I don't know. Things are getting bad. It's been about ten days since it all went down. People will be getting desperate. Most people will be out of food. With the grid down, I doubt water treatment plants will be running. There's about a million of people between where I'm at and where you're at. I can't imagine they'll all let me waltz through their neighborhoods."

"Travel at night. It will be safer," she said.

"Maybe. Maybe not. I'll have to play it by ear. Is Sierra around? I want to say hi to her before I hang up.

"She's out at the stream washing clothes."

"Then tell her I love her," he said. "Liz, I love you. I know I don't say it enough, but I do. You're the greatest thing that ever happened to me. I'd be a broken man without you. If you need to fight, fight. If you need to kill, do it. You have to stay alive, and you have to keep the kids alive. Promise me you won't give up."

"I promise. I swear it. We're going to live until

we're one hundred and then we'll die together on the same day, right?"

His throat tightened. How many times had they made that joke? They'd never really considered the possibility that one of them could die so young.

"Right," he choked.

"The battery's running low."

"Tell the kids I love them. I love you. I'll be home soon."

After he ended the call, he sat down on the back porch. Brock came back outside and handed him a glass of water.

"Are they okay?" Brock asked.

"As good as they can be considering the circumstances."

"Will you be heading out at first light?"

"Yeah."

"I'll put together some supplies," Brock said. "It might not be enough to get you all the way home, but it should help."

"I appreciate anything you can give me. Thanks for all of your help. You don't know what that call meant to me. When things get back to normal, if I can find a way to repay you—"

"Not necessary," Brock interrupted. "This is what I do. I'm glad I could help you out. Just pay it forward someday. Deal?"

"Deal." Luke shook his hand.

In the predawn light, Luke rose and mentally prepared himself for a full day on the trail. According to Brock, he had about twenty-five miles to go before he made it to Highway 15. As Luke hiked back to the Pacific Crest Trail, he replayed his conversation with his wife over and over again in his head. He didn't know what kind of trouble he might run into, but he was ready for anything. Even the devil himself couldn't keep Luke from his family.

When Luke finally stepped on the deserted highway, he took a deep breath. The relative safety of the trail wouldn't protect him now. If he could use his sheer will to get home, he'd make it. But he had no illusions about the journey. The city would be rife with desperation, strangled by roving gangs of militant people. Overrun by people with nothing to lose and everything to gain from his death. As he trekked down the freeway, he walked toward an unknown future in a society on the edge of collapse.

NEWSLETTER

Don't miss the next book in the American Fallout series: *Edge of Fear*. Want to know when it's coming out? What to find out if Luke ever makes it home or if Liz is able to defend the cabin?

My newsletter subscribers will be the first to find out about the new release. Sometimes I'll send out cover reveals and sneak peaks of chapters from the next book.

Sign up at www.alexgunwick.com

Please consider leaving a review. Authors rely on honest reviews to help spread the word. Readers like you are what makes it possible for me to continue writing edge of your seat suspense books. You don't have to write a huge paragraph, a few words is plenty. I'd really appreciate it.

I never give away email addresses. I personally hate spam so I would never sell your email.

ABOUT THE AUTHOR

Alex Gunwick started researching post-apocalyptic scenarios for book ideas. When she realized how unprepared she and her husband were for a disaster, she launched into prepping. Now she's armed and sitting on enough beans to rocket her to the moon and back. She's already mastered her Mossberg 500 and can't wait to put her HK P2000 through its paces at the range.

Her fantasy of moving to Montana to live in a cabin in the woods has become an obsession. Her husband's totally on board and can't wait to wrangle grizzly bears with his bare hands. We'll see how that works out. ;)

To find out more about her including what she's shooting these days, visit her online at:

www.AlexGunwick.com
AlexGunwick@gmail.com
Facebook.com/AlexGunwick

Made in United States
Orlando, FL
03 July 2024